The Elijah Project

Other Bill Myers Books You Will Enjoy

The Forbidden Doors Series
The Dark Power Collection
The Invisible Terror Collection
The Deadly Loyalty Collection
The Ancient Forces Collection

Teen Nonfiction
The Dark Side of the Supernatural

The Elijah Project

Bill Myers

with James Riordan   *bestselling author*

ZONDERVAN.com/
AUTHORTRACKER
follow your favorite authors

ZONDERKIDZ

The Elijah Project

On the Run
Copyright © 2009 by Bill Myers

The Enemy Closes In
Copyright © 2009 by Bill Myers

Trapped by Shadows
Copyright © 2009 by Bill Myers

The Chamber of Lies
Copyright © 2009 by Bill Myers

This title is also available as a Zondervan ebook.
Visit www.zondervan.com/ebooks.

Requests for information should be addressed to:
Zonderkidz, *Grand Rapids, Michigan* 49530

Library of Congress Cataloging-in-Publication Data

Myers, Bill, 1953-
    The Elijah project / by Bill Myers ; with James Riordan.
      p. cm.
    Previously published in 2009 in 4 vols.: On the run; The enemy closes in; Trapped by
shadows; and Chamber of lies.
    ISBN 978-0-310-72077-5 (softcover)
    I. Riordan, James, 1949- II. Title.
PZ7.M98234El 2010
[Fic]—dc22   2009048442

Published in association with the literary agency of Alive Communications, Inc., 7680 Goddard Street #200, Colorado Springs CO 80920, www.alivecommunications.com.

Zonderkidz is a trademark of Zondervan.

Art direction: Merit Alderink
Cover illustration: Cliff Nielsen
Cover design: Merit Kathan
Interior design: Carlos Eluterio Estrada; Greg Johnson/Textbook Perfect

Printed in the United States of America

11 12 13 14 15 16 /DCI/ 22 21 20 19 18 16 15 14 13 12 11 10 9 8 7 6 5 4 3 2 1

On the Run

For Lee Hough:
Friend and fellow servant

"Lo, I am with you always ..."

Matthew 28:20

Chapter One

Beginnings ...

Zach Dawkins headed for the schools.

Schools—as in the high school, middle school, and elementary school—that were all lined up side by side on the same street. He called it "Death Row."

Zach was sixteen, with dark hair that stuck out in so many directions it looked like it got cut by a lawn mower gone berserk. It's not that Zach was sloppy, he just had better things to do than worry about his looks, especially when he was late for school ... which was just about every day.

Zach wasn't exactly the responsible type.

Unfortunately Piper, his thirteen-year-old sister, was.

It seemed her job was to remember everything Zach (and the rest of her family) forgot. Like her brother, she was good-looking (though you couldn't convince her of that). She had beautiful chocolate brown eyes, but you had to work hard to find them beneath all that hair she hid under.

Piper was a bit on the self-conscious side.

At the moment, she was trying to keep up with Zach, while also shouting back to her little brother. "Elijah, come on. Hurry up!"

As usual, six-year-old Elijah dragged behind them. Nothing new there. The guy was always lost in his own world, and he hardly, if ever, talked. Piper loved him fiercely, and she always looked out for him.

But there was no getting around it—the kid was weird.

"Come on," she called. "We're going to be late!"

Elijah nodded, then immediately slowed to watch a butterfly.

Piper blew the hair out of her eyes and stopped with her hands on her hips. "*Elijah* ..." She was about to traipse back and get him, when she heard Zach use that voice he reserved only for making her life miserable.

"Well, well, lookie here."

With a certain dread she turned to her older brother ... and cringed.

Cody Martin, the all-school heartthrob, walked on the other side of the street. He was tall with deep blue eyes and a smile that made it hard for Piper to breathe. Of course he didn't know her from Adam ... or Eve ... but that didn't stop her from pulling up her sweatshirt hood or ducking further under her hair whenever he was around.

Unfortunately, she had stupidly asked her brother about him when the two had played baseball together. And that was all the ammunition Zach needed.

"Look who's across the street," he teased.

"Who?" Piper asked, trying to sound bored. "Oh, you mean Cody. What do I care?"

"Yeah, right," Zach snorted. "So you don't mind if I call him over?"

Suddenly her heart was in her throat. "Zach!"

With a sly grin, he shouted, "Yo, Cody. What's up?"

Cody turned and spotted them. "Hey, Zach." Then, nodding to Piper, he added, "How's it going, Patty?"

"Piper," Zach corrected.

She turned away, whispering between her teeth. "Zach!"

"What?" Cody asked him.

"My sister's name. It's Piper. Actually, it's Naomi Sue, but if you don't want her to beat the tar out of you, I'd stick with Piper."

"Gottcha." Cody grinned.

Zach turned to her and whispered, "So do you want me to call him over?"

"Please, no!" she begged.

"Then you admit you've got a crush on him?"

"No, I just—"

He turned back to Cody and yelled. "So, Cody—"

"Yeah?"

"All right," Piper whispered, "All right, I admit it!"

Zach grinned. "Nothing. Just wondering if you were going to play ball this spring."

"Probably. You?"

"Yeah, probably."

"Cool." Then, spotting a friend, Cody sped up to join him. "Take care," he turned to say.

"Right," Zach called.

"You too ... Piper."

Piper's head snapped up to him. The only thing

more startling than hearing him speak her name was the grin he flashed her before moving on.

He had *grinned* . . . at . . . *her*.

Suddenly, Piper's hood was up, her hair was down, and her knees were just a little wobbly.

It wasn't until she heard Zach snicker that she came to earth and turned on him. "Is it your goal to be the jerkiest brother on the face of the planet?" she demanded.

Zach laughed. "It's not a goal. It's a duty."

She blew the hair out of her eyes. Looking back to their little brother, she called, "Elijah, *please* hurry!"

Elijah came to attention and ran toward them. That was when Piper noticed the KWIT-TV news van heading up the street.

So did Zach, which explained why he immediately waved and shouted, "Hey, TV news guys! Over here. Check me out. Your next TV star is right here!"

Piper gave another sigh. What was God thinking when he made older brothers?

Suddenly, she noticed a small cocker spaniel puppy running into the street in front of them. It was followed by a little girl, probably in kindergarten.

Neither of them saw the car coming from the opposite direction.

"Watch it!" Piper shouted.

The little girl looked up, but it was too late.

The driver hit the brakes, tires screeching. The car's right front wheel ran over the dog with a sickening *KA-THUMP* while the front bumper hit the little girl. It knocked her hard to the ground, causing the back of her head to slam onto the concrete.

Neither the girl nor the dog moved.

The driver opened the car door, his mouth hanging open in shock and horror. The crossing guard, who had seen the whole thing, ran toward them. The news van jerked to a stop as the woman reporter leaped out of the still-rolling vehicle.

"Get the camera rolling!" she called over her shoulder.

"I'm on it!" the cameraman shouted just behind her.

Students quickly gathered, pressing in around the car and little girl. By the time Zach and Piper arrived, the crossing guard was already shouting, "Stand back! Give her air! Everybody, stand back!"

Piper glanced around for her little brother, but he was nowhere to be found.

"Elijah?" she called. "Elijah?"

She turned to Zach, but he was too busy trying to get a look at the girl to pay attention.

"Elijah!"

The news crew pushed past them for a closer shot.

"Hey, check it out," the reporter pointed. But she wasn't pointing at the little girl. She had noticed some-thing across the crowd and on the other side of the street.

Piper followed her gaze to see ... Elijah.

He sat on the curb holding the dead puppy. But instead of crying, his lips quietly moved — almost like he was whispering to it. And then, to Piper's dismay, the puppy began to move. A little at first, but it soon began wiggling, squirming, and even lifting up its head to lick Elijah's face.

"Did you get that?" the reporter cried.

"I've got it!" the cameraman shouted.

"It's like he healed it or something!" she exclaimed.

With a grin, Elijah set the dog down. It began jumping and running around like it had never been hurt.

"Get in closer," the reporter ordered. "I'm going to talk to him."

Only then did Piper realize what she had to do. "Elijah!" She brushed past the reporter and raced for her little brother. "Elijah, come on!"

The little boy looked up, grinning even bigger.

"Excuse me?" the reporter called from behind her. "May I ask you a few questions?"

Piper ignored her. "Come on, little guy," she said as she arrived. She put her hand on his shoulder, looking for a way to get out of there. "Mom and Dad won't like this. Not one bit."

"Excuse me!" the reporter shouted.

Spotting the school, Piper figured it was better than nothing, and started toward it. "Let's go."

"Excuse me?"

They walked faster.

"Excuse me!"

They started to run, neither turning back.

●

Judy Dawkins was struggling with the vacuum cleaner when her husband burst through the front door.

She looked up, startled. Seeing the concern on his face, she asked, "What's wrong?"

He tried to smile, but something was up.

"Mike, what is it?"

He walked over to the TV remote. Without a word, he snapped it on and found the news. Finally, he spoke. "They've been playing this all morning."

A white-haired anchorman addressed the camera: "Carly Taylor, our Newsbeat reporter, is still on the scene in Westwood. Carly?"

A young woman appeared on the screen. She stood

perfectly poised in front of the news van. "Thank you, Jonathan. As we've been saying, something very strange happened over on Walnut Boulevard this morning. Let's roll the footage, please."

The scene cut to an accident sight where medics loaded a little girl into an ambulance.

The reporter continued. "At approximately eight o'clock this morning, LeAnne Howard ran into the street after her dog and was struck by an oncoming car. From there she was taken to St. Jerome's Hospital, where her condition is reported as critical. There is speculation that she will shortly be transported to the Children's Surgical Unit at Eastside Memorial. But there is another side to this story that we found most interesting ..."

The scene cut to a cocker spaniel lying in front of a car.

"This footage was taken immediately after the accident. As you can see, the dog looks ... well, it looks dead ... or, at least severely injured."

Again the picture changed. This time a little boy sat on the curb holding the dog and whispering to it.

"Oh no," Mom brought her hand to her mouth. "It's Elijah!"

The reporter continued. "But moments later, as people were trying to help the girl, this small boy picked up her dog and ... you'll have to see for yourself. This is simply unbelievable."

Tears filled Mom's eyes as she watched the dog suddenly sit up in Elijah's lap and then lick his face.

"That's amazing," the anchorman said. "Let's see it again."

While the scene replayed, the reporter continued. "We tried to interview the boy, but a girl, the girl you see here, rushed him away."

Mom stared at the screen as Piper appeared and hurried Elijah away from the camera and toward the school.

The report continued, but Mom no longer heard. Tears blurred her eyes as her husband wrapped his arm around her.

"Don't cry, sweetheart," he said. "We knew this day would come, didn't we?"

She tried to answer, but her throat was too tight with emotion.

Dad repeated the words more softy. "Sooner or later we knew it would come."

●

Monica Specter and her two assistants sat in the dingy, cockroach-infested hotel, staring at the same newscast.

With a sinister grin, she switched off the television. "All right, team, the objective's been sighted." She rose and started for the adjacent room. "Pack up. We're leaving in fifteen minutes."

Bruno answered. He was a hulk of a man whose neck was as thick as most people's thighs and whose upturned nose looked like he'd run into a brick wall as a child (several times). "Uh ... okay. Where are we goin'?"

Monica stopped, flipped aside her bright red hair, and stared at him in disbelief. "Westwood, you dolt. You saw the news. The boy we're tracking is in Westwood."

Bruno nodded. "Uh ... right."

She looked at him another moment. Then, shaking her head, she disappeared into the other room.

Silas, their skinny partner, shut down his laptop and

gave a sniff with his long, pointy nose. "You shouldn't ask stupid questions like that," he said to Bruno.

Bruno nodded, then stopped. "But how do I know they're stupid if I don't ask 'em?"

Silas sighed. "Because you're going to try something brand new."

"What's that?"

"You'll try thinking before you speak."

Bruno frowned, not completely sure he understood the concept. Then, summoning up all his brain cells, he answered, "Huh?"

Silas answered. "We've been looking for this kid eight months now—checking newspaper articles, surfing the Net—and then, out of the blue, he suddenly winds up on TV?"

Bruno grinned. "Yeah, some coincidence, huh?"

"Yeah, right. That was no coincidence."

"You think Shadow Man had something to do with it?"

Silas shrugged. He never liked talking about the head of their organization. To be honest, the man gave him the willies.

"Come on," he said, changing the subject. "Let's get packed and grab the kid."

Chapter Two

On the Run

Mom furiously threw clothes into each of her three children's suitcases.

They'd been discovered. Found out. And in a matter of time they'd be taken.

No, not all of them.

Just one.

Just Elijah.

She heard car tires screech outside. She raced to the bedroom window to see a strange trio leap out of a green van and start down the sidewalk. First, there was a red-headed woman. Somehow she had learned the delicate art of stomping in high heels. Behind her was a giant of a man. And, last but not least, was a short, skinny man with a long, pointed nose ... who was carrying a gun!

"Honey!" her husband shouted as he raced up the stairs.

"I see them," she called.

He entered the room. "We'll have to draw them off."

"As decoys?"

He nodded. "I'll leave a note. The kids can meet up with us tonight."

"Oh, Mike . . ." Once again, tears filled her eyes.

"It's the only way, sweetheart." His own voice thickened with emotion. "For now, it's all we can do."

•

Monica sent Bruno to the back of the house while she and Silas knocked at the front door.

There was no answer.

She knocked harder.

Still no answer.

She turned to Silas. "You may have to break it in."

Silas squirmed. "I'm not the break-down-the-door guy. That's Bruno's department." Suddenly he brightened. "But I'll be happy to shoot off the lock if you want."

Monica gave him a look.

It's not that Silas was a gun nut; he just had this thing about blowing things up first and asking questions later. The worst was the time Bruno brought home a battery-operated puppy for Monica's birthday. (It really wasn't her birthday, but it was the thought that counted. Actually, in Bruno's case it wasn't the thought, either, since thoughts were not exactly something he specialized in.)

Anyway, once Monica rejected the gift (she always rejected Bruno's gifts), Bruno pretended it was *his* birthday. After a rousing chorus of "Happy Birthday to Me," he unwrapped the toy.

"Oh, what a wonderful surprise," he shouted.

Next came the hard part—figuring out how to put the batteries in. Once he accomplished that, Bruno turned on the toy and let it loose on the floor. Immediately, the mechanical puppy began prancing around and barking.

Silas, who was trying to watch a baseball game on TV, wasn't impressed.

"Will you turn that thing off?" he demanded. "I'm watching the game!"

"Oh, sorry," Bruno said.

But before he could turn it off he had to catch it. And since the only thing worse than Bruno's brain function was his coordination, he was never quite able to grab hold of the crafty little toy.

"Turn it off!" Silas shouted.

"I'm trying, I'm trying," Bruno said.

Finally, Silas saved him the effort.

The first shot sent the mechanical puppy into the air.

The second blew its little head off.

The third turned it into a pile of gears, fake fur, and a warranty label they somehow suspected was no longer valid.

Yes, Silas definitely had a thing about blowing stuff up.

Back at the house, the garage door behind them began to rise. Monica spun around to see a blue Jeep Cherokee backing out.

"They're trying to get away!" she cried.

The gang took off for the garage but were too slow. The car barreled backward down the driveway and onto the road, where it skidded to a stop. Then, with tires squealing, it peeled out and zoomed up the street.

"Get 'em!" Monica screamed as she turned for their van.

Unfortunately, Silas didn't turn as quickly as she did, which meant he crashed into her ... and fell onto the driveway ... where they got tangled up together.

After flopping around a bit, Silas finally pulled his foot out of her purse, and she pulled her arm out of his shirt. At last they scrambled to their feet and raced for the van.

"Don't let them get away!"

●

As they headed home from school, Zach was his usual irritating self.

"So you're a big TV star now," he teased his sister.

"What?" Piper asked.

"Couple kids saw it at lunch—you and Elijah were all over the news."

"Great," Piper sighed. "Mom and Dad aren't going to like that."

Zach nodded. "It's not exactly the low profile they tell us to keep."

Piper threw a look over her shoulder to Elijah, who was his usual fifty steps behind. This time he'd been stopped by three older kids.

"Hey, it's Miracle Boy," one of them taunted.

"Yeah," another said. "How 'bout doing a trick for us, Freako?"

Without thinking, Piper launched into her attack mode. It made no difference that there were three of them and one of her, or that their backs were to her so she didn't know how tough they were.

The point is, they were going after Elijah, so she was going after them.

"Leave him alone!" she shouted.

She grabbed the nearest kid, who had just arrived. She spun him around only to see that it was ... Cody.

"Hey ... uh, Piper."

She swallowed, then croaked, "Leave my brother alone!"

"Right, I was just—"

"You heard me!"

"I know, that's what I was telling—"

"I don't care how gorgeous you think you are, you don't mess with my brother!"

She pulled up her sleeves and glared at the other two boys like she was ready for a fight. They exchanged nervous glances, as if they were dealing with a crazy person.

"That goes for you too!"

Not wanting to tangle, particularly with a crazy person, they backed away. Then they turned and sauntered off. They fired off the expected insults, but Piper didn't care. She'd made her point. No one messed with her little brother.

It was about this time that she noticed Elijah tugging on her sleeve. She turned to him. "What?"

He pointed to Cody and shook his head.

"What?" she repeated.

Cody coughed slightly and explained, "I think he's telling you I was trying to help."

"Wh ... what?" She looked to Cody, then back to Elijah, who nodded broadly.

"Those two goons were giving him a rough time, so I came over to—"

"Hey, Cody," Zach strolled up to them. "I see Holster and Larson were trying to be tough guys again."

"Yeah," Cody agreed. "They'll never learn."

Zach nodded. "Looks like you scared them off."

"Actually, I think Piper did most of the scaring."

All three turned to Piper, whose ears were suddenly

burning red hot. "You ... you were trying to help?" She stammered. "I thought—"

"Yeah, I figured," Cody said. He flashed her that killer grin.

Piper tried to answer, but it's pretty hard talking with your jaw hanging open.

Cody cranked up his grin even brighter. "Don't sweat it. Truth is, I like people who stand up for others. *A lot*."

Piper may have nodded. She wasn't sure. All she knew was that her mouth was still hanging open (and she was praying there was no drool).

"Maybe I can give you a call sometime?" he asked. "I mean, if you don't mind."

If her jaw was hanging open before, now it was dragging on the ground.

"Piper?"

She tried moving her mouth, but nothing happened. He spoke again. "Piper?"

"Uh-huh," she heard herself croak.

"If I'm going to call you ... I'll need your cell number."

"Uh-huh."

He paused, waiting. Was it her imagination or was his friendly smile turning into a look of pity?

At last, Zach came to her rescue. "It's 484-1601, right, Pipe?"

"Uh-huh."

"Great." Cody grabbed a pen and wrote it on the back of his hand.

"Thanks for helping out," Zach said. "With Elijah, I mean."

"No prob." Cody answered as he turned and started up the sidewalk.

Piper wasn't sure how long she stood there. All she remembered was Zach putting his arm around her shoulder and easing her in the direction of their house.

"Come along now," he said gently. "Everything will be all right."

●

Mom and Dad sped down the entrance ramp and merged onto the freeway. The green van was close behind . . . and getting closer by the second.

"They're closing in," Dad said, looking in the rear-view mirror.

"Can we outrun them?" Mom asked.

"I doubt it. But we can stay ahead of them long enough for the kids to see the note and get away."

●

"What happened?" Piper said as they stood in the middle of the kitchen. The vacuum cleaner was out, unwashed dishes sat in the sink, and the floor was covered with clothes from the dryer.

"Looks like they were in a hurry," Zach said as he opened the fridge to get some milk.

"Thank you, TV news!" Piper drolled. "They also left the garage door open."

Grabbing a dirty glass from the sink, Zach asked, "You don't think anything serious could have happened, do you?"

Piper cringed as he poured the milk into the filthy glass.

He looked at her. "What?"

She started to explain and then stopped. With Zach, it would do no good.

Elijah spotted a note on the counter. Silently, he scooped it up and handed it to Piper.

"What's that?" Zach asked between gulps.

"It's from Mom and Dad," Piper said. She began reading. " 'No time to explain. Meet us at Aunt Myrna's tonight. Take everything you need in case we can't come back.' "

Zach stopped drinking. "Can't come back?"

"Oh no," Piper groaned. "It's happening again, isn't it?"

Zach frowned. "Maybe ... but Aunt Myrna's all the way in Pasadena. We don't even know her address."

Piper tapped the note. "It's right here."

"Anything else?"

"Just a Bible verse." Since they were kids, Mom and Dad always ended their notes with a verse from the Bible.

Zach finished the milk and belched. "Which one?"

Piper read the verse:

" 'Lo, I am with you always ... ' Matthew twenty-eight, verse twenty."

"That's it?" Zach asked.

"Almost." Piper swallowed. "There's one last word."

"Which is ...?"

"Hurry!"

●

Monica Specter squinted through the dirty wind-shield as Silas drew closer to the Jeep.

"I don't see no kids in there," Bruno called from the backseat.

"Neither do I," Silas said. Turning to Monica, he asked, "Should I force them off the road?" (Silas liked crashing into cars as much as he liked blowing up battery-operated puppies). Unfortunately, Monica had a better idea.

Unfortunately, because the last thing in the world she wanted to do was put a call in to her boss. He was creepy. And not as in a little weird. He was creepy as in a *lot* weird.

Maybe it was his voice—the way it sort of slithered around your mind and hissed in your ears. Slithered and hissed the way rattlesnakes do.

Or maybe it was his tremendous size. He wasn't a little overweight, he was *really* overweight. Picture Jabba the Hutt from *Star Wars*. Yeah, that was pretty close to his size.

Actually, neither his voice nor his weight was a problem compared to his face. The reason? She never saw it. Well, it was there and everything, stuck on top of his neck like everyone else's. But she could never quite make it out. It always seemed to lurk and hide in shadows. Even in the brightest light, she still couldn't see his face.

But despite all these reasons she didn't want to call, she knew the time had come. Whether she liked it or not, she knew what she had to do.

Monica took a deep breath, reached into her purse for her cell phone, and began to dial.

●

The office was black. Not black as in dark with no lights, but black as in all black—black carpet, black desk, black phones. Even the pens and paper clips were black.

The phone rang only once before a shadowy form reached over and picked it up.

"Yesss," it hissed in a strange, quivering voice.

"Got them in sight, sir," Monica said over the phone. "But I'm not sure the kid is with them."

"What?!" the dark form demanded.

"We're coming up on Lankersham Boulevard. Should we force them off the road?"

"Leave that to me. I shall contact otherssss."

"But—"

"Jussst find the boy!"

"Yes, sir," Monica said.

Without another word, the shadowy creature slammed down the phone.

●

"They're peeling off," Dad called as he looked through the mirror.

Mom turned to see the green van taking the exit ramp behind them. "Do you think they've given up?" she asked.

He said nothing, and she turned to him. The weary expression on his face said more than she wanted to know.

They drove in silence through the traffic—five, ten minutes—lost in their own thoughts, recalling memories of how time after time they had to pull up stakes and leave. In the early days, they'd tried going to the police. But what could they tell them? That their son had been born with strange gifts? That there was an organization connected to a dark, sinister force that would stop at nothing to get their hands on him?

Not exactly the type of thing police would believe.

Dad slowed the Jeep, and Mom looked up as they came to a stop.

"What's wrong?" she asked.

"Looks like an accident ahead. An overturned truck or something."

She nodded and returned to her thoughts. Even before he was born, she knew Elijah was different. To this day, she remembered the crazy man on the street who stopped her when she was pregnant. The one who started telling her all the things her baby would do and how he was even mentioned in the Bible. Then there was the—

The banging on the Jeep window jarred Mom from her thoughts. She spun around to see a good-looking man in a suit.

He motioned for her to roll down the window.

Throwing a look to Dad, who nodded, she reached for the button and rolled it down.

"Hello, there," he said in a thick Australian accent. "Leave everything and walk away with me. We've got a car waiting on the other side of the freeway."

"Who ... who are you?" Dad demanded.

"Oh, I think you know who we are, mate. Now come on."

"You just can't grab us in the middle of traffic!"

"You'll be coming with me. That is, if you want to see your children alive again."

Mom froze. "Our children? What have you done with the children?"

"There's only one way to find out." He turned and walked away from the car.

Mom twirled to her husband. "What do we do?"

He frowned.

"Maybe it's a bluff," she said. "Maybe the kids are safe."

"Maybe ..." Dad let out a heavy sigh. "But is that a risk we're willing to take?"

She looked at him a moment then shook her head. Then they both reached for the door handles and climbed down out of the car.

●

"Elijah . . ." Piper looked down into her little brother's suitcase. "You can't take all this stuff! The lid won't close."

He crossed his arms and scowled.

"Sorry, buddy."

She began pulling things out. First went the photos. Not just those from his room, but also from the hallway, the mantle, next to Mom's bed, and on Dad's dresser.

"Didn't you pack any clothes?" she asked.

He scowled harder and pointed at the shirt, pants, and shoes he was wearing.

"You have to pack more than those."

He lifted up his shirt to show his underwear.

Piper smiled and reached back into the suitcase. The next thing she pulled out was a heavy book—the family Bible. He loved that thing. And even though he couldn't read, he'd stare at the printed pages for hours. He especially liked the last section, the book of Revelation.

Piper continued to dig.

This was their fourth move in six years. And, like the others, it was always last-minute with no explanation. When they tried to get their parents to tell them why, the answer was always the same: "When you're older we'll explain. Right now, the less you know the better it will be."

Piper blew the hair out of her eyes. It wasn't anything illegal, she knew that. The family always went out of their way to do the right thing. So what could it be?

She looked back into Elijah's suitcase and pulled

out Zach's baseball card collection. Next she felt fur and pulled out her koala bear — the one she'd slept with since she was a baby. She'd wanted to pack it in her own suitcase but didn't have room.

"Oh, Eli," she said softly. "That is so sweet. But you have to pack something for your—"

She was interrupted by Zach shouting from downstairs. "Looks like we've got company!"

She moved to the window with Elijah. Sure enough, a green van had pulled up and the door was sliding open. The first person to step out was a skinny man with a funny nose . . . and a gun.

That was all Piper needed to see.

"Come on, Eli," she whispered. "Let's get out of here."

"The back door!" Zach called. "Let's sneak out and head across old lady Hagen's yard!"

●

Monica was surprised to see the front door unlocked. Instead of breaking it down (or allowing Silas to shoot it) she simply pushed it open, and they walked inside.

She turned to the men. "Bruno, check the back door. Silas, look upstairs."

They nodded and went to work, just as Monica's cell phone rang. She flipped it open and answered, "Hello."

"We have the parentsss," the voice hissed through the phone. "You were correct. The children are not with them."

Monica nodded as she moved through the kitchen. "It doesn't look like they're here, either."

"You have lossst them?" the voice hissed, sounding even darker than before.

Monica spotted a note on the counter and silently read it:

No time to explain. Meet us at Aunt Myrna's tonight. Take everything you need in case we can't come back.

"Lo, I am with you always ..." — Matthew 28:20

At the bottom was an address.

"No, sir, I haven't lost them." Monica's thin lips curled into what was a cross between a snarl and a smile. "In fact, I know right where they're going."

Chapter Three

A Close Call

Zach lugged Eli's suitcase and his own down the sidewalk.

Piper pulled hers on little attached wheels. When she'd picked it out with Mom, she'd known the wheels were a good, efficient feature.

Piper had a thing about being "efficient."

"I wish Dad would've left us some money for a cab," she said with a sigh. "The bus will take forever."

"Actually," Zach explained, "he probably figured we had enough."

"Why's that?"

"He gave me a bunch of money for football equipment and stuff, but I ..." Zach came to a stop.

Piper turned to him. "But you what?"

"But I, well, um ..." He fumbled, looking for a way out. Finally, he shrugged. "All right, so I bought lunch for a few of my friends. Big deal."

"You bought lunch for a few of your friends?!"

"All right, for *a lot* of my friends."

Piper groaned. "Zach ..."

"Don't sweat it." He reached into his pocket. "We've still got almost three bucks left."

"Great. We get to walk a thousand miles to the bus stop, then ride the smelly thing all the way across town just so you could be B.M.O.C."

"Big Man on Campus?" Zach asked.

Piper shook her head. "Big Moron on Campus."

Elijah began tugging on Zach's sleeve.

"What is it, little buddy?"

Elijah pointed at a sign that read *Hospital*, with an arrow pointing down the street.

"You want to go to the hospital?" Zach said.

"Are you feeling sick?" Piper asked in sudden concern.

Elijah shook his head.

"Sorry, pal," Zach said. "No field trips today. We gotta keep moving. Hey, there's the bus now."

"Yeah," Piper agreed. "I can smell it from here."

Piper didn't dislike riding busses, per say. It was more like a deep hatred, a powerful loathing. In short, she despised it with every bone in her body.

It wasn't just the smelly exhaust, the sticky seats, or the sweet old ladies that always wound up sitting next to her and talking her ears off. The loathing went deeper, and it had started a long time ago. When she was seven, to be exact. That was when little Billy Hutton thought it would be great fun to sit behind her on the school bus and play "flick the girl's ears."

Yes, sir, lots of fun ... at least for the first couple days. But after a week or two it got a little boring—and painful. So, after asking him to stop for the hundredth time and complaining to the bus driver for the hundredth and one time, little Piper took matters into her own hands.

Translation: She leaped over the seat and beat the tar out of him.

Billy didn't laugh much after that. It's too embarrassing to laugh when you've been beaten up by a girl. (Even more embarrassing to laugh when you no longer have front teeth because of it.)

Of course, Mom and Dad weren't fond of paying for the dental bills. And Piper was even less fond of them taking it out of her allowance for the next thousand years. But Billy never showed interest in her again.

Unfortunately, neither did any of the other boys.

Ever.

●

Monica sat in the passenger seat of the green van looking for any sign of the kids.

"They can't be too far," she grumbled. "They're on foot."

Silas nodded from behind the wheel and turned the van up another street. A block later they came to a stoplight.

"There they are!" Bruno shouted from the backseat.

"Where?" Monica demanded.

"Across the street! At the bus stop!"

"Great." Silas grinned.

"And there's the bus!" Monica pointed.

Silas looked up the street and saw the approaching bus. It was half a block away. "No problem," he said.

"We've got plenty of time to get over there and grab them before it gets here."

The light changed, and he started to make a U-turn to cross the street when, suddenly, a homeless man appeared in front of them.

Silas slammed on the brakes. "Hey!"

The man didn't move.

Silas blasted the horn. "HEY!"

The homeless man looked up and smiled.

Silas blew the horn again. "Get out of the way!"

The man raised a hand to his ear as if he couldn't hear.

"The bus is coming!" Monica yelled.

"Come on, pal!" Silas shouted, motioning for him to move.

"Hurry!" Monica cried.

"What can I do?!" He hit the horn again.

The bus entered the intersection and pulled to a stop in front of the kids.

"They're getting on!" Monica yelled.

Silas continued honking. The man continued smiling.

"Run over him!" she shrieked.

With a belch of black smoke, the bus began to pull off.

"They're getting away!" Monica banged on the dashboard. "They're getting away!"

Silas turned back to the homeless man ... only to discover he was no longer there. "Where'd he go?"

"Who cares?" Monica screamed. "Follow that bus!"

Silas resumed the U-turn, only to have another car pull out in front of him. Again he slammed on the brakes, and again he blasted the horn.

But the car wouldn't move. Actually, it couldn't move. The homeless man had crossed the street and now blocked the traffic coming from the opposite direction.

"Unbelievable," Silas said with a sigh as he watched the bus head off down the road.

"Now what do we, uh, do?" Bruno called from the backseat.

"We meet them at their aunt's," Monica said. She pulled out the note she'd picked up from the counter. "If we can't grab them here, we'll grab them there."

Silas nodded. When the traffic finally cleared, he hit the gas. He drove like a madman to make sure they arrived before the kids.

Thirty minutes later, they pulled up in front of the aunt's house.

"You guys wait here," Monica said as she opened the van's door.

"Don't you want us to go with you?" Silas asked.

"Yeah, you might need, like, a protector or somethin'," Bruno said.

Monica looked at him for a long moment. For weeks she figured Bruno had been getting a crush on her. And now, by the way he tried to suck in his gut, grin, and smooth down his hair all at the same time, she was sure of it.

Finally she spoke. "I don't want any trouble here."

"Gotcha." Bruno grinned. Both he and Silas reached for their doors.

"No, listen to me," Monica said. First she pointed at Silas. "Too creepy looking." Then she pointed at Bruno. "Too stupid."

They both stared.

"Understand?"

The big guy looked down and nodded. He seemed to wilt before her very eyes.

She continued. "Just wait here for me."

Neither answered.

With a heavy sigh, she stepped out of the van and closed the door behind her.

Quickly, she hurried up the walk. As she arrived at the door, she took a compact from her purse and checked her face in the mirror. She tried smiling to soften her hardness. But no matter how she smiled, her face always looked as strained as a tortoise with a migraine.

She finally gave up and rang the bell.

A kind, older woman with silver hair opened the door. "Yes?"

Monica tried her best to look pleasant. "Are you … Myrna?" she asked, suddenly realizing she didn't know Aunt Myrna's last name.

But Myrna saved her. "Dawkins. Yes, I am."

Monica tried smiling again. Her attempt to smile caused her physical pain. "I'm sorry to have to tell you this, but your brother's family was in a car accident up north. They're at Bellevue Hospital in Ventura."

"Oh no!" Aunt Myrna cried. "Are they all right?"

"It's too early to tell. I'm a friend of your sister-in-law. She wanted me to ask you to come to the hospital right away."

Aunt Myrna nodded. "Thank you, thank you." She turned and called up the stairs to her husband. "Tom! We've got to go to Ventura right now! Mike's family has been in an accident!"

Thanking Monica once again, she shut the door.

Monica sneered as she headed back to the van.

"Any luck?" Silas called from the window.

She nodded and climbed inside. "Park down the block, in a place where we can watch the house without being spotted."

Silas dropped the car into gear. But as they pulled away, Bruno let out a forlorn sigh with a couple sniffles.

Monica turned and asked, "What's the matter with you?"

Silas explained. "He's upset because you said he was stupid."

Monica turned back to Bruno and said in her most comforting and understanding voice, "Bruno ... dear, dear Bruno?"

He looked up, hopefully. "Ye ... yes?" he answered between sniffles.

"Knock it off!"

●

After three bus transfers (and more than a little complaining from Piper), the kids finally approached their destination. Or so they hoped.

"You sure you remember how to get there?" Piper asked Zach for the hundredth time.

And for the hundredth time, Zach sighed. "Sure I'm sure. Their house is just down the street from that park."

"Which park is that?"

Zach shrugged. "You know, the park."

Piper looked at him.

"What?" he asked.

"Can I see the note please?"

"What note?"

"The one with the address."

"Oh, that note." Zach reached into his shirt pocket, but only found a flyer for a concert at a local coffee-house. He checked his back pocket. It was his history assignment. He tried his left pocket and found two one-dollar bills and forty cents in change.

Piper looked at him in disbelief.

He tried his right pocket and found two pieces of gum and half an eraser.

Piper rolled her eyes.

"What?" he repeated.

"You lost the note?"

"What do I need a stupid note for? Her place is on Jasmine Drive, just down from the park."

"*Which* park?" she repeated.

"How should I know? I mean, how many parks can there be in the city?"

Just then, the bus slowed as the driver called out, "Rutherford Park. Next stop, Cantrell Park, followed by Gelford Park."

If looks could kill, Zach would be making funeral arrangements for himself.

Suddenly, Elijah leaped to his feet and pointed out the window toward a large statue of a horse.

"This is it!" Zach cried. "The park with the horse!"

"Are you sure?" Piper asked.

"Sure I'm sure!"

Seconds later, all three piled out of the bus and headed down the street toward Aunt Myrna's.

"I'm starved," Zach said. "I hope she's got dinner for us."

Piper gave another one of her world-famous sighs. "I'd just settle for a hug. Do you think we'll go back home tonight?"

Zach shrugged. "I doubt it. Remember the last time we had to move?"

"How could I forget? It was in the middle of the night."

"Yeah," Zach said. "We had to keep the TV on so people would think we were still there watching it."

"And you wanted it to be on some stupid football game."

"Well, it was better than your America's Top whatever it was."

"It was the middle of spring, Zach. They don't play football in the spring."

"Details, details."

Piper gave up on sighing and tried one of her world-famous eye rolls. She still remembered that night vividly. Once they had decided on the TV show, an old *CSI* rerun, they had to push the car out of the garage without turning on the lights ... or the engine. It was supposed to be so no one would hear them leaving. And, for the most part, they were pretty successful—except for the part where Zach pushed the car by holding onto the steering wheel. Actually, that wasn't the problem. It was the horn on the steering wheel. The horn he accidentally pressed again and again, and again some more. The horn that managed to wake up the entire neighborhood—and all their dogs.

So much for silence. Maybe that's why this time Mom and Dad decided to leave without their help.

"Anyway," Zach said, bringing her back to the present. "I'm betting it's the same thing now. You know, them having to leave at the last minute."

"Why won't they ever tell us what's happening?" Piper complained.

He gave another shrug. "You know what they say— we're better off not knowing. At least for now."

She nodded and looked back to Elijah. She knew there was a connection between their sudden moves and her little brother, but what?

Suddenly, her cell phone—which Zach had programmed for her—rang to the tune of "If I Only Had a Brain," from *The Wizard of Oz*.

She pulled the phone from her pocket and checked

the caller ID. It was a number she didn't recognize. She flipped it open and answered anxiously. "Hello?"

"Hey, it's Cody," a voice on the other end replied.

Piper's heart sank and swelled at the same time. "Uh ... hi," she stammered.

"So, what're you up to?" he asked.

She swallowed nervously. The last thing she wanted to do was cut him off, but she didn't have much choice. "Listen ... Cody. Now's not such a good time. We're kinda busy and—"

"Where are you?" he asked. "I dropped by your place, but nobody was home."

"Yeah ... we're on the way to my aunt's in Pasadena. We took the bus."

"The bus!" Cody exclaimed. "All the way out there? Where are your folks?"

Zach pointed across the street. "There's the house."

"Uh, listen, Cody ..." Just saying his name made her mouth dry. "I'm sorry, but I really gotta go. I'll talk to you later."

"Yeah, sure, but—"

Piper cringed as she closed her phone on him.

"Where's Dad's car?" Zach asked.

"Maybe ..." She cleared her throat. "Maybe he went to get pizza. We always have pizza when we come here."

They moved across the street and up to the front door. Zach knocked and waited. Piper blew the hair from her eyes and reached over to ring the bell.

A moment later, the door swung open. The woman standing before them was in her thirties, with long red hair and a strangely forced smile. "Hello. You must be Mike and Judy's children."

Zach and Piper exchanged looks.

"I'm ... Elaine, a house guest of your Aunt Myrna's. They went to pick up some dinner." She opened the door wider. "Won't you come in? They'll be back anytime."

Chapter Four

Extra Sausage

Cody stared at his cell phone. "She hung up on me."

Willard, his geeky, overweight friend, replied, "Perhaps she is too enamored of your fabled charm to speak directly to you."

Cody frowned. "And in English that would mean ...?"

Willard translated. "Maybe she thinks you're too hot."

Cody shook his head. "Don't be stupid."

Willard smiled to himself. Cody was the best friend a guy could have. Thoughtful, modest, and always there when the chips were down. But when it came to girls, he was clueless. The guy had absolutely no concept of his incredible looks or the effect he had on girls ... which was probably why they were all nuts over him.

Willard remembered the time in third grade when they were playing dodgeball and two girls were chosen to be captains. To say that they were each crazy to get him on their team was an understatement. To say that it involved screaming, a fist fight, and huge clumps of pulled-out hair on the gym floor when they were through was at least the truth.

The fact that Willard was always chosen last was another truth. But one he was used to.

At the moment the two of them were working in Willard's dad's garage, tinkering on Willard's latest invention. In the past he had created other mind-numbing devices:

ROCKET-POWERED BOWLING BALLS—a lot of fun, except for the holes they put in the back walls of bowling alleys.

MAKE-YOU-INVISIBLE ELECTRON BEAMS— a useful invention, except it only worked on skin and muscle, leaving folks walking around like human skeletons (not one of humankind's more attractive features).

Finally, there was the ever-popular AUTOMATIC HAIR CURLER—a hit with the girls, except that it fried their hair and made them permanently bald.

Now Willard was working on his latest ... the HELIO-HOPPER. It was made of three big ceiling fans—one on top to work as helicopter blades, and the other two on opposite sides to steer it. Below the fans were two side-by-side wheelchairs to sit in. And on the bottom of the chairs were plenty of springs (just in case the fans didn't work so well).

Cody's frown deepened as he said, "I'm just afraid Piper might be in trouble."

"Why's that?" Willard said as he returned to tightening the bolts on the helio-hopper.

"She said they took a bus to Pasadena."

Willard agreed. "That alone is an indication of something being incorrect."

Cody nodded. "Who would take a bus to visit their aunt all the way in Pasadena *without* their parents?"

Willard continued to tinker.

Cody nodded to the hopper. "I wish that thing was working so we could fly over there and check on her."

"You are in luck." Willard tightened the last bolt and looked up. "I believe we are ready for our first test flight."

"Cool!" Cody exclaimed. "Start her up."

Willard climbed aboard the helio-hopper and turned the key. It gave a grinding noise until the engine coughed to life.

"All right!" Cody shouted.

That was the good news. Unfortunately, there was also a little bad . . .

The whole machine leaped suddenly into the air and crashed down onto the floor. Then it leaped higher and crashed harder.

"What's going on?" Cody yelled.

"It appears to be over-oscillating!"

"What does that mean?"

It shot up, nearly hitting the roof. "It means you better hurry and get on before we take off!"

Once again it slammed to the ground. This time Cody jumped into the empty chair just before it shot up and grazed the ceiling.

"Hang on!" Willard shouted as they crashed back down. "I suspect the next couple leaps will be the ones!"

"The ones for what?" Cody yelled.

Again they slammed into the ceiling. This time the wooden planks gave a sickening *CRACK* before the helio-hopper fell back to the floor.

"The ones for what?" Cody repeated.

Again, they shot up, hitting the ceiling with such force that it finally gave way. The wood splintered into a thousand pieces as the boys and machine shot through the roof and up into the sky.

●

Piper stood at Aunt Myrna's doorway beside Zach and in front of Elijah. She couldn't put her finger on it, but something was stopping her from entering.

Maybe it was the forced smile on the woman's face—a smile that looked more painted than real.

Maybe it was the fact there were no cars parked out front—not Aunt Myrna's, not Dad's.

But she suspected the real reason was that Elijah had grabbed the back of her belt and held her, not letting her go inside the house.

"Please," the woman repeated. "I really think it's time to come in, don't you?"

"Oh, yes," Piper agreed. Once again she tried moving forward, and once again Elijah held her back.

Finally, she turned to him. "What is the matter with you?"

The little guy gave no answer but narrowed his eyes and pulled even harder.

Just then the phone rang from inside the house.

"Oh, that must be your parents now," the woman said.

Zach stepped inside. "Probably calling to see what we want on our pizza," he offered.

Piper looked at her little brother and decided she'd had enough. She reached back, grabbed Elijah by the hand, and pulled him inside with her. "Tell them I want extra sausage," she said.

"Yes." The woman smiled painfully as she shut the door. "Extra sausage."

●

By now, Willard and Cody were fifty feet in the air—dipping and diving, spinning and twirling—all the time hanging on for dear life.

Cody yelled, "Can't you—*WOAHH, WHAAA, WOOO*—steer this thing?!"

"Of course!" Willard shouted back. "Just as soon as I get a little—*WOOO, WHAAA, WOAHH*—practice!"

And practice he did as they dove this way and that, then that way and this . . . barely missing trees, telephone wires, and more than one angry seagull.

After twenty or thirty minutes of these fun and games, Willard finally started getting the hang of it.

"Isn't this cool?" he shouted.

Cody would have been happy to answer, but he was too busy hanging his head over the side of his chair, trying not to throw up. When he finally looked over to Willard, he saw his friend managing the controls with one hand while at the same time pressing buttons on a small box.

"What's that?" Cody yelled.

"My GPS tracker!" Willard shouted.

"Your what?"

"I believe there is a way we can find Piper's location!"

"How?"

"With a few modifications to this device, it is possible to locate her cell phone signal and trace it."

"Great!" Cody shouted. "That's just—" He wanted to finish the sentence, but it was more important he throw his head back over the side and hope there was nobody standing directly below him when he barfed.

•

Zach, Piper, and Elijah stood in the living room as the woman answered the phone.

"Hello, Mike? Good. The kids are here." She looked at them and tried another smile. "Yes, they seem fine."

Piper felt a wave of relief and smiled back.

The woman continued talking. "Yes, I'll tell them. Oh, and remember your daughter likes extra sausage on her pizza. Yes, we'll see you soon."

At last she hung up. "They'll be here in a little while."

"Great," Zach said as he plopped down on the sofa.

Feeling better, Piper joined him. Only Elijah remained standing. "C'mon, Eli." Piper held out her hands. "Come sit with me."

But Elijah refused. Instead, he turned and walked back to the front door.

The woman tensed. "He's not leaving, is he?"

"Nah," Zach assured her. "He'll stay with us."

The woman continued to watch.

"You'll have to excuse him," Piper explained. "Sometimes he acts a little ... strange."

"Yes." The woman nodded, not taking her eyes from Elijah. "So I've heard."

"Hey, pal," Zach called. "What are you—"

Elijah reached up and locked the front door with a loud *CLICK*.

Piper shrugged. "Guess he's afraid of burglars."

"Yes." The woman nodded again. "That must be it."

Suddenly the door knob rattled. Someone was trying to get in.

Zach rose from the sofa to take a peak out the window. Concerned, Piper joined him.

"It's probably just those annoying Girl Scouts," the woman said. "They're always trying to sell those awful cookies."

But they were not Girl Scouts. Instead, one was a big hulk of a man with a funny face. The other was the skinny guy with the long, pointed nose that Piper had seen pulling out a gun in front of her house—the very same gun he was pulling out now!

Without a word, Piper spun around and headed for the kitchen.

The woman turned. "Is everything . . . all right?"

"Oh, yes." Piper fought to keep her voice even. "I was just wondering—" She silently motioned for Zach to follow. This time, for whatever reason, he decided to listen. So did Elijah. "*We* were just wondering if there was anything we could snack on while we waited?"

The woman looked unsure whether to follow them or unlock the door. She voted for the door. And that was all the time they needed.

Piper raced for the back kitchen door and threw it open. Her brothers followed right behind.

They leaped off the porch and dashed to the tool shed their dad had helped build a couple summers back.

Zach tugged at the shed's door. "Locked!" he whispered.

They turned, searching the yard. Elijah pointed at the old RV beside the house some twenty feet away. Zach nodded. "It's worth a try."

They ran to it and barely arrived on the other side when the porch light flooded the yard. "They're out here!" the woman shouted.

"I knew she was up to something," Piper whispered as she tried the RV door. It wouldn't budge.

"Try jiggling the handle," Zach said. "Maybe it's stuck." Piper tried again with no luck.

They heard footsteps coming down the porch stairs.

"What'll we do?" Piper whispered. She spotted Elijah feeling under the front bumper. "Elijah!"

The voices began to approach.

"Look in that shed," the woman ordered. "I'll check the RV."

"Elijah, what are you—"

Suddenly her little brother held up the hide-a-key he'd found under the front bumper. Zach quickly grabbed it and unlocked the door. "Everyone inside," he whispered.

They didn't have to be asked twice.

When they were all in, Zach locked the door behind them. "Crouch down so they can't see," he whispered.

The voices drew closer.

Zach reached over and silently pulled Elijah out of the light streaming in through the RV's windshield ... just as the door rattled.

Piper caught her breath.

"It's locked," the woman called. "Shine your light inside."

A flashlight beam blazed through the windshield. Piper pressed flat against the wall. So did Zach and Elijah. They watched, frozen, as the beam moved across the floor and walls.

Another light appeared through the side window. Piper prayed silently as it crept toward them. They were going to be spotted any second.

Zach motioned them under the kitchen table. Piper

nodded. It was their only hope. Silently, Zach and Elijah darted under it without a problem.

But Piper was a fraction too slow. The beam caught her arm and she froze. It passed her, hesitated, and then darted back.

Chapter Five

Hide-and-Go-EEK!

On its next pass through the RV, the beam caught the edge of Piper's arm just as Zach grabbed her and dragged her under the table.

The light continued to shoot back, then forward, then back again, just inches from them. But it found nothing.

All while this happened, the red-haired woman continued yanking and pulling at the door.

Piper prayed quietly. She threw a glance to Zach and noticed he was doing the same. But not Elijah. Instead, the little guy was sitting there actually grinning. Weird.

The shaking of the door handle stopped.

"They musta gone down the alley," a man's voice said.

"Check it out," the woman ordered. "Bruno, go the other way."

"What are you going to do?" the other voice asked.

"Call the Compound. Now hurry! We've got to find them!"

The beams of light disappeared, and the footsteps began moving off.

●

Willard zipped over houses, roads, and a freeway or two. The good news was Cody had nothing left to throw up. The bad news was he was still sicker than a dog.

Willard's flying had improved quite a bit. And, other than that one close call with the 747 coming in for a landing (never fly a helio-hopper near a major airport) he did pretty well. Soon, they were soaring over the homes in Pasadena.

"We're getting close!" he shouted, looking at the GPS tracker. "She's in this neighborhood."

"I hope she's okay," Cody yelled back. "There was something about her voice."

Moment's later, Willard shouted, "I'm landing! The last transmission was on this block!"

Cody nodded as Willard reduced power. Unfortunately, he reduced it just a little too much. They fell like a rock.

"AUGH!" Cody yelled.

"AUGH!" Willard agreed.

They slammed hard onto the road and—*BOING!*— bounced back up. And slammed hard and—*BOING!* And slammed hard and—Well, you get the picture. Finally, after a couple minutes of the pogo-stick imitation, they came to a stop.

"Well," Willard said as Cody threw up again, just for

old time's sake, "that was rather exciting." He turned to Cody and said, "You appear somewhat pale, my friend. Might I suggest you get a bit more sun?"

Cody said nothing. He was just grateful to be back on the ground. When he finally did speak, he managed to squeak out the words, "Are you sure this is the right place?"

"I'm double-checking," Willard said as he pressed more buttons on his GPS. "I'm triangulating the signal at this present time and ..." He hesitated.

"And what?" Cody asked.

Willard scowled hard at the numbers. "The call was transmitted within five feet of this very location."

Cody glanced around. "So where did they go?"

"Perhaps one of these houses is their aunt's residence."

"Yeah, but which one?"

"Why don't you call her and ask?" Willard said.

"Because ..." Cody came to a stop. "Because ..."

"What?" Willard asked.

"Why didn't we just call in the first place?"

Willard looked at him and shrugged. "An excellent observation, and one we should consider the next time we encounter a similar situation."

"You mean when we're not hanging on for our lives, trying not to die?" Cody said.

"Yes, something to that effect."

Cody shook his head and reached for his phone to dial Piper's number.

●

Inside the RV, Piper held her breath as the voices continued to fade.

Suddenly, her cell phone began playing, "If I Only Had a Brain."

"Shut it off!" Zach whispered.

She fumbled in her pocket and pulled out the phone. It nearly slipped from her hands as she struggled to turn it off.

●

Silas came to a stop at the porch steps. "Did you hear that?"

"Hear what?" Bruno asked.

"It was like music." He listened again. "It's gone now."

Up on the porch, Monica was pacing. There was nothing she hated worse than calling Shadow Man—especially when it came to giving him bad news.

The two men watched as her left eye began twitching the way it did whenever she became nervous.

"She's pretty upset," Silas whispered.

"Really?" Bruno replied. "Her foot ain't tapping."

"Not yet, but—"

Suddenly, her right foot began to tap.

"There it goes," Bruno whispered.

Silas nodded.

Both men looked on—Silas, because he was nervous; Bruno, because he was in love. Of course, Silas had tried to warn Bruno that it wasn't such a good idea falling in love with your boss. But whenever she was around, all fourteen or fifteen of Bruno's brain cells went into *hyper ga-ga*.

The third phase of Monica's nerves kicked in. She began swallowing . . . hard.

Twitch, twitch, tap, tap, swallow, swallow.

Swallow, swallow, tap, tap, twitch, twitch.

"She's sooo beautiful," Bruno said with a sigh.

"Not now, you dork," Silas warned.

At last, Monica reached for her phone and hit the speed dial.

●

In the dark mountain compound, the phone rang. A long, shadowy arm reached for the receiver. "Yesss?" a voice hissed.

Monica answered, "We're still looking for them, sir."

A strange screeching sound escaped from Shadow Man's throat. Then, after taking a deep breath, he asked, "Did they not come to the houssse?"

"Yes ... they came in the front door and went out the back."

"You let them get away?"

"No, I mean, yes. I mean, we're looking for them right now and—"

Another screech leapt from Shadow Man's throat. Then, with a wheezing breath, he shouted, "You know what will happen if you fail!"

"Yes, sir."

"Then fiiiind themmm!!"

●

The kids huddled beneath the table in the dark. They could hear the woman shouting instructions. It sounded like she was leaving, but they couldn't be certain.

Always the "mom" of the group, Piper turned to see how Elijah was doing. But when she spotted him, he was grinning even bigger than before.

She glanced at Zach, who also saw it.

Then, ever so softly, Elijah began to hum.

Zach and Piper exchanged worried looks.

The humming grew louder until, very softly, Elijah began to sing. A hymn! Like they sang in church!

"Shh!" Zach warned. "Quiet, Elijah."

The boy opened his eyes. It almost looked like he was about to say something when, all of a sudden, someone banged on the door.

Zach and Piper froze. Elijah quit singing.

Someone banged on the door again.

"Maybe they'll go away," Piper whispered.

Elijah slipped out from under the table.

"Elijah!" Zach whispered.

But he didn't listen. Instead, he started for the door.

"Eli, get back here!"

Elijah reached for the handle and unlocked it.

Zach sprang toward him. But instead of stopping the boy, he tripped and slammed into him. The two fell into the door, which flew open. Unable to catch themselves, they tumbled out of the RV and onto the ground right in front of ... Cody and Willard!

Zach looked up at them in surprise. "What are you guys—"

"Shh!" Cody whispered. "They're searching the neighborhood for you."

Piper watched wide-eyed as the boys climbed back into the RV silently and shut the door.

"What are you doing here?" she whispered.

"I thought you were in some kind of trouble," Cody said, his blue eyes shining even in the dark.

Piper opened her mouth, but no words would come.

Willard explained. "We flew my helio-hopper over."

Before Piper could ask what a helio-whatever was, her brother had moved to the windshield and was looking outside.

"What do you observe?" Willard asked.

"They must have gone around front. They're nowhere in sight ... at least for now."

"What do we do?" Piper asked, still unable to take her eyes from Cody's.

Zach sighed heavily. "We can't stay here."

"Maybe we should make a run for it," Cody offered.

"I do not believe that is advisable," Willard said.

Piper nodded. "Willard's right. We can never out-run them ... at least not on foot."

As Cody's looked at the driver's seat, a thought began taking shape. "Who said anything about using our feet?" He moved to join Zach at the front of the RV. "Does this thing run?"

Zach looked to him, then back to the driver's seat. "I guess there's only one way to find out." He fished into his pocket to pull out the key Elijah had given him.

Piper's heart raced. "Zach, you're not going to try and start it?"

"You got any better ideas?"

Once again she opened her mouth, and once again there were no words.

Zach slipped into the seat, bent over to find the ignition, and inserted the key. "Well, here goes nothing."

And "nothing" is exactly what happened—except for the dull click of the starter.

He tried again.

Another click.

"Battery's dead," Cody said.

Zach nodded.

"Now what?" Piper groaned. She glanced back to Cody, who'd already turned to Willard.

"Well ..." Willard cleared his throat. "It is perhaps possible to connect the battery of my helio-hopper to the battery of the RV. That may generate enough electrical power to—"

"Right," Cody interrupted. "But we need jumper cables."

"There might be some in the shed," Zach suggested.

"It's locked," Piper reminded him.

"Perhaps we could reroute the starter to my battery," Willard suggested, "then onto the RV's battery—provided we can secure enough wire from the accessories panel."

The group traded looks.

"What are we waiting for?" Zach blurted. "Let's get to work!"

●

Mom and Dad had no idea where they were—it was some sort of storeroom with office supplies. They were tied together, back to back, in two wooden chairs. And, even though their backs were to each other, Dad could still hear his wife's quiet tears.

"Sweetheart, we've got to be strong," he said.

"I know," she answered hoarsely. "I just can't stop worrying about the kids."

"They'll be all right. Zach is tough. And Piper is smart."

She softly sniffed. "I just wish we could contact them. Let them know we're okay."

"And make sure they don't come looking for us," Dad added.

"Oh, Mike." She sucked in her breath. "You don't think they would, do you?"

To be honest, he wasn't certain. He wished he could warn them and tell them not to fall for any tricks. To help calm his wife, he tried changing the subject. "Let's see if we can get out of these ropes."

"How? They've got us tied so tightly I can barely move. No way can we break free of these chairs."

For the hundredth time, he tried moving his own arms and legs, and for the hundredth time he failed. She was absolutely right. There was nothing they could do. Unless ... An idea began to form. "Maybe we can't break free of the chairs," he said, "but ... maybe they can break free of us."

"What?"

"We can't move in these chairs. But if we could break one, it might give us room to wiggle. Here, start rocking with me."

"What do you—"

"The floor is concrete. If we fall over hard enough and slam the chairs into the concrete, we might be able to break them."

"Or our backs."

"It's worth a try," he said. "What else can we do?"

Mom had no answer.

He started to rock slowly. "Come on, join me."

She hesitated, and then finally began to rock with him.

"That's it," he said.

They rocked harder.

"Keep it up. And when we fall, smash as hard as you can onto the floor."

"Right."

Seconds later, it happened. The chairs tipped to the left. The couple leaned as hard as they could until they crashed onto the floor near the wall.

There was a loud CRACK.

"Did you hear that?" he asked.

"Yes."

"It was the arm. It's loose. Now if I can just wiggle my hand free."

Another moment and he shouted, "Got it!" With his loose hand, he moved the ropes until he freed his other. Next, he worked on his feet.

"Mike?" his wife asked in concern.

"Hang on, sweetheart, I'm just about there."

Chapter Six

The Escape

The RV was a mess. The protective cover between the front seats was off. The engine was exposed. And there were so many wires it looked like a spaghetti factory had exploded.

"How's it coming?" Piper asked, holding their one and only flashlight.

Cody looked up and gave her that killer smile of his. "Well, I think we've done as much damage as we can."

"Actually," Willard cleared his throat, "we have stripped the wires from the accessories panel in the RV and are quite certain it will carry the low voltage emitting from my helio-hopper battery. Then, of course, we must splice it back from the RV's starter into the RV's battery to maintain engine performance."

Piper looked at Cody.

Cody looked at Zach.

Finally, Zach cleared his throat. "Great. And once we're out of here, let's get something to eat. I'm starved."

"You're always starved," Piper said.

"Hey, I'm a growing boy."

"Who'll eat everything," Piper agreed.

"Not everything."

"What do you mean?'" she asked. "Name me one thing you won't eat."

"Remember the macaroni and cheese you tried frying up in mustard and ketchup?"

"Zach ..."

"And covered in horseradish?"

Piper felt her ears growing hot. "It was an experiment."

"Tell that to Molly."

"Who's Molly?" Willard asked.

"Our dog," Zach explained. "Nobody would eat it so we gave it to her."

"What happened?"

"We had to take her to the vet."

"Zach ..." Piper repeated her warning.

But her brother was on a roll and there was no stopping him. "To the emergency room—"

"Zach, please ..." She stole a look over to Cody.

"Where they had to pump her stomach so she wouldn't die!" Zach broke out laughing. He could really crack himself up at times.

Piper would have joined in if she wasn't busy giving him one of her death ray stares ... until she spotted Cody looking at her ... until she suddenly changed it to a smile, trying to look all pleasant and polite.

Unfortunately, the look on Cody's face said she failed on both accounts.

After a lengthy pause that redefined the term *awkward*, Willard said, "I have half a burger and some fries left over in my sweatshirt pocket."

"Left over from what?" Zach asked.

"Lunch."

The group exchanged glances.

Willard reached into his pocket and explained, "Waste not, want not."

He pulled out the bag and handed it to Elijah, who sat the closest. But instead of passing the bag over, Elijah held it a moment. In the dim light it almost looked like he was moving his lips.

Paying no attention, Zach grabbed the bag from him and opened it. "I don't care what you got, I could eat a—" He came to a stop.

Cody looked over to him. "You okay?"

Zach stared into the bag but said nothing.

"Yo, Zach."

Finally, Zach spoke. "I thought you said there was only half a burger here."

Before Willard could answer, Zach pulled out an entire hamburger. Then he reached in and pulled out another. And another.

For the first time in his life, Zach was speechless.

Piper reached across the aisle and grabbed the bag. She stuck her hand inside ... and pulled out another burger!

"I don't get it," Willard said. "Where did I get those?"

Without a word, Piper passed the bag to Cody.

Cody took it and pulled out one, two, three bags of French fries.

No one said a word.

Piper coughed nervously. Finally, she cleared her throat and asked, "So ... anybody want to say grace?"

●

Dad had wiggled out of the ropes and was helping Mom get free.

"There we go," he said as he pulled her last rope away. He reached to her arm and gently helped her to her feet. "You okay?"

She nodded, rubbing her wrists. "You?"

"Yeah." He moved across the room quickly and tried the door.

Locked.

No surprise there.

"Now what?" Mom asked.

He looked to the ceiling, to the walls, searching for any type of opening, any type of air duct.

Nothing.

Mom had moved to a shelf of stationery supplies. "Maybe there's something here."

He turned to her. "Like what?"

"I don't know. But we've got to do something."

Without another word, she reached for the nearest box and started to tear it open. Dad crossed the room and joined her.

●

Willard looked over the mass of wires and duct tape that led from the helio-hopper battery on the RV's kitchen table to the RV starter, and back to the RV's battery. "I believe we are ready for our first test."

"It better be a good one," Zach said as he pulled

away from the window, "'cause they're headed back this way!" He turned to Piper and motioned for her to shut off the flashlight.

She nodded, but was too late.

Outside, the heavier male voice asked, "Did you see that?"

"A light in the RV!" the other man answered.

"Let's get 'em!" the first cried. Louder, he shouted, "We found 'em, Monica! They're in the RV!"

Get down, Zach motioned to everyone in the motor home. *Down.*

The door suddenly rattled. Zach had luckily had the good sense to lock it.

"A rock!" one of the men shouted. "Get that rock!"

There was a moment's silence. Then, a rock smashed the right door's window directly above Piper's head.

Piper gave a stifled scream and everyone stopped breathing.

The rock hit the window again ... and again, until finally the glass exploded.

Piper cried out as glass rained down all over her.

A hand reached inside, trying to unlock the door.

"What do we do?" Willard yelled.

"The only thing we can do!" Zach shouted. He jumped behind the wheel of the RV.

The hand had nearly found the lock. Without stopping to think, Piper pulled off her shoe and slammed the hand with it.

The man yelped in pain and the hand disappeared.

Zach tried the engine. There was a very faint whine, then nothing.

Everyone groaned.

The hand came back inside.

Piper hit it again, and again, as hard as she could.

But this time, it remained.

"It must work!" Willard exclaimed. "Everything is in place." Only then did he see Elijah pointing to a loose wire.

"Yes!" Willard lunged forward and reattached it.

Finally, the hand found the lock. It unlocked the door.

Again, Zach turned the key. This time the engine sputtered to life ... just as the door flew open.

The big man reached inside. Piper was the closest, and he managed to grab hold of her sweatshirt. She screamed, trying to break away, but it did little good.

He had her.

Cody leaped into action. He plowed into the man as hard as he could. The man gasped and lost hold of Piper as Zach dropped the RV into gear and hit the gas.

Tires spun, spitting mud and gravel. The RV drifted to the right until Zach fought the wheel and straightened it.

The man's arms and head were still inside as he ran, trying to keep up.

The side gate lay dead ahead.

Zach pushed the pedal to the floor.

Piper screamed as they crashed through the gate, stripping the man away while driving right over what was left of Willard's helio-hopper.

They bounced onto the street as Cody shut the door.

Piper raced to the back and looked out the window. She saw the two men and the woman racing for their green van.

"They're coming after us!" she yelled.

"Let 'em," Zach shouted as he looked in the rear-view mirror. "No way will they catch us!"

Chapter Seven

The Hospital

Zach swerved crazily down the city street.

"Watch out!" Piper shouted as he barely missed his fourth (or was it fifth?) parked car.

"This thing drives like a house!" Zach complained.

"You don't even have your license!" Piper cried.

"Details, details."

"You barely know how to drive!"

"Relax," he said with a grin. "It's just like a video game."

"Video games give you three crashes for a dollar!"

Zach turned to her. "How much money we got?"

"Stop joking!"

Zach continued to laugh. He could be so clever sometimes. At least he thought he could.

"Look out!" Piper cried as they drifted into the wrong lane. (Normally this wouldn't be a problem, except for the cement truck heading straight for them.)

"Zach!"

He turned just in time and yanked the wheel hard to the right so they barely missed crashing into it.

The mailbox on the other side of the road wasn't so lucky. Nor was the rosebush, or the pink plastic flamingos that were arranged on the front lawn. Well, they *had* been on the front lawn. Now they were crunching under the RV's tires, flying over the RV's roof, or hitching a free ride on the RV's bumper.

Once the fun and games were over, they bounced back onto the street and continued their little suicide ride.

"Excuse me," Willard interrupted, holding up his handheld computer. "If my calculations are correct, they will be catching up with us in roughly one minute and thirty-two seconds."

"Willard's right," Cody agreed. "There's no way we can outrun them in this thing."

"So what do we do?" Piper asked.

Willard answered. "Since the RV is so visible, I suggest we hide it."

"But where?"

Suddenly, Zach threw the RV into a hard left, tossing everyone to the side.

"Zach, what are you—" Then Piper saw it. He'd found an underground parking lot and was racing inside.

"They'll never find us here," he shouted.

"Uh, excuse me, Zach?" Willard called. "What is the maximum clearance of this structure and what is our vehicle's height?"

"Huh?"

Before he could repeat himself, the RV gave a sickening shudder as its plastic skylight was sheered off by one of the low-hanging concrete beams in the garage ceiling.

Zach hit the brakes and threw them all forward to the floor.

"Oh no!" Piper groaned. She staggered back to her feet. "Did you just do what I think you did?"

"Perhaps we should ascertain the damages," Willard suggested.

"Yeah," Zach agreed. "Perhaps we should."

As they stepped from the RV, Piper spotted a sign that read *Eastwood Hospital Parking*.

"Well, at least we know where we are," she said.

They boosted Zach up to the top of the RV to see what had happened.

"Doesn't look too bad," he called over his shoulder. "Where did all these pieces of flamingos come from?"

"What about the RV?" Piper asked. "Is the RV okay?"

"The roof might leak a bit, but we could stuff a blanket in to stop that."

Willard and Cody helped Zach back down as Piper asked, "So what's our plan now?"

"Go to the police?" Cody offered.

Zach shook his head. "Kids against adults—who do you think they'd believe?"

Piper nodded. "Especially when one of those kids has just stolen an RV, driven it illegally, and crashed it into a parking-garage ceiling."

"Hey," Cody asked, "where's your little brother?"

Piper glanced around. He was nowhere in sight.

"Eli?" Zach stuck his head into the RV. "Little buddy, you in here?"

Nothing.

"Where could he have gone?" Piper asked. She tried unsuccessfully to keep the fear out of her voice. "You don't think that they, they—"

"We'd have seen them, Pipe," Zach said. "Nobody grabbed him. But why would he just slip off?"

Piper glanced up at the Eastwood Hospital Parking sign. "Wait a minute."

"What?" Cody asked.

"Earlier today," she turned to Zach, "remember he wanted to go visit a hospital?"

"So?" Zach asked.

"So maybe he's doing that now."

Zach began to nod slowly.

"But why?" she asked.

"Why does he do half the things he does?" Zach said.

Piper shrugged. Zach had a point.

"Perhaps we should commence searching for him?" Willard offered.

No one disagreed. But nobody suggested how to begin either.

Finally, Cody spoke up. "Why don't Willard and I check out everywhere on this block?"

Zach nodded. "I'll check the block across the street and behind us."

Cody continued. "And Piper, why don't you look in the hospital?"

"But what if . . ." Piper's voice was suddenly clogged with emotion. "What if we can't find him?" She looked down, letting her hair drop over her face.

Cody waited until she looked back up. Then, holding her eyes, he said softly, "We'll find him, Piper. Don't worry. We'll find him."

"But what if — " Her voice cracked and she couldn't continue.

Ever so gently, Cody put an arm around her shoulders. Then he turned to the group. "Let's all meet back here in one hour. If we don't find him by then ..." He hesitated. "Then we'll call the police."

●

Five minutes later, Piper arrived at the Information Desk in the hospital lobby. A silver-haired woman was frantically answering phones while pointing out directions to various visitors.

"Excuse me?" Piper asked. "Excuse me?"

A third phone rang. The woman motioned for Piper to wait as she answered it.

Piper blew the hair out her eyes and glanced around the lobby. The place was huge, and modern art covered the walls. In the middle of the room stood the world's ugliest statue. She couldn't figure out if it was supposed to be a spiderweb, a boney hand, or some stringy alien spacecraft visiting from another planet.

It made no difference. Piper was not crazy about visiting hospitals. Actually, it wasn't the hospitals, it was the people suffering in them. She'd never forget the time she volunteered as a candy striper. On her first day of the job, a nurse asked her to help change the dressing on an old man's wound.

It wasn't too bad—just a deep gash along his belly where a piece of metal had dug in from a car crash. And Piper didn't have to do any of the work. All she had to do was hold the bandages as the nurse unwound them.

No problem.

The problem came when they peeled back the old bandages and Piper saw the open wound. Actually, it wasn't the "seeing" that was the problem ... it was the getting sick to her stomach, the feeling her face break out in a sweat, and the fainting right there onto the floor that was a bit embarrassing.

When she woke up, the nurse was helping her to her feet.

"Sweetheart, are you okay?" she'd asked.

Of course, Piper had pretended nothing was wrong, that she'd tripped or stumbled or something. And she might have pulled it off ...

Except for the part of seeing the open wound again, breaking out in a sweat again, and, you guessed it, hitting the floor again.

So much for her career in the medical field.

"May I help you?"

The voice drew her out of her memories and back into the lobby. She looked at the silver-haired lady and cleared her throat. "Did you see a little boy come in here? Six years old, dark hair, and glasses that are—"

"Is he lost?"

"Well, no. I mean, maybe. I don't know."

The woman's smile froze slightly.

Realizing how lame she sounded, Piper tried again. "Actually, I'm not even sure he's here."

The frozen smile cracked slightly.

Luckily, another phone rang. The woman reached for it and answered it. "Good afternoon, Eastwood Hospital. How may I help you?" Then another rang. "Would you hold, please? Good afternoon, Eastwood Hospital. How may I help you?"

Piper glanced around. It was pretty obvious that the only way she could find Elijah was to look for him herself. With a sigh, she turned from the desk and started for the elevators. But she'd only taken a few steps before she heard, "Miss . . . Miss."

She turned to see the woman at the desk calling to her. "I'm sorry, but children are not allowed to visit without an adult."

"Child? I'm no child. I'm almost—"

"Sorry, those are the rules." The phone rang again, and she answered it. "Good afternoon, Eastwood Hospital, how may I help you?"

Across the lobby, the doors to the elevator opened. For a second, Piper thought of racing into it—rules or no rules. But knowing the woman was keeping an eye on her, and that she had broken more than the daily minimum requirement of rules for one day, Piper turned and slowly started for the exit.

With each step she took, her heart grew heavier. Things were finally catching up with her—leaving the house, losing Mom and Dad, and now . . . her baby brother. Why was everything so hard? What was the big secret her parents kept hiding from her? And why, just when things started to get normal, did stuff like this always happen?

She stepped out the hospital doors and into the sunlight. Tears filled her eyes. She blinked them back. She would not cry. Not now. Not when Elijah needed her. She swallowed hard, then thought back to the Bible verse Mom and Dad had left them: "I am with you always."

It sure didn't feel like anybody was with her. It felt more like she was lost and alone. Very, very alone.

"Where are you, God?" she whispered to herself. "Where are—"

"Excuse me?"

She turned and saw an old man holding his chest, leaning against the building.

"I think … I'm … having a heart attack," he said.

Piper rushed to his side.

"Hospital," he gasped. "I must get to—"

"It's here!" she said. She searched the building. "You just passed the emergency exit. It's back there!"

The man turned, but could barely stand.

"C'mon." She slipped her shoulder under his arm. "I'll help you!"

"Thank …" He could say no more.

They headed down the sidewalk as fast as they could. But even as Piper helped the man, she sensed there was something familiar about him. She'd seen him somewhere. They were a dozen feet from the hospital doors when she heard Zach shouting across the street.

"Piper? What's up?"

She turned as he ran to join them. "This man, he's having a heart attack," she shouted.

Zach arrived and moved to the man's other side.

"Thank you," the man gasped. "Thank you."

Zach nodded. Glancing to Piper, he asked, "Any sign of Eli?"

Piper shook her head no. "You?"

"Nothing."

They reached the emergency entrance. The doors hissed open, and within seconds an orderly was at their side. Grabbing a wheelchair, he eased the man down as a nurse arrived with a clipboard.

"What's your name, sir?" she asked.

"Gabriel," he wheezed.

"Like the angel?"

He nodded.

The nurse wrote it down and turned to the orderly. "Get Mr. Gabriel inside, stat."

They rolled him toward a pair of frosted-glass

doors. But when the doors slid opened, Piper caught her breath. For there, just inside the hallway, stood her little brother.

"Elijah!" She called.

The boy looked up and smiled.

Zach saw him too.

But when they started toward him, Elijah turned and raced down the hall.

"Elijah!" Zach called. "Eli!"

By the time they got inside the door, their little brother was nowhere to be found.

●

Monica, Silas, and Bruno cruised the streets in their van.

"How could a huge motor home just vanish?" Monica demanded.

"Well ... uh ... maybe we can't see it," Bruno offered.

"I know we can't see it," Monica snapped. "Otherwise we'd ... *see* it."

"Uh, yeah." Bruno gave a giggle. "That's what I thought too."

Monica looked at him, thought of saying something, then figured it would do no good.

"Maybe they're hiding it," Silas suggested.

"Where do you hide a motor home?" Monica grunted.

Silas immediately hit the brakes, and they all flew forward.

"What are you doing?!" Monica demanded.

He said nothing but pointed to the building directly beside them—the one with the sign reading *Underground Parking*.

"Yes!" she exclaimed. "Yes! They could have hidden it in a parking garage. Let's check them all out. There can't be that many. Let's search every parking garage until we find them!"

●

Mom and Dad continued rummaging through the storage room, tearing through box after box of stationery supplies.

"These people must sure like notes," Mom said as she tossed another box of sticky notes to the side.

Dad nodded and glanced to the door. "What we really need is something to help us pop that lock. If they hadn't taken my wallet, I could have used a credit card or at least a—" He stopped, seeing a look of hope cross Mom's face.

"What about a metal ruler?" she asked. "I've got a whole box of them right here."

"Let's see one."

She handed him a ruler and he headed for the door.

Mom followed as he crouched down to peer through the small crack between the door and the frame. Then, ever so carefully, he slipped the ruler into the crack and tried to catch the underside of the bolt.

A moment later the door gave a click.

"Got it!" he said.

"Now what?"

"Now we try to find a way out of here."

●

The children's surgical unit was on the fourth floor of the hospital. There, in a small conference room, an older doctor spoke to some very frightened parents.

"We feel that brain surgery is the only chance for LeAnne's survival. But, at best, it's only a fifty-fifty chance."

A long pause followed before the father cleared his throat. "Those aren't great odds, Doctor."

The doctor nodded. "I understand how you feel. But, as you know, we have the best surgeons in the city for this kind of procedure."

The father nodded. "That's why we had her transferred here. But only fifty-fifty . . ."

Another pause followed.

Finally the doctor answered. "A fifty-fifty chance is better than no chance. And that's what she'll have if we don't operate."

Across from the room an elevator dinged. The father looked into the hall to see the elevator's door open and a six-year-old boy with dark hair and glasses appear. The boy stepped into the hallway, looked both directions, and then headed for the children's ICU.

●

The green van entered the hospital's parking garage.

"There it is!" Silas shouted.

After three garages, they'd finally found the right one.

Silas brought the van to a stop and stepped out. Pulling his gun from his waistband, he silently approached the RV. He opened the door carefully and looked inside. No one was in sight.

"It's empty!" he called back to Monica.

Monica nodded. "All right then. Let's you and I comb the area. Bruno, you stay here in case they come back."

Bruno replied. "Yes, dear Monica. Your wish is my command."

Monica gave him a furious look, then shouted, "Knock it off!"

Chapter Eight

The Noose Tightens

Elijah peered around the corner into the ICU.

There were a dozen beds with all sorts of hanging bottles that were dripping and electronic gadgets that were beeping. At the far end, two nurses were speaking to a young doctor. But it was the third bed that caught Elijah's attention.

The girl he'd seen hit by the car was lying in it.

She looked awful. There were tubes running into her nose, mouth, and arms. Her skin was as pale as paper.

Slowly, Elijah made his way toward her. But he didn't get far.

"You there," a bald orderly called out from behind him. "Little boy."

Elijah froze a moment and then continued forward.

The voice continued. "You're not supposed to be in here."

Elijah was only a few steps from the bed when the orderly's huge hands grabbed him by the collar.

Within seconds, he was back outside the ICU with the orderly waving his finger in his face. "Children are not allowed in there. Where are your parents?"

Elijah shrugged.

The orderly grabbed him by the arm and escorted him down the hall to the reception desk. Here he spoke to an angry-looking nurse. "I caught this kid in ICU. Do you know who he belongs to?"

The nurse shook her head and eyed Elijah suspiciously. "How'd you get up here?"

Elijah turned and pointed at the elevator.

"I see," the nurse said. "He probably just wandered on and pushed a button. Call Security. They'll find his parents."

The orderly nodded. He pointed to a chair next to the desk. "Sit there!" he ordered as he reached for the phone. "We'll find your parents."

Elijah sat with a quiet sigh. He only wished that the man were right.

●

Dad looked around the corner and down the hall toward the exit.

Two burly guards stood at the front door. They didn't wear uniforms. In fact, they looked more like thugs than security guards. Both wore shoulder holsters with guns.

"Someone's coming," Mom whispered softly from behind him.

Dad pulled back, took her hand, and together they darted to the nearby stairwell. "Upstairs," he whispered.

They stole up the steps silently until they reached the second level, where Dad checked out the hall, making sure the coast was clear.

"C'mon," he said.

They stepped into the hallway and moved past a bunch of offices. The first two were lit and had people talking inside. The third was dark. He reached for the knob and gave it a try.

It opened with a quiet creak, and they stepped inside.

The office was small with only a desk, metal filing cabinet, phone, and computer. There were no windows.

Spotting the phone, Mom reached for it, but Dad stopped her. He pointed to the blinking lights on it. "Someone will see the light. Let's try the computer instead."

Mom nodded as Dad sat down in front of the computer and worked the keys. She began to pray quietly.

Moment's later the email screen popped up.

"Yeah, baby!" Dad whispered. Then turning to Mom he asked, "What do we say?"

"Write the kids first," she whispered. "Tell them we're okay. *And* tell them not to try and find us."

Dad started typing. "Got it."

"And after that ..." Mom took a breath. "After that, have them call the police."

●

In the dark room, Shadow Man stared at the photo of Elijah Dawkins. He drummed his fingers on his jet-black desk. "So young," he muttered. "And already such a threat."

Just then, a tiny green light lit up on the signal board

next to his computer. Frowning, he picked up the phone and pressed a key.

"Who isss usssing the sssystem in room 211?" he demanded.

"I don't know, sir," came the reply.

"Find out and report to me at onccce. There should be no one in that officcce."

"Yes, sir."

Shadow Man stared at the green light a moment, his suspicions growing.

"Is there anything else, sir?"

"Yesss. Kill the computer line in Room 211."

"The computer line, sir?"

"Yeesss! Shut it down, now!"

"Yes, sir."

Shadow Man slammed down the receiver and glared at the light. A moment later it went dark.

●

Elijah fidgeted in his seat.

The nurse gave him a nasty look.

He fidgeted again.

She looked at him again.

Finally, she picked up the phone, dialed, and spoke. "Hello, Security. Have you found the boy's parents yet? He's driving me nuts." She listened a moment. "Well, keep looking. Oh, and send someone up here to take him off my hands. He can wait in *your* office."

She hung up the phone and glared at Elijah.

He fidgeted.

She glared some more.

Moments later, a gray-haired orderly arrived.

"That was fast," the nurse said. "Are you here for the kid?"

The orderly nodded.

"All he does is stare at me with those huge eyes of his and fidget. Stare and fidget. Stare and fidget. He's driving me crazy."

The old man nodded again and held out his hand. Elijah smiled, slipped out of his chair, and grabbed onto the man's hand.

They headed down the hall. But instead of going to the elevator, the orderly took him directly to the children's ICU.

Elijah looked up at him and grinned wider. The old man smiled back.

Suddenly, the double doors opened, and a doctor and several nurses walked by. But for some strange reason they didn't even notice Elijah and the orderly. Then, from the opposite direction, the bald orderly also passed.

But, again, he didn't see either one of them.

The gray-haired orderly released Elijah's hand and nodded. Elijah returned the nod and entered the ICU.

He approached the third bed, the one where the little girl slept. Then, ever so gently, he reached over and touched her head.

●

"Something's wrong," Dad said. "I've lost the signal."

Mom looked alarmed. "Did you get a message out?"

"I think so . . . at least to the kids. But—"

The office door exploded open, and two big thugs entered.

"Don't move," the first ordered. "Don't touch the keyboard."

Dad nodded. "The signal's shut down anyway."

Finally, a third man came into the room—the strangest person Mom or Dad had ever seen.

He was huge, a good four hundred pounds. Somehow his head didn't quite match his body. But there was something even stranger. Even in the light, parts of the man could barely be seen. It was like he was constantly cloaked in shadow. It made no difference how directly the light shown on him; parts of his body, especially his face, could never be seen completely.

"Very clever, Mr. Dawkinsss." The man seemed to hiss more than speak. "I sssee you have sssent a message. "

Stepping closer to the computer, the man stared at what Dad had been writing.

Of course, Dad turned, trying to delete the message. The man made a horrible sound like a screaming, suffering animal. Dad was then thrown across the room as easily as if he were a rag doll.

He crashed into the filing cabinet and slid to the floor. Mom screamed and ran to him.

The man of shadows hunched over the computer. "Ssso. Sssending messagesss, are we? Perhapsss I can asssist you."

He stared hard at the computer. Then, to Mom and Dad's amazement, the keys suddenly began moving on their own.

The man read the words as they appeared on the screen:

DEAR KIDS,

DISREGARD PREVIOUS MESSAGE. NEED HELP.

BEING HELD AT COMPOUND IN MOUNTAINS.

COME FOR US. MAKE SURE ELIJAH IS WITH YOU.
DIRECTIONS ARE BELOW.

MOM AND DAD

The man turned to the couple and laughed at the look of alarm on their faces. "Don't worry. I'll give them very clear directionsss. They'll have no trouble finding usss."

•

"This is one big hospital!" Zach complained as he plopped down on the sofa in the third-floor waiting area.

"He's gotta be here," Piper said. "We both saw him."

"But where? And why is he hiding from us?"

Piper shook her head and glanced at her watch. "Oh, great, we were supposed to meet up with Cody and Willard four and a half minutes ago."

Zach snorted at her exactness.

"Well, we were," she insisted.

"Right."

"We should get them. See if they'll help us look."

Zach nodded and lumbered to his feet. "All right. I'll go. You keep looking." He started for the stairs.

"And tell them we're sorry for being late," she called.

Without turning, Zach gave a wave and continued toward the stairway.

•

Elijah slipped out of ICU and into the hall. He made his way quickly toward the elevator. Now he would find Piper and Zach. He pushed the call button, and moments later the elevator door opened. He checked the hall one last time as he backed inside.

"Can you believe this?" a man behind him said. "Right into our hands."

Elijah spun around to see the skinny man with the pointed nose ... and the woman with bright red hair.

Chapter Nine

Race for Your Life

Zach spotted Cody standing next to the RV in the garage.

"Hey," he shouted. "Elijah's running around somewhere in the hospital. We need you guys to help us find him."

"Uh ..." Cody raised his eyebrows, blinked twice, and nodded his head to the right. "We can't, uh, come right now."

"Why not?" Zach asked as he approached. "And where's Willard?"

"He's, uh ..." Cody did the same weird eyebrow raising, blinking, and nodding. "We're working on the RV."

Zach frowned. "Why do you keep blinking like that?"

"I'm not blinking," Cody said as he blinked, raised his eyebrows, and nodded to the right.

"You're blinking right now. What's the matter with you?"

"I'm—"

"What's the matter?" the big guy who had been chasing them said as he stepped out from behind the RV. In his hand he held a gun pointed at Cody.

"Why didn't you say something?" Zach asked Cody. "Or try to signal me? And what was with all the blinking and nodding?"

Cody shook his head in dismay. "That *was* me signaling you."

"Oh," Zach said, suddenly feeling anything but smart.

"So, uh, your brother's in the hospital, and your sister's looking for him?" the big man asked as he flipped open his cell phone.

"What?" Zach exclaimed. "Where'd you get that idea?"

Unfortunately, the only thing Zach was worse at than understanding blinking and nodding signals was his ability to act. And, even though the big guy wasn't the brightest candle on the cake, he saw through it in a second. He pushed a number on his cell phone. After a moment, he spoke into it.

"Yeah, it's me, Bruno," he said. "The older brother came back. His sister's looking for the kid in the—What? You got him already? Great ... Yeah, we'll, uh, wait right here."

Zach and Cody exchanged nervous looks as the big man hung up and flashed them a menacing grin.

●

Piper had gone downstairs to the lobby to meet the others when she froze. There, coming off the elevator, was the woman with the bright red hair. Next to her was the skinny assistant. And between them, holding their hands, was ...

"Elijah!" she gasped.

She ducked around the corner and watched from across the lobby. Desperately, she looked for a policeman, for any security.

There were none. Only—

She had another surprise. There, coming from the opposite direction, was the old man they had helped who had been having a heart attack. Only now he looked perfectly healthy!

He spotted her and gave a nod. But not a "hi-there, good to-see-you" nod. No, this was more like an insider's nod, the type that said, "You and I know something those others don't."

Piper stared at him, not understanding, as he continued walking ... straight toward Elijah and the two grown-ups.

When he was ten feet from them, he suddenly broke out coughing—huge, violent coughs, like he was choking. He grabbed his throat as if he couldn't breathe.

The woman and man tried to sidestep him, but he suddenly reeled as if he was going to fall. And he did. Right into the woman with red hair.

She let out a yelp and lost her grip on Elijah as she and the old man tumbled to the ground. Her assistant tried to grab the boy, but the old man went into another coughing spasm and threw himself onto the assistant.

Suddenly, Piper understood. She darted around the corner and raced at them.

"Run, Elijah," she shouted. "Run!"

Her brother looked up and grinned as Piper arrived and grabbed his hand. But as they turned for the door, she spotted something. The woman's cell phone had spilled out of her purse and onto the floor.

In one quick move Piper scooped it up, and they raced for the exit.

●

Back on the fourth floor, the little girl's parents stepped out of the conference room. They looked worn, tired, and very scared. Beside them was the doctor.

"I'll have the nurses begin prepping her for surgery right away," he said. "We'll begin in one hour."

The couple nodded sadly, and the husband did his best to support his wife.

Then, a young nurse from ICU rounded the corner.

"Nurse," the doctor said, "I want you to start prepping LeAnne Howard for surgery. We're going to—"

"But Doctor," she interrupted. "That's why I was coming to see you. LeAnne's awake. She's out of the coma!"

"What?" the doctor exclaimed.

"She seems to be fine. I know it's hard to believe, but there's absolutely nothing wrong with her!"

The doctor traded looks with the parents. Then, without a word, all four broke into a run toward the ICU.

●

Piper raced down the street toward the parking garage. She glanced over her shoulder, but neither the redhead nor her assistant had left the hospital yet. That old guy must really be keeping them busy.

Piper noticed the woman's cell phone had begun to vibrate. She looked at it in her hand and hesitated. Should she answer it?

It vibrated again.

Approaching an alley, they ducked into it and she came to a stop.

The phone vibrated again.

She stared at it. Then, with a deep breath, she opened the lid and listened.

The voice on the other end paused a moment, then asked. "Monica?"

Piper fumbled with her shirt sleeve and brought it up to the phone. In a deep voice, she answered, "Yes?"

"I'm, uh, just checkin' in," he said. "You about here?"

Using her deepest voice, she answered, "Yeah, we're on our way."

"That's, uh, real good. 'Cause I got them other three all tied up nice and neat in the RV."

Piper's mind raced. They'd found the RV! They'd tied up Zach, Cody, and Willard! Now what? Where could she go, how could she help them, and what should she say?

Fortunately, the guy on the phone saved her the trouble.

"You, uh, want me to come pick you up?"

Piper's heart skipped. "Yes!" she cried. Then, remembering to lower her voice, she repeated, "Yes, leave the others, and pick us up in the van at the front of the hospital."

"Good, and then maybe we can buy you some cough drops."

Piper frowned. "Cough drops?"

"For your voice. It sounds like you're getting a cold."

"Uh, yes," Piper said, then gave a couple coughs for good measure. "Cough drops would be nice."

"Okay. Roger, ten-four, over and, uh ... uh ..."

"Out?" Piper suggested.

"Yeah." He giggled. "And out."

Piper pushed the *End* button and leaned against the wall with a huge sigh. Reaching down for Elijah's hand, she poked her head back out of the alley to check for the redhead, and then she turned and started for the parking garage.

Thirty seconds later, she arrived at the entrance only to hear a car racing down the ramp. She pulled Elijah out of sight just as the green van sped out and screeched a hard left toward the hospital.

As soon as the coast was clear, she raced into the garage and down the ramp where they'd parked the RV.

As she came closer she thought she heard muffled sounds from inside.

Once she arrived, she opened the door and, sure enough, there were Zach, Cody, and Willard all tied together with duct tape over their mouths.

"We've got to get out of here fast," she said as she and Elijah clambered inside.

"Hmmmph! Hummmph!" Zach said.

"Hang on," Piper said as she kneeled down and tore off his duct tape.

"Ow!" Zach cried. "That hurt."

Grabbing a knife from the kitchen drawer, Piper quickly cut through his ropes. She then turned to remove Cody's tape—much more carefully.

"Thanks." Cody flashed her that heart-melting grin.

Piper nodded.

Zach was already up and heading over to start the

RV. "You guys hold on," he said. "Going up this ramp might be bumpy."

He fired up the RV, hit the gas, and they lurched forward.

"Zach!" Piper cried as she nearly fell.

But that was only the beginning. They hit the first speed bump and the RV's roof slammed hard into the ceiling, knocking the rest of the sky light off.

"*Zach!*" everyone shouted.

He slowed but paid no attention to the concrete beam hanging down in front of them ... until there was the sickening *SCREEETCH! K-THUNK!* as the RV wedged itself underneath the beam and completely stopped.

"*ZACH!*"

He gunned it, but the RV wouldn't budge.

He threw it into reverse and revved the engine.

Still nothing.

●

Finally Monica and Silas broke free of the coughing old man and raced outside the hospital ... just in time to see Bruno pulling up in the van.

"What is he doing?!" Monica cried.

"Maybe he caught the kid," Silas said.

Monica threw him a look. Somehow, she suspected that wasn't the case.

●

Back in the RV, Piper shouted, "What're we going to do? They'll be here any minute!"

"Let's all get out and push," Cody suggested.

It was as good an idea as any. Everyone but Zach piled out of the RV and lined up behind the rear bumper.

"Ready," Cody shouted. "One, two, three ... push!"

They pushed, and Zach revved the engine.

Nothing happened.

"Harder!" Zach called out the driver's window.

Again he revved, and again they pushed. But nothing seemed to work. They were stuck for good.

"Maybe we should run for it on foot!" Piper shouted.

"Five youngsters running on foot," Willard said. "I am afraid that will draw far too much attention."

"I'm open to other suggestions," Piper snapped.

Unfortunately, everybody seemed to have one ... all at the same time.

As the noise and shouting continued, Piper looked for Elijah. She spotted him kneeling at the front wheel.

"Eli!" she called. "What're you doing?"

The group came to a stop and looked.

"He's letting air out of the tire!" Cody said.

"Eli, stop that!" she shouted.

"No, no," Willard said. "That's a good thing. A little air out of each tire may lower the vehicle enough to allow the appropriate clearance."

The kids exchanged surprised looks ... and then each raced for a different tire.

●

"I didn't tell you to pick us up in front of the hospital!" Monica shouted.

"On the phone ... you, uh, said to hurry," Bruno argued. "You said you had the kid and..."

"You idiot! I don't even have my cell phone! How could—" Monica stopped in mid-sentence, suddenly realizing who *did* have her phone.

"Hurry!" she screamed. She threw open the van door and crawled inside. "Get back to the parking garage!"

Bruno frowned. "Does this mean we won't be getting you the cough drops?"

"*Hurry!*"

●

"That should do it," Zach called from the driver's window. "Now everyone get back inside!"

The group climbed back into the RV, and Cody had barely shut the door before Zach pressed his foot on the gas.

There was another crunching sound, but this time it was different—more *scraping* and less *screeching*.

The RV finally began to move, and everyone cheered. Zach picked up speed and headed for the exit.

Congratulations were given and high-fives shared until the green van bounced into view. It squealed to a stop directly in front of the exit.

"What do we do?" Piper shouted. "We're blocked!"

Zach gave no answer, but punched the gas harder.

"Zach?!"

They picked up speed ... heading directly for the van.

Piper screamed, "*Zach, what are you—*"

They plowed into the side of the van with a loud CRASH, pushing it four or five feet to the side.

Zach shifted the RV into reverse, rolled back several yards, and shifted into first. Again he hit the gas.

"*ZACH!*"

And again they hit the van—this time smashing its front side and spinning it around until it slammed into the wall. Water began spewing out of its radiator. The people inside seemed okay, but their van was definitely not going anywhere.

Everyone cheered as Zach squeezed the RV past the van, gave a wave to the red-haired woman, and bounced onto the street. He gunned it, and they took off, throwing Piper backward. She would have hit the floor had Cody not been there to catch her.

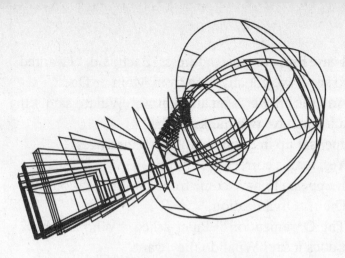

Chapter Ten

Wrapping Up

Once they were far enough away, Zach pulled into a gas station to put air back into the tires.

"I'll take care of it," Cody said as he hopped out of the side door.

Piper leaned back in her seat. It had been a long, hard day that had taken its toll on everyone. Well, everyone but Eli. He just sat there beside her, humming away like everything was peachy keen. But it wasn't, not by a long shot.

"Hey, Willard," Zach called from up front. "Any luck on that computer yet?"

"Yes, I believe so," Willard said as he stared at his handheld device.

Piper looked over to him. "What are you doing?"

"I gave him our email address," Zach said. "I wanted him to see if we got anything from Mom or Dad."

"And the answer is an affirmative," Willard said. "It appears you have two messages."

Piper sat up in excitement. "Two messages?"

"Yes, that is correct."

"It appears to have come from an organization entitled The ... Organization."

"The Organization?" Piper asked. "Who are they? What does it say? What do they want?"

"Probably just spam mail," Zach called back.

Willard snorted. "With my latest in software technology? Highly improbable."

"What do they say?" Piper asked.

"Patience, child. Patience." He took a moment, cleared his throat, and finally read the message.

DEAR KIDS.

WE ARE FINE! WE WILL CONTACT YOU SOON. DON'T TRY TO FIND US! IT'S TOO DANGEROUS. DON'T SEND ANY MESSAGES THAT REVEAL YOUR LOCATION. THEY MAY BE CHECKING OUR MAIL.

"They?" Piper asked. "Who's *they?*"

Trying to ignore the interruption, Willard again cleared his throat and continued:

WE WILL FIND YOU. WE WILL CONTACT YOU WHEN WE CAN. PLEASE TAKE CARE OF EACH OTHER. KEEP ELIJAH CLOSE. WE LOVE YOU.

MOM AND DAD

—ROMANS 8:28

Willard looked up. "What is a Romans eight, verse twenty-eight?"

"It's a Bible verse," Zach explained. "Mom and Dad always end their messages with some Bible quote. But what are they saying—that we're just supposed to go on like this?"

There was a moment of silence broken only when Cody opened the door and climbed back inside. "All set to go," he said.

"Right," Piper nodded. "But where?"

"Say what?"

Zach explained. "We can take you and Willard back home, but what are *we* supposed to do?"

"What about the other message?" Piper asked Willard. "You said there were two?"

Willard scrolled down to the second message. Once again he cleared his throat and read.

DEAR KIDS. DISREGARD PREVIOUS MESSAGE. NEED HELP. BEING HELD AT COMPOUND IN MOUNTAINS. COME FOR US. MAKE SURE ELIJAH IS WITH YOU. DIRECTIONS ARE BELOW.

MOM AND DAD

With a heavy sigh, Zach turned forward in the driver's seat, reached for the key, and started up the RV.

"What are you doing?" Piper demanded.

"Mom and Dad need our help," he called back as they pulled from the station.

Piper frowned. "Yeah, but ..."

"But what?" Cody asked.

"That second message doesn't even sound like Mom and Dad."

Willard added, "And there is no Bible reference, like you say they always include."

Silence stole over the RV.

Finally, Zach called back. "It doesn't matter who sent that second message. The point is Mom and Dad are in trouble."

Piper agreed. "And we're the only ones who can help them."

"So what are you going to do?" Cody asked.

"The only thing we can do," Piper answered. "Look for them."

"Way up in the mountains?" Willard asked.

Zach nodded. "If that's what it takes."

"There is a high probability that you may be walking into a trap," Willard warned.

"I know," Zach said. "But at least we'll know it's a trap. And like Piper says, what else we can do? We'll just have to be careful."

"Yeah," Piper nodded in thoughtful agreement. "*Very* careful."

●

Monica watched as the tow truck hooked up their van and prepared to take it to a garage for repairs. Her left eye was twitching, her right foot was tapping, and she kept swallowing. Translation: She was on the garage's phone with Shadow Man.

"You ssshall come to the compound immediately," Shadow Man hissed. "Follow the route you think they will take. They are coming here, sssearching for their parentsss. If you misss them on the road, we ssshall grab them here."

"Yes, sir," Monica replied. "There's just one thing."

"Yesss ..."

"There's this man. Twice when we came close to nabbing those brats, he appeared from nowhere and blocked us."

There was no answer, only a loud, raspy gasp.

"Sir?"

Still no answer.

"Sir, are you there?"

When the voice returned, it was a harsh whisper. "And ssso it has come to thisss."

"Excuse me?"

"The enemy . . . He is sssending reinforcementsss."

Monica gulped. "Enemy, sir?"

"SSSILENCE!" he shouted. Then more calmly, he continued. "You will sssearch for them as you make your way here. And, thisss time, you will make no more missstakesss."

"Y-yes sir. No mistakes."

"We have no room for failure. Sssoon the boy will be oursss to control or kill as we sssee fit."

Monica gulped harder.

"Sssoon. Very, very ssssssoon."

The
Enemy Closes In

For Drew Sams: A man of compassion with
a heart for youth.

For our struggle is not against flesh and blood, but against
the rulers,
against the authorities, against the powers of this dark
world and against
the spiritual forces of evil in the heavenly realms.

—Ephesians 6:12

Chapter One

The Chase Continues

The tires of the old RV squealed around the turn.

Piper flew across the motor home, slamming hard into the door. "Zach, slow down!"

Of course her big brother didn't listen. What else was new? But this time he had an excuse. Driving the RV up the winding mountain road was tricky. Especially when people were chasing them.

Especially when those people wanted to kidnap their little brother.

Especially when they had guns.

He took another corner, throwing Piper the opposite direction. "Zach!"

He grinned, pushing aside a lock of his handsome black hair—handsome if you like haircuts that look like they were trimmed by a lawn mower.

Throwing a look out the back window, Piper saw the green van closing in.

She glanced at six-year-old Elijah. He was sound asleep. Although she loved him dearly, the kid was definitely odd. He seldom, if ever talked, but he always seemed to know things no one else did.

Then there were the miracles—healing a girl in the hospital, raising a puppy from the dead. Of course they tried to keep the stuff secret, but people always found out.

Which was probably why the bad guys were after them.

Which was probably why their parents had been kidnapped and hidden in these mountains. Someone very evil was using them as bait. And Piper and Zach were the only ones who could save them.

"What if it's a trap?" Piper had asked as they started out on the journey. "What if Mom and Dad didn't send that message wanting us to rescue them?"

"Then it's a trap," Zach shrugged. "What other choice do we have?"

Of course he was right. It was just hard to remember little details like that when you were being thrown around a motor home like a human ping-pong ball.

They took another corner, faster and sharper than all the others.

"ZACH!"

●

The driver of the green van was a skinny guy by the name of Silas. He was shouting to his red-haired passenger, Monica. "Are you sure they're going to break down?"

"That's what Shadow Man said."

"Right, but—"

"Has he ever been wrong before?" she asked.

"No, but—"

"Then shut up and keep driving!" (Monica was not exactly the polite type).

A third voice called from the back. "Shadow Man— he's like my hero."

Silas and Monica rolled their eyes. They always rolled their eyes when Bruno spoke. He was a huge man with a tiny brain.

"Wanna know why?" he asked.

"Why?" Silas said.

"'Cause he brought me and Monica together."

Monica stole a look over her shoulder. As always, the man was all misty-eyed and ga-ga over her.

As always, she felt her stomach churn.

And, as always, she answered in her most pleasant screech. "Put a sock in it!"

"Yes, my sweet." He sighed dreamily. "Whatever you say."

●

The RV gave a loud *clunk*.

"Oh, no!" Piper cried "What's that?"

"I don't know." Zach pressed on the gas, but it did no good. *CLUNK! CLUNK!* They were definitely slowing down.

"There's a gas station," Piper pointed to the right. "Pull in there."

"And just wait for those creeps to grab Eli?" Zach argued.

CLUNK! CLUNK! CLUNK!

Piper glanced to her little brother, who was now wide awake and looking out the side window. Not only looking, but grinning and waving.

Piper followed his gaze to the road. No one was there.

CLUNK! CLUNK! CLUNK! CLUNK! Finally, the engine stopped.

Zach dropped the RV into neutral and coasted the rest of the way into the station.

●

"LOOK OUT!" Monica screamed.

Silas looked up just in time to see a hitchhiker standing in the middle of the road. He hit the brakes. They skidded out of control and swerved, barely missing the old man.

"WATCH IT!"

Now they slid toward the guardrail and a 200-foot drop-off.

Silas cranked the wheel hard and the tires smoked ... until they hit the rail and bounced back onto the road.

"WHAT WERE YOU DOING?!" Monica demanded.

"I'm trying to keep us alive!"

"You almost got us killed!"

"I'm not the one standing in the middle of the road!"

"The old coot!" Monica looked back over her shoulder. "He could have gotten us all—" She stopped. "Wait a minute, where did he go?"

Silas glanced into the mirror. Try as he might, he could not see the old man.

"Did we, uh, squash him?" Bruno asked.

"I don't think so." Silas started to slow.

"What are you doing now?" Monica said.

"We better go back and check."

"We're not checking anything!"

"But—"

"If he wants to get hit, that's his business. We got some brats to catch!" Monica turned back to the RV in front of them. There was only one problem.

"Where is it?" she asked.

Silas searched the road before them and saw the same thing.

Nothing.

The motor home they'd been chasing all this time was nowhere to be seen. "Where'd it go?" Bruno asked.

"I don't know." Silas frowned. "They were right in front of us a second ago."

"Well step on it!" Monica shouted. "Don't let them get away!"

●

"Did you see that?" Zach asked. He watched as the green van continued up the highway, passing them and the gas station.

"They didn't even see us!" Piper said. "They were too busy swerving and skidding."

Zach searched the road. "I wonder why."

"Maybe they were trying to miss a deer or something."

Zach shook his head. "No, there was nothing there." He glanced into the mirror to see Elijah sitting in his seat smiling back at him.

Piper spotted him too. "Looks like the little guy knows something we don't."

Zach nodded and let out a weary sigh. "So what else is new?"

●

Mom and Dad sat chained to opposite walls in the cold, dark room.

"How are you holding up?" Dad asked. His voice was hoarse and cracked from lack of water.

"I just can't stop thinking about the kids," Mom said.

He heard the worry in her voice and nodded. "We just have to ..." He swallowed back the emotion in his voice and tried again. "We just have to be strong."

Outside, there was the rattling of keys. The door creaked open, and a guard just slightly smaller than a semi truck entered the room. "Time to see the boss," he grunted as he stooped to unlock their chains.

"Please ..." Mom's voice quivered. "Not again. There's nothing we can tell him."

"It'll be all right," Dad said. But inside he didn't believe it for a second.

"I just can't face him." Mom began to cry. "The way he burrows into my thoughts with those awful eyes."

"Stop your whining." The guard hoisted each of them to their feet. "It'll be over soon enough." He pushed them into the dimly lit hall. "If you're lucky."

Chapter Two

The Plan

"I just feel like we deserted them," Cody said as they entered the cluttered garage.

"Them?" Willard said. "Or *her?*"

"Her, who?" Cody asked.

"Her, *Piper,*" Willard answered.

"What are you talking about?" They walked around another one of Willard's failed inventions:

The Nuclear Powered Dental Flosser—a giant, two-storey machine designed to automatically floss your teeth while you slept. Not a bad idea, except instead of cleaning your teeth, it sort of yanked them out.

"I see the way she looks at you," Willard teased. "Course, it's no big deal 'cause all the girls do that."

"Yeah, right," Cody scoffed.

Willard had to smile. Cody was clueless about his good looks and the effect he had on girls, which was probably why the two of them were still best friends.

"There's only one difference," Willard said.

"What's that?"

"I also see the way *you* look at *her*."

Cody glanced down embarrassed. "It's just that she ..." he caught himself and tried again. "It's just that *they* are all alone in that motor home up in the mountains."

"Not exactly." They stopped in front of another gigantic pile of junk. Willard reached in and dug out a laptop computer and a pair of night-vision goggles.

"Cool," Cody said. "You get those goggles from the Army?"

Willard shook his head. "It's another one of my inventions."

"Uh-oh ..."

"No, listen, these are way cool. Check 'em out." Willard pulled a cable from the pile and began attaching it. "These will let us watch Piper and her brothers wherever they are."

"I hope they work better than your helio-hopper."

"Why's that?"

"'Cause that almost killed us ... twice."

"No," Willard insisted. "These are perfectly safe. You just plug them in, like so ..." He finished attaching the cable to the computer and then the goggles.

"Willard, I don't think—"

"Then you put them on, like so ..." He fitted the goggles over his thick glasses. "Then you enter a cell phone number, like so ..." He typed Zach and Piper's email address into the computer.

"Willard, are you sure—"

"And then finally you turn them on, like so." He flipped a switch on the side of the goggles and waited.

Fortunately, nothing happened.

Cody gave a sigh of relief.

Unfortunately, Willard wasn't done. "Maybe there's a short." He looked to the keyboard. "Maybe ... Wait a minute! Of course! I forgot to hit Enter."

"Willard, I really don't—"

He pressed the key, and the goggles lit up like a Christmas tree. Only it wasn't just the goggles. It was also ...

"Willard!" Cody shouted.

The boy's face glowed like a nightlight. And his body shook like a bowl of Jell-O on a jackhammer.

"T-t-t-turn i-t-t-t offfff ..." he cried.

"How?" Cody yelled. "Where!?"

"D-d-d-de-leeet-e!" Willard shouted. "Hit-t-t-t D-d-de-lete!"

Cody reached over to the computer and hit the Delete key. Instantly the goggles went off and everything was back to normal.

Well, almost everything...

It seemed Willard's hair was still smoldering. Actually, it wasn't so much hair anymore. Now it was more like smoking peach fuzz.

"Are you okay!?" Cody asked.

Willard pulled off his goggles and sighed. "I hate it when that happens."

●

"Boy, you did a number to this baby." The old mechanic slammed the RV's engine compartment shut.

Zach and Piper traded nervous looks.

"How much is it going to cost?" Zach asked.

"Well, first you got your alternator. That's a hundred sixty bucks. Then you got your battery. That's gonna be—"

"Whoa, whoa, whoa." Zach held up his hand. "We don't even have the one sixty."

"Then I'd say you got yourself a problem." The mechanic wiped his hands on an oily rag and limped away. Zach and Piper ran to catch up.

"There must be something you can do," Piper said.

"I can let you use my phone to call your folks."

"I wish it was that easy," she mumbled.

The old man blew his nose into the oily rag, then checked it for results. "If I ain't fixin' it, you ain't leavin' it here," he said.

"Right." Zach looked around, trying to figure out what to do.

"Can we get back to you?" Piper asked.

The old-timer shrugged. "If you ain't got the money, you ain't got the money. 'Less you're expectin' some sorta miracle."

The word touched off an idea in Zach's mind, and he turned to Elijah. As usual, his little brother was clueless—unless you call playing with a caterpillar on a nearby tree having a clue. Still ...

Zach glanced over to the roadside diner next door. "Can we grab a bite to eat before we give you an answer?"

"Suit yourself. Just don't take too long." The mechanic blew his nose again and checked for results. This time he was more pleased.

●

Mom and Dad entered the dark office. In the shadows, a huge man sat behind his desk. They'd seen him before—felt his chilling power.

"Welcome," he hissed.

Mom shifted, trying to get a better look. But no matter how she moved, his face seemed to stay in shadow, even when light hit it.

"What do you want from us?" Dad demanded. His voice sounded strong, but Mom could tell he was terrified. Who wouldn't be?

"SSSILENCCCE!" the man shouted. "I am the one who assksss the quessstionsss." The room grew very, very still. Ever so slowly, he rose from his desk. "Where isss he?"

"You'll get nothing from us." Dad said.

"Really ...?"

Mom didn't like the man's tone. She liked it even less when he started toward them. Maybe he walked, maybe floated. She couldn't tell in the dark.

"Oh, but I will get sssomething from you," he hissed. "If not your cooperation ... then at leasst their weaknessesss."

"Their weaknesses?" Dad asked.

"Yesss." He arrived and hovered over Mom. She pulled back. "You will tell me their weaknessesss, and I will ussse them."

"What do you mean?" her voice trembled. "Use them for what?"

"Why, to dessstroy them, of courssse." His long fingers shot out and wrapped around her head. She tried to scream but could not find her voice. Suddenly, her eyes began to shudder.

"Ssshow me," he hissed. "Ssshow me your oldessst."

Before she could stop herself, thoughts of Zach raced through her mind. Memories.

First there was his weird sense of humor. She remembered the time he was in second grade and he had the entire class believing he came from the strange and mysterious planet of Whatcha-ma-call-it. He said he'd been sent as a scout to observe and report what he saw on Earth. If he reported that Earthlings were a kind and generous race (by giving him all their spare change and any cool deserts their mom packed for lunch) then his boss, the mighty warlord of Whatcha-ma-call-it, might let them live. If they didn't, well Zach couldn't promise what their fate would be.

"No," Shadow Man growled. "Ussselesss." His hands tightened around Mom's head. "Ssshow me sssomething elssse."

Another memory shot through her mind. Suddenly she recalled the time the newspaper called them on the phone.

"Hello?" she answered.

"Hi," the voice on the other end said. "This is the Los Angeles Times."

"The Los Angeles Times?" she had asked.

Of course, that was all Zach had heard. In a flash he ran up the stairs, showered, and put on his hottest clothes. He was so sure that they were going to do a front page story on him that he even combed his hair (well, as much as you could comb that type of mess).

It wasn't until he headed back downstairs that he learned the newspaper just wanted Mom to renew her subscription for another year.

"Worthlesss," the man hissed. "I need sssomething I can ussse to control him!"

He moved his hands to another part of her head and another memory flashed before her eyes. Only this time there were several images . . .

Images of Zach strolling up to pretty girls in the lunch line and introducing himself. Images of him sucking in his stomach and looking all buff when he sauntered past the girls' locker room. Images of him catching a reflection of himself in a store window and smoothing back his hair (if you could call it smoothing) before turning to a nearby girl and piling on the charm.

"Yesss," the evil voice seemed to come from inside her head. "Hisss weaknesss for girlsss. Yesss, I ssshall ussse that." Then he started to laugh. Ugly. Menacing. "Yesss ... yesss ..." His laugh grew louder and louder, filling her head until she collapsed onto the floor and heard nothing at all.

●

"So what do we do?" Piper asked. She and Elijah sat in a booth across from Zach in the diner. "I saw a Help Wanted sign in the window. Maybe I could get a job."

"You don't know how to be a waitress," Zach said.

"I could learn." Zach gave her a snicker and she gave him a look.

"What's that for?" she demanded.

"Sorry," he shrugged, "it's just that you and food, well, you're not always the best of friends."

"Meaning?"

"Remember the last time you tried to fix dinner?"

"Yeah."

"And you served us canned peas?"

Piper felt her ears growing warm. "Alright, so I over-cooked them a little."

"Not if you like chewing on bee-bees," Zach teased.

Piper ears grew a lot warm.

"Or what about that time Dad broke his tooth eating your oatmeal?"

"Okay, so it was a little lumpy."

"And remember the time everybody got sick when you fixed us hamburgers?"

"Not everybody," Piper argued. "You never got sick."

"That's because I fed mine to Molly, the wonder dog."

Piper's eyes widened. "Is that why we had to take her to the vet?"

"That's why we had to take her to the vet *that time*," Zach said. "And that's why they had to pump her stomach. *That time*."

"You're not going to bring up the other time when you fed her my mac and cheese, are you?"

"The stuff you fried in mustard and ketchup, then smothered in horseradish?" Zach shook his head. "Never."

Piper looked at him suspiciously. "Why not?"

"Because I'm a sensitive kinda guy."

She snorted and blew the hair out of her eyes. Changing the subject, she asked, "So what do you suggest? For making money, I mean?"

"I've got something right here." Zach pulled his hand from his coat pocket and produced a wadded gum wrapper and their life savings of $1.47.

"Great," Piper groaned. "That'll do us a lot of good."

But Zach wasn't listening. Instead, he turned to Elijah. "So what do you think, little guy?"

Elijah looked at the money and smiled.

Zach held it closer.

"What are you doing?" Piper asked.

"Remember back in the RV how he multiplied the burgers and fries so we had enough to eat?"

"Yeah ..."

"So, if he can multiply burgers and fries, he can multiply money."

"Zach ..."

"What?" He held the money closer. "Come on fella, do your thing."

"Isn't that kind of ... dishonest?"

"What's dishonest about it?"

At last, Elijah reached for his hand.

"There we go, that's right. Just touch it and ..."

But instead of taking the money, the boy picked up the wadded gum wrapper.

"No, no, no," Zach said, "the money ... we need *money*."

Elijah looked at him, grinned, and set the paper on the table.

"No." Zach shook the money in his hand. "*This!*"

Elijah began playing with the wrapper.

"This! Eli, we need more of THIS!"

But Elijah was too busy playing to hear.

Piper covered her mouth, trying not to laugh. Elijah looked up at her. His eyes sparkled like he understood. Maybe he did.

"Hi, there."

Piper turned to see their waitress. She was about Zach's age, with black hair, black clothes, black fingernail polish, and some major black eyeliner. She was definitely Goth, but underneath all that makeup she was probably cute. And by the way she flirted with Zach, she was definitely interested.

"Can I take your order?"

"Yeah," Zach shrugged. "I guess we'll just ... uh ..." he glanced down at his money. "We'll just split some fries."

"That's it?"

"All we have is a dollar forty-seven."

"But you're hungry, right?"

"Oh yeah, big time."

"Right." She gave him another smile and started scribbling on her pad. "That's three deluxe burgers, three sides of fries, three milkshakes, and one hot apple turnover."

"No, you don't understand. We can't afford—"

She flipped her hair to the side. "I understand perfectly. And what the boss doesn't know won't hurt him."

"What?"

"It's on the house, big guy."

Zach could only stare. Come to think of it, that's all Piper could do too.

The waitress flashed another smile. "It's the least I can do for a hottie like you." She turned and started off. "I'll be back."

Zach broke into a grin and nodded. "Right. We'll, uh, see you soon."

"Zach," Piper whispered, "we can't do that."

"Why not?" Zach said, still impressed with himself.

"Because she's ripping off the restaurant to feed us."

"Oh well." He shrugged.

"Oh well? That's all you can say?"

"Hey, it's not my fault I'm such a hottie."

Piper rolled her eyes and groaned.

"Hey, it beats green peas, oatmeal, or mac and cheese."

She gave him a slug in the arm.

"Ow."

And then another in the other arm.

"What's that for?" he complained.

"In case I'm not around the next time you're mean."

Chapter Three

A New Friend

"Faster!" Monica yelled. "Faster!"

"Uh, guys?" Bruno called from the backseat.

"I don't understand," Silas said. "The brats were right in front of us!"

"Guys?"

"It's your fault they got away!" Monica yelled. "If Shadow Man finds out, it's your neck, not mine!"

"Guys!?"

They both turned and shouted in unison. *"WHAT!?"*

"That hitchhiker back there ... Wasn't he the same homeless guy we saw back in Los Angeles?"

"Bruno," Silas sighed, "that was a hundred miles ago."

"Yeah ..."

"And I've been driving eighty miles an hour the whole time."

"Yeah ..."

"So there's no way somebody's going to walk faster than I'm driving!"

"Oh, yeah," Bruno giggled. "I get it."

"Good," Silas muttered. "I'm glad."

"Except ..."

Silas tried to ignore him. He would have succeeded if Bruno hadn't drilled his finger into his back.

"Excuse me ... Excuse me?"

"What is it, Bruno?"

"What if he was, like, magical or something?"

"There is no magic."

"Right ... but what if he was, like, an angel."

"Bruno ..."

"Yeah, Silas?"

"Don't be stupid."

"You know I can't help it," said Bruno.

"I know." Silas shook his head. "Believe me, I know."

●

"Sure you don't need some more fries?" The waitress asked. "Maybe some onion rings?"

"No," Zach said, pushing back the remains of his third hamburger. "I'm stuffed."

"A big guy like you needs his nourishment," she said.

The line was so corny, Piper had to look away. Unfortunately, there were more coming.

"You work out, don't you?"

Zach gave a little flex. "You can tell?"

Piper couldn't help snickering. "The only time he works out is when he's reaching for the remote."

Zach shot her a glare.

The waitress laughed. "My name is Ashley. You guys just passing through?"

"Our RV broke down, and we don't have the money to fix it," Zach said. "Unless you know a mechanic who'll work for a dollar forty-seven." Zach chuckled at his little joke, and Ashley laughed like it was the funniest thing she'd ever heard.

Piper glanced away, thinking she might get sick ... and it had nothing to do with the food. That's when she saw the tears in Elijah's eyes. The kid was looking directly at Ashley and getting all misty.

"Hey, little buddy," Piper asked, "you okay?"

Elijah didn't hear. Instead, he slowly reached out and touched Ashley's arm.

"Whoa!" The girl stepped back. "What's with him?"

"He's our little brother," Zach said. "He doesn't mean anything."

"Yeah, well I'm really not into being touched. Kinda creeps me out."

"Really?"

"Long story." Ashley raked her hands through her hair and turned to Piper. "Listen, if you need some cash, why not work here a couple days? I could use a day off, and we really need the help."

"You think they'd hire me?" Piper asked.

"They're so desperate, they'd hire anybody."

Piper nodded and then stopped, not exactly sure it was a compliment.

Ashley motioned to the back. "Go talk to Stan. He's the owner and cook."

"What?" Piper asked. "*Now?*"

"Sure. We're closing up soon. Now's the perfect time."

Piper looked to Zach. "What do you think?"

But Zach was so busy staring at Ashley, he wasn't thinking of anything.

"Zach!"

"What? Oh yeah, sounds good to me."

Piper hesitated. "I really don't—"

"Go ahead," Ashley said. "It'll only take a minute. And while you're doing that," she turned to Zach, "you can walk me home."

"Really?" His voice squeaked like a rusty hinge.

"Well, it's not really home. But it's where we all stay."

"We?" Piper asked.

"Another long story. It's just a few hundred yards from here."

As she spoke, Elijah quietly slipped off the bench and started toward the back door.

"Elijah," Zach called. "Where you going? That's the wrong door!" Elijah didn't turn but arrived at the back door and opened it, patiently waiting.

Ashley chuckled. "Well, I guess you're *both* taking me home."

"Why's that?" Zach asked.

"That's the way to my place." She shrugged. "Strange kid. I wonder how he knew."

Piper and Zach exchanged looks and then answered in unison. "Long story."

●

"Well, that didn't work out so well," Cody said as he finished brushing the ashes off Willard's bald head.

Willard nodded. "Good thing that was only Plan B."

"Plan B?"

"Yup."

Cody swallowed nervously. "Is there a Plan A?"

Willard smiled an even geekier smile, which always meant trouble. "Knowing where they are isn't going to be all that helpful."

"It isn't?"

"Not really."

Cody wasn't thrilled to ask, but he had little choice. "What *would* be helpful?

Wilbur cranked up his smile to super geek. He motioned for Cody to follow. "I was afraid you were never going to ask."

Cody gave a quiet groan. "And I was afraid I would."

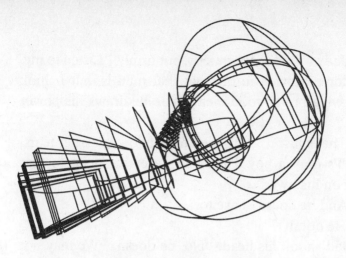

Chapter Four

Real Power

Mom sat on the cell floor with her head on her knees. "I've betrayed him," she softly wept.

Dad called over to her, "Sweetheart ..."

"Our own son. And I've betrayed him." She sniffed. "I don't know who or what that thing is, but I told him."

"You did the best you could."

Somehow his words only made the tears come faster. "I let him read my mind." She looked up, her eyes red and swollen. "I let him know Zach's weaknesses."

At that moment Dad would have given anything to break the chains holding him to the wall, not to be free, but just to reach out and hold her.

She buried her face back into her knees. "I'm sorry, Zach ... I'm so sorry."

"Judy." Dad spoke quietly, but firmly. "Listen to me. We don't know who or what that man is, but I think we have a pretty good idea where he draws his power from."

"That's just it." She tried to swallow back her tears. "Zach's only a boy. He could never stand up to that thing on his own."

"And he doesn't have to."

"He doesn't?"

Dad shook his head. "No, he doesn't. We may not be there to help him, at least physically. But there's another way ... and it's more powerful than any other."

"You mean ... are you talking about prayer?"

"That's where the real battles are won or lost. That's where the real power lies."

"But ... he's just a teenager."

Dad nodded. "And so was David when he beat Goliath. And Mary. And some of the disciples."

Mom sniffed and slowly started to nod. "Then we'd better get to work."

"I hear that," Dad said. "And in Zach's case, the sooner the better."

Mom gave a quiet chuckle, which warmed Dad's heart. Then, all alone on the hard stone floor, husband and wife bowed their heads and started to pray.

●

Elijah clung to Zach's hand as they followed Ashley up the wooded trail. The little guy wasn't scared, but something was definitely going on in his head.

"Jason's place is right there." Ashley motioned to a broken-down house in definite need of a paint job.

"Who's Jason?" Zach asked.

"He's this real cool guy who lets a bunch of us stay with him."

"Where are your parents?"

"My stepdad's a junkie who beats me, and my mom's an alcoholic who doesn't care."

"So you ran away?"

Ashley shrugged. "Wouldn't you?"

"I'm . . . sorry."

"No biggie," Ashley said. "If I hadn't left them, I'd never have met Jason."

Elijah tugged on Zach's hand. Zach glanced down and saw him motioning for them to head back to the restaurant. But if it came down to spending time with Elijah or Ashley . . . well, let's just say there wasn't much competition.

Turning back to Ashley, he asked, "Who exactly is this Jason?"

"Our spiritual advisor."

"Spiritual advisor? You mean like a pastor?"

Ashley broke out laughing. "No way."

"What's so funny? We've got a cool pastor at home."

"Yeah, I'm sure. But Jason, he knows the deeper mysteries, like contacting spirits — that sort of stuff."

Zach tensed. More than once his folks had warned them about fooling around with those types of things. He knew he should probably say something, but Ashley was so beautiful.

Elijah tugged harder. Again, Zach ignored him.

At last they reached the porch steps leading to her door.

"Well, here we are." Ashley turned to face Zach just as Elijah yanked on his arm with all of his might.

"What's with him?" she asked.

Zach acted like he hadn't noticed. "Who?"

"Him?"

Again he tried ignoring Elijah, but it's hard to ignore someone when he's yanking your arm out of its socket.

"Is he okay?"

"Oh, yeah," Zach said as casually as possible. "Probably just has to go to the bathroom or something."

Elijah continued yanking and tugging and pulling.

"He looks kinda desperate."

"Yeah, probably," Zach said.

Elijah tucked his legs up and completely hung from Zach's arm.

"There's a restroom back at the restaurant," Ashley said. "I'd hurry and get him there if I were you."

Zach nodded, feeling very much like a human monkey bar.

"So . . ." she turned and headed up the steps. "I guess I'll see you tomorrow."

Zach nodded.

Elijah began swinging back and forth on his arm, like it was a trapeze.

Ashley gave one last smile, mostly out of sympathy. "Good-night."

"Good-night," Zach answered, still pretending nothing was out of the ordinary.

She opened the door, stepped inside, and quietly closed it behind her.

As soon as it shut, Elijah dropped back to the ground, acting perfectly normal. Zach looked down at him and glared.

Elijah looked up at him and grinned.

Then, without a word, but maybe a little giggle, Elijah turned and skipped back toward the restaurant.

Zach shook his head and started to follow. "I tell you, you're one strange dude, dude."

Cody and Willard rounded another pile of junk and came face-to-face with an old-fashioned telephone booth.

"Here we go," Willard said proudly.

"Here we go, what?" Cody asked.

"Here is the solution to all of our problems."

Cody was afraid to ask, but knew he had no choice. "How will this solve all our problems?"

"Instead of just viewing Piper and her brothers, this will actually send us to visit them. It's my new and improved teleporter machine."

Cody simply stared at him.

"What?" Willard asked.

"Sounds like you've been watching too many Star Trek reruns."

"No, seriously," Willard said. "You just step inside and punch in Piper's email address."

"And then?"

"And then it will send you to wherever she is."

"Willard?"

"Yes, Cody?"

"Are you taking your medication?"

"Laugh all you want, but there's only one way to find out if it works."

"And that is ..."

"Step inside and try it out."

Cody turned to Willard and gave him one of his world-famous *are-you-crazy-or-am-I-just-having-a-nightmare* looks.

Unfortunately, it was no nightmare. Instead, it was much worse.

Chapter Five

A New Day

The next morning, after sleeping in the RV, Piper started work in the restaurant. Not only did she not know what she was doing, but she didn't know enough about what she was doing to know she didn't know what she was doing.

Translation: The girl was in trouble.

"Miss!" some fat guy shouted at her for the hundredth time. "I wanted these eggs scrambled!"

Actually, he was lucky to get eggs at all. The first time she had brought him pancakes, the second time three jars of mustard.

"I'm sorry, sir, I'll be right with—"

"Where's my syrup?" an old lady demanded from the next table over.

"And my creamer!" her husband shouted.

"Sorry, I—"

"It's been twenty minutes since I ordered my coffee!" a skinny guy behind them whined.

"Sorry!" She raced to the coffee pot, grabbed it, and headed toward him.

"What about these eggs?"

"I'll be right there." She arrived at the skinny guy's table just in time to hear a familiar voice.

"Hey, Pipe."

She spun around and bumped into Zach and Elijah, sloshing a little of the coffee onto the floor. "Where have you two been?" she asked.

"Lady!" the guy beside her complained. "You spilled coffee on the floor."

"Yes, I know. I'll clean it—"

Zach gave a lazy stretch and answered her question. "I thought we'd sleep in."

"Sleep in?" Piper couldn't believe her ears. "It's—" she turned her wrist to check her watch. Unfortunately, it was the wrist that was connected to the hand that was holding the coffee pot, which explains why the scalding liquid dumped all over the skinny guy's lap.

"Aughhh …" He jumped up. "Look what you've done! Look what you've done!" He turned and raced for the restroom.

"Sorry!" Piper called after him.

"Where's my syrup?" the old lady shouted.

"Listen," Zach said, "I see you're kinda busy. I'm just going to leave Elijah here and go visit Ashley."

"Zach!" Piper demanded.

"Where's my creamer?"

"Relax," Zach told his sister. "He's got his Bible. You know how he likes lookin' at the pictures and stuff."

"Miss, I want these eggs scrambled!"

Piper turned to her customers, then back to Zach, who was already heading out the door.

"Zach!"

"Could I please have my syrup?"

"Where's my creamer?"

"Sorry." Piper raced back to the counter and grabbed the syrup and creamer. She joined the old couple and apologized as she poured the containers for them. A nice idea ... except the old lady's pancakes were suddenly covered in creamer, while her husband's coffee swam in syrup.

"What are you doing?!" they cried in unison.

Piper was so startled that she leaped back and slipped on the coffee spill ... which sent her sliding across the floor ...

"Miss, I want these eggs—"

... and landing on the fat man's table, her elbows jabbed in his plate, squirting the yolks from his eggs onto his shirt while she dumped the rest of the creamer and syrup on him.

"My shirt!" he screamed. "Look at my shirt!"

Piper could only stare at his shirt in horror, while at the same time thinking, *Well, at least your eggs are scrambled.*

●

On her best days, Monica Specter was not a happy camper. On her worst days, she was a major terror. And on her worst days without sleep? Don't ask. Let's just say she wouldn't be winning any Miss Congeniality contests.

No one's sure what made her so ill-tempered.

Some say it was growing up as the only girl with six brothers. In most families that would make her a little princess—the sweet, darling girl everybody loved and treated with gentle tenderness.

In Monica's family that meant she was the human guinea pig.

If her brothers wanted to know what would happened if you shoved a hundred fire crackers into the soles of somebody's tennis shoes and lit them, Monica would be the one to find out.

If they wanted to know if an umbrella really worked as a parachute when you jumped off the roof, Monica would provide the answer.

And if they wanted to know what would happen if you stuffed a little girl into an inner tube and rolled her off a 2,000 foot cliff ... well, you probably get the picture.

By the time Monica was seven, she learned how to protect herself from any bully.

By the time she was thirteen, the bullies learned how to run for their lives to protect themselves from her.

It's not that she was mean. She was just ... well, all right. She *was* mean.

Real mean.

At the moment she was proving that meanness by screaming at Silas, their driver. "Turn back! We've missed them! Turn back!"

"What makes you so sure?" Silas said. It had been a while since he'd gotten any sleep and he'd been busy just trying to keep his eyes open.

"The brats were supposed to be rescuing their parents in the mountains!"

"Right."

"So look around you!"

Silas opened his eyes wider. He'd been so tired he hadn't paid much attention to anything the past several hours.

"What do you see?" Monica demanded.

"I know, I know!" Bruno cried eagerly from the back.

"Yes," Monica sighed wearily. "What does Bruno the Brainless see?"

"Sand!" Bruno shouted triumphantly. "Miles and miles of sand."

"Very good. And where do we find miles and miles of sand?"

"Uh ... um ... "

"Come on, Bruno, think. I know it's a new concept, but give it a try."

"I've got it!"

"Yes ..."

"A litter box for giant kitties?"

Monica dropped her head and covered her eyes.

"We're in the desert," Silas said. "We passed over the mountains, and now we're in the desert."

"And what do you suggest we do now?" Monica asked.

"Buy sunscreen!" Bruno exclaimed.

Monica gave a quiet groan.

But Silas knew exactly what to do. Before Monica could blow a major blood vessel, he brought the van to a stop, turned around, and headed back up into the mountains.

●

Zach leaned against the back wall with Ashley. The room was dark except for the single candle that lit a table where three teen boys sat. They were dressed pretty much the same as Ashley—all black with plenty of tattoos and body piercings.

Earlier, Ashley had introduced Zach to them. The skinniest one they called X-Ray. The short one was Stump. And the big one with red hair was called—what else?—Big Red. They seemed nice enough but, unlike Ashley, they were way too cool to smile.

They had set up a board game—something called a Ouija Board—and had just started to play.

"What's it supposed to do?" Zach asked.

"It helps them contact the dead," Ashley whispered.

A chill crept over Zach's body. "The dead?"

"Pretty cool, huh?"

Zach swallowed but did not answer.

"What's wrong?"

"It's just that, well, doesn't the Bible say not to mess with that stuff?"

"Does it?" Ashley asked.

Zach tried to nod, but he wasn't sure he pulled it off.

Ashley moved closer and whispered into his ear. "Why do you suppose it says that?" Her presence felt good, and for the moment Zach couldn't think of an answer. Unfortunately, somebody else did.

"Because the Bible is an outdated book of superstitions." The voice was so close that Zach jumped. He turned to see a skinny, black-haired guy in his thirties standing beside him. Every square inch of his arms and neck were covered in tattoos.

"Oh, hi, Jason." Ashley leaned past Zach and smiled. "I wondered where you were."

"I see you brought a friend," the man said.

"Yeah," Ashley answered. "Zach, this is our spiritual leader, Jason. And Jason, this is my friend—"

"Zachary," the man spoke slow and soft. "Yes, the

driver of the RV. The one helping his younger sister and brother."

If Zach had felt a chill before, he was downright freezing now. "How," he cleared his throat, "how did you know that?"

"Oh, there's a great deal I know about you Zach. A great, great deal."

Chapter Six

Darkness Closes In

Zach tried his best to stay cool. It would have helped if his heart wasn't pounding a thousand times a second and if he wasn't breathing like he'd just sprinted a dozen miles.

"You don't mind, do you?" Jason asked. "My sensing those things about you?"

Ashley giggled, "I told you he knows stuff."

"But . . . how?" Zach managed to croak.

Jason chuckled. "I just talked to Gus, the garage mechanic."

Zach relaxed, but only slightly.

"But you could have learned it other ways too," Ashley said.

"Oh, yes, I'm frequently in contact with the spirit world," Jason said.

"And that's what he's teaching us," Ashley explained.

"Teaching you?" Zach asked.

Jason merely smiled. "Can I get you guys a beer?"

"Uh, no thanks," Ashley said.

Zach cleared his throat. "None for me."

"Are you sure?"

Zach couldn't tell if Jason was sneering at him or just smiling. "No, I'm good."

"Suit yourself." Jason disappeared into the darkness as Ashley gave another giggle. "Isn't he cool?"

Before Zach could answer, Big Red asked from his seat at the table, "Why isn't it moving?"

"Yeah," Stump complained, "it's never taken this long before."

Zach turned back to Ashley. "What's supposed to happen?"

"Usually that plastic thing they have their hands on starts to move."

"Move?"

"Yeah. See those letters on the board? The spirits move the plastic thing to spell out messages from the dead."

Zach gave a nervous snicker, but Ashley was serious. He glanced around the room, feeling more and more like this was a place he didn't belong.

Jason appeared at their side, sipping a beer.

No, he definitely didn't belong.

"Hey, Jason," Big Red called from the table. "How come it ain't moving?"

"Yeah," Stump said. "It's almost like something's stopping it."

"Might be a negative force," Jason said.

"A negative force?" Stump asked.

"Yes, someone who is not open to our powers. Someone afraid to give in to the dark forces."

Zach fidgeted.

Jason continued. "Not only afraid, but actually fighting it. Fighting the darkness."

"Who would do that?" the skinny kid asked.

"Oh, I don't know." Jason turned toward Zach. "Maybe our guest has a clue?"

Zach swallowed. "About what?"

"About who might be stopping our powers? About who in this room is opposed to the powers of darkness?"

By now all eyes were on Zach. And they were not happy eyes.

Again, Zach tried to swallow, but his mouth was bone dry. "Listen," he coughed. "I'd better be going. It's getting late." He looked at his watch. It would have been more convincing if he actually wore one, but it seemed a small detail.

"Yes," Jason spoke so softly that it almost sounded like a threat. "I think that would be a fine idea. A very fine idea indeed."

●

Cody watched as Willard grabbed the cord from the back of the telephone booth and looked for an outlet.

"Uh, listen, Willard. I don't want to be a spoilsport, but the last time we tried one of your inventions it almost made me a permanent part of the street pavement."

"Right," Willard said as he pushed aside some old TV sets, a bunch of ancient computers, and piles of electrical junk. "That's the price one pays for being a genius."

"Actually, that's the price *I* pay for you being a genius," Cody said.

"Don't tell me the great Cody is scared," Willard teased.

"Scared?" Cody asked. "No way. Terrified? You bet. Horrified? Absolutely. Wondering if I should ask my mom and dad to take out a life insurance policy on me? Most likely. But definitely not scared."

"Relax," Willard chuckled. "This will be a piece of cake."

"I'm just saying I'm not crazy about having my body sent through the Internet."

"Ah, here we go." Willard found the outlet and plugged in the cord. Immediately the garage lights dimmed as the phone booth lit up.

Cody continued. "All I'm saying is that maybe we should run a few tests first."

"No problem."

"Really?"

"Sure. Just stand over there at my laptop, and I'll send something to you."

"Like what?"

Willard thought a moment before turning and starting out of the garage.

"Where you going?" Cody shouted.

"I'm going into the garden to grab one of my mom's tomatoes. Turn my laptop back on."

Cody nodded and strolled over to Willard's combination laptop/hair remover. Moments later, Willard returned and placed a tomato on the floor of the phone booth.

"Now turn the speakers up nice and loud," Willard said confidently.

Cody reached over to the laptop and turned the volume up to high.

"You ready?" Willard called.

Cody looked at the laptop, took a step back just to be safe, and shouted, "Ready!"

Willard punched a series of buttons on the phone, quickly stepped out of the booth, and shut the door. "Stand by!"

The booth started shaking. Then rattling. Then it started to make strange sounds:

GIRRR-GIRRR-GIRRR

like a coffee grinder gone berserk. Then it started another sound:

DING-DING-DING-DING

like a railroad crossing on too much caffeine. And, finally, it began the ever-popular sound of a:

KERUGACHA-KERUGACHA-KERUGACHA

cement mixer stuck on high.

All of this as the light inside grew brighter and brighter. Suddenly there were more sparks than the Fourth of July and:

POP!

it was all over. (Well, except for the cloud of smoke).

And, there, in front of the computer and speakers, sat a lovely, ripe tomato.

Well, sort of.

The good news was the tomato had transported across the Internet. The bad news: it had transported into a pile of steaming ketchup.

"Uh, Willard?"

The pudgy inventor raced toward him in excitement. "How'd we do?"

"You might want to make a couple adjustments."

Ashley tried to follow Zach outside, but Jason blocked her. "I'd like to see you in my office for a moment."

"I should really check on Zach and—"

"This *is* about Zachary."

Ashley looked up into his coal-black eyes. The man was deadly serious. And when he got that way, she knew it was best not to argue. She'd seen the way he'd humiliated other kids who gave him trouble. Sometimes he made fun of them in front of the entire group. Sometimes he gave them the worst jobs, like cleaning the toilet. And sometimes he completely ignored them like they weren't even there—for days or even weeks.

Without a word, the two of them walked toward his office and entered.

Since Jason liked darkness, there were no lights in the room, and the drapes were drawn to keep out the sun. He pulled up a chair at the end of a long table and sat. "So ... tell me *all* you know about Zachary."

Ashley shrugged. "There really isn't much to tell. He's a nice guy, and he's got a sister and a strange little brother."

"Yes," Jason nodded and lit up a cigarette. "The brother. Tell me about the brother."

"I can't really explain it. It's like there's something different about him. Like he's really simple but at the same time he seems to know stuff."

Jason remained sitting in the dark for a long moment. Only the glow of the cigarette illuminated his face. Finally, he spoke.

"I think it is time to elevate you, my dear."

"Elevate me?" she asked.

"The spirits have confirmed to me that you are very special."

"Me?" Ashley's heart began to race. Wasn't that the whole reason she'd been attracted to Jason and his group in the first place? No one else accepted her, but his group did. Not only accepted her, but there was always the hint that she just might have special powers.

And now ... wasn't that exactly what Jason was saying?

"Yes," he whispered. "Very, very special."

"But how—" She could barely find her voice. "How so?"

"You have the ability to draw people ... to lead them to us for enlightenment."

"Like who? I don't know anybody."

"You know Zachary. He is special, don't you agree?"

Ashley nodded, almost smiling. He *was* special ... at least to her.

Jason continued, "He will draw other special people— like his sister and, most importantly, his little brother."

Ashley continued to stare at the glowing cigarette.

"Tell him he is invited to our séance this afternoon."

"But, you saw how freaked he was with the—"

"Yes ... and I'm afraid I didn't help. Please apologize to him for me. And tell him I am specifically holding the event in his honor."

"And if he still doesn't want to come?"

"You'll see to it that he does."

"But I don't want to pressure him. I mean, if he feels uneasy, maybe—"

Jason pounded the table. "You'll see to it that he does!"

The outburst shocked Ashley. She wasn't sure what to do. But Jason's voice quickly softened, becoming as quiet and mysterious as it always was. "That is your destiny, my dear. Your high calling. That is why you have been chosen."

Almost against her will, Ashley felt herself beginning to nod. Part of it was the excitement of being so special. Part of it was fear of what would happen if she disobeyed.

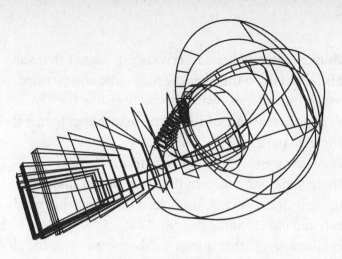

Chapter Seven

A Strange Customer

It had been a long, tiring morning as Silas retraced their route back up the mountain road. They stopped at every turnout and rest stop along the way. The kids' RV had to be somewhere.

It wasn't any easier with Bruno the Belching Machine sitting in the back. Apparently he'd eaten something that didn't agree with him. Silas couldn't imagine what. It was just the usual five double cheeseburgers, four greasy tacos, a couple sides of onion rings, three apple turnovers, and one supersized soda.

And if all his burping and belching wasn't enough, there was the little call Monica got from Shadow Man.

"You lossst them, didn't you?" he hissed through her cell phone.

Monica's face twitched nervously. It wasn't that she was afraid to talk to the Shadow Man. She was terrified. Come to think of it, so was everybody else in the van. It wasn't the *shadow* part of his name that scared them. It was the *man* part.

They just weren't sure if it was true.

There were parts of him that were like a man. You could see him and everything. And there was his need to sleep and eat ... and eat ... and eat.

But there were other things ... like the way you could never quite see his face. The way he always seemed to be in shadow, even on sunny days.

And there was something else ...

The way he always knew what others were thinking. Or what they were feeling. Sometimes, even from a great distance, he knew what they were doing. Definitely weird. In fact, on the Freaky Scale of one to ten, he was definitely an eleven. Someone whose good side you wanted to stay on. If such a thing was ever possible.

"The bratsss are at a truck sssstop," he hissed. "I sssee a garage and diner."

Monica swallowed. "Sir, are you sure? Because, we've been—"

"Sssilenccce!"

Monica closed her mouth.

"You will find the little boy, and you will bring him to me!"

"What about the others—the brother and sister?"

"They are of no interessst. Disssspossse of them as you sssee fit."

"Yes, sir." Monica waited until the man hung up and then, with shaking hands, closed her phone.

"What did he say?" Silas asked.

"What do you think he said?" she snapped. Talking

to the Shadow Man always put her a little on edge. "Find them!"

Another hour had passed before Silas slowed the van.

"Why are we stopping?" Monica demanded.

"We're coming up to where we first lost them."

"How can you tell?"

Silas pointed ahead. "There's the railing we bounced off of when I almost hit that guy."

"Let me see!" Bruno leaned forward from the seat behind them. Unfortunately he leaned just a little too far, just a little too fast, considering how queasy his stomach was. Which would explain his sudden ...

BLAAHH!

as he threw up all over Silas and Monica.

Of course Monica did her usual screeching and name-calling. Silas, on the other hand, was too busy jerking away and yanking the steering wheel. No problem, except that he threw the van completely out of control. So, just like old times, the vehicle skidded and the tires squealed.

"Look out!" Monica shouted.

"I got it!" Silas yelled.

BLAAAAHHHH!

Bruno threw up again.

They slammed into the exact same railing as before. For a moment it looked like they were going over the cliff, but Silas fought the wheel and, after a few more skids, squeals, and screechings from Monica, he regained control.

The good news was they had once again missed seeing the garage and the diner.

The bad news was, Bruno still had a little food left in his—

BLAAAAAAHHHHHH!
Never mind, it's gone now.

•

If Piper thought the breakfast folks were demanding, they were nothing compared to the lunch crowd. The place was packed with twice as many customers, who were twice as rude.

"Where's Ashley?" Piper called to Stan, her boss. He was cooking at the grill. "When does she come in?"

"Not till tomorrow."

"Tomorrow!? You mean I'm all by myself?"

"Don't worry, kid." He set out three more hamburger platters for her. "You're doing great."

Piper grabbed the platters and turned. Unfortunately they were hot, and one slipped from her hands. It crashed to the floor, sending hamburger, fries, and ketchup in all directions. Of course, everyone stopped and stared. And, of course, Piper felt her ears turning their usual beet red.

Stooping down to clean the mess, she muttered, "This is obviously a new definition of 'doing great.'"

When she rose, she saw that a gray-haired gentleman had entered and was sitting next to Elijah. He was pointing something out in the Bible, and Elijah was nodding, eagerly listening.

Feeling a surge of panic, Piper made a beeline past the other customers to her brother's table. When she arrived she asked, none too politely, "May I help you?"

The man looked up, and Piper caught her breath. "Aren't you ... aren't you the guy who had the heart attack in Pasadena?"

The man smiled kindly. "Lots of folks mistake me for other people."

"Yes, but—"

"I guess I just have one of those faces."

Piper frowned, not entirely convinced. She wasn't sure how to ask the man to leave her brother alone, especially since Elijah was so excited over what they were studying. So she tried another approach. "Can I get you something?"

"No, thank you." He pointed to the cherry pie and cup of coffee in front of him. "This should do me."

Piper's frown deepened. "But I ... I didn't wait on you."

The man's grin broadened. "Maybe you just don't remember."

"No, I—"

"Actually, I think you're a lot better waitress than you give yourself credit for."

"Yeah, right." She rolled her eyes and turned to the customers behind her. "Tell that to all these—"

She came to a stop. To her amazement, every customer had their food. Not only that, but they were all perfectly content.

Her mouth dropped open as she slowly turned to the man.

But he was back in the book studying with Elijah.

"How ... how ..."

He looked up. "I see your little brother likes to read the Bible."

"Yes," she answered numbly. "He likes Revelation."

"Especially Revelation 11," the old man acknowledged.

"Revelation 11?"

"The passage about the two prophets."

Piper scowled, trying to remember. "You mean the two guys that come out of heaven?"

"Not exactly," he corrected.

"What do you mean?" Piper asked.

"I mean prophets usually start off as little boys, don't they?"

"Miss," a customer called out politely.

Reluctantly, Piper turned to a young mother.

"May I have a refill on my iced tea? When you have the time, I mean?"

"Oh, sure." Piper turned back to the gentleman. "I, uh, have to get back to work."

"Certainly," he smiled.

Her mind spinning, Piper headed over to the iced tea pitcher. She heard the little bell above the door ring and turned to see Zach enter. He looked a little tired and a lot pale. She picked up the pitcher and moved to refill the young mother's glass.

"Thanks," the woman said.

Piper nodded and looked back to Elijah's table just as Zach sat down beside him.

The gray-haired gentleman was nowhere to be found.

●

Dad turned to Mom in the dark cell. They'd been praying off and on throughout the night and on into the morning. It was harder work than either had expected.

"How are you doing, sweetheart?" he asked.

"Fine," she said. "It's just—"

"Just what?"

"I feel like all I'm doing is asking for the same thing over and over again—for the children's protection, for their safety, that we get out of here and help them."

Dad nodded. "I know what you mean."

"It seems like there should be more."

"More?"

"More than just asking the same thing over and over again."

Dad thought a moment then answered. "Maybe there is."

"What do you mean?"

"Instead of just asking ... maybe we should also be worshipping."

"What, *here? Now?*"

"God's still in control, right? Whatever happens, he still deserves our love."

"Right."

"So maybe part of our prayers should also be worship."

"Like a song or something?

"I know it sounds crazy, especially in a place like this, but ..." He dropped off, feeling a little embarrassed. But when he turned to Mom, he saw she was starting to nod.

"Maybe ... maybe you have a point."

He shrugged. "I mean, that's what they did in the Bible, remember? Even when they were thrown in jail, they sang songs to God."

"I'd almost forgotten."

There was a long moment's silence. Then, in the dark, Mom started to hum.

Dad recognized the tune immediately. It was one of his wife's favorites. He smiled as the humming turned into words:

Amazing grace, how sweet the sound
That saved a wretch like me ...

Eventually he joined in.

I once was lost, but now I'm found,
Was blind but now I see.

Together, their voices grew louder and louder. And, although they were tired and exhausted, they soon filled the room with their singing.

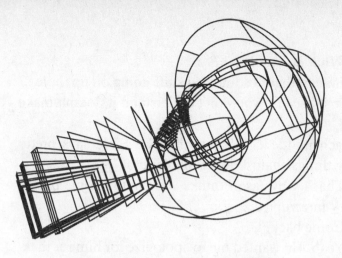

Chapter Eight

Conflicts Grow

"Zach . . ."

Zach looked up as Ashley approached their table. "Can I talk to you a moment?"

"Oh, hi. Sure." He noticed Elijah reaching out to her. So did Ashley.

"Outside?" she said. "Alone?"

Zach nodded and stood. "I'll be right back, little buddy."

Elijah nodded and watched as Zach followed Ashley to the door.

Once they were outside in the afternoon sun, she turned to Zach. "Look, I'm really sorry about what happened back at the house."

"No, that's okay." He shrugged. "It was my fault. I should never have gone in the first place."

"What do you mean?"

"I mean there's some bad stuff going on up there."

"Just because you don't understand it doesn't make it bad."

Zach nodded. "It's just that the Bible says pretty strong things against doing that kind of —"

"That's why Jason thinks you should come back," Ashley interrupted.

"Come back?"

"Yeah. He wanted me to apologize for him for making you feel so bad."

"He said that?"

"He thinks you're real special and that you deserve to be treated a lot better."

Zach arched an eyebrow. Maybe this Jason wasn't such a bad guy, after all.

Ashley took a step closer. "He wanted you to better understand what we're about."

Zach frowned.

"I mean," she moved closer, "how do you know something's wrong, if you don't really know what it is?" She looked up at him with those big, beautiful eyes.

He swallowed.

"You know," she reached out and took his hand. "He thinks you and me ... he thinks we both have potential."

Zach's voice cracked. "Potential?"

She smiled and nodded. "He's going to do something special in your honor, and all he wants is for you to come back so he can show you." She glanced down and then looked back up with those incredible eyes. "That's all I want too."

"Well ..." Zach cleared his throat. Most of him knew that he shouldn't. But there was another part that figured it wouldn't hurt. Besides, like she said, how could he know something was wrong if he really didn't understand it? He cleared his throat again. "We'll, uh, we'll see."

"Great!" She rose up on her toes and gave him a peck on the cheek. "We'll see you at five o'clock."

Before he could answer she had turned and started up the hill.

"Ashley ..."

She turned and flashed him that killer smile. "Don't be late."

Zach wanted to say something, to tell her not to get her hopes up. But at the moment, he couldn't think of any words.

●

It was late afternoon by the time Piper finally got her lunch break. She dragged herself over to the RV to see what progress the mechanic had made.

"It's the weirdest thing," the grizzly old guy said. "I fired her up 'bout an hour ago, and she ran like a top."

Zach and Piper exchanged looks and then glanced over to Elijah, who was playing with a ladybug on a bush.

Zach turned back to the mechanic. "What exactly do you mean?"

"I mean, as far as I can tell, there ain't nothin' wrong with your vehicle ... at least now."

Piper's excitement grew. "You're saying it runs?"

"As good as new."

"You mean, we can just go?"

"Anytime you want. Now if you'll excuse me, I got some real work to get to." With that, the old-timer limped off.

Piper turned to Zach and practically squealed. "Can you believe it? We can leave! I don't have to work at that place anymore! We can get out of here now!"

Zach nodded.

She turned toward the diner and then back to Zach. "I'll finish my shift, though. I owe Stan that much. But afterward, we can get out of here and—"

She came to a stop. Zach was shaking his head.

"What's wrong?" she asked.

"There's something I gotta do first."

"What do you mean?"

"I promised Ashley I'd go back to Jason's."

"Jason's?"

He glanced to the ground. "Yeah."

"You said they were messing with spirits and witch-craft and stuff."

"They are."

"But—"

"But Ashley's different. I think I can help her."

"Why? 'Cause she's pretty and thinks you're cool?"

He gave her a scowl. "Get real."

"What then?"

"She's just trying to find herself and be liked."

"So?"

"So she's going to the wrong place for it."

Piper blew the hair out of her eyes. "And what are you going to do, point her to the right place?"

He shrugged. "I should at least try."

Piper couldn't believe her ears. She put her hands on her hips. "What are you saying? You're going to tell her about God and stuff?"

Another shrug. "I'd be a jerk if I didn't."

Piper's anger grew. She couldn't tell if he really wanted to help the girl or if he really liked her. Either way, going back to that house was stupid. And dangerous.

"Hey Piper!" She turned to the diner. Stan stood at the door calling after her. "Break time's over, girl!"

She turned to Zach who was still staring at the ground.

"Piper!"

She called back to Stan. "All right! I'll be right there!" She turned to Zach. "Going back there is stupid, real stupid."

He nodded. "Yeah, probably."

"And you're still going to do it?"

It seemed like forever before he looked up. When he did, she saw his eyes were shiny with emotion. "What else ..." His voice caught and he tried again. "What else can I do?"

●

Jason's house was packed. Zach counted at least a dozen kids, all teens. But only five of them had been chosen to sit at the round table with Jason.

As the guests of honor, two of the chosen ones were Ashley and Zach.

Jason called out to Big Red. "Pull the drapes, please, if you will."

The big guy obeyed, and the room instantly fell into darkness. Now it was lit only by a single candle on the table. The good news was there was no Ouija Board before them. The bad news was ... well, Zach was about to find out.

"Place your hands on the table," Jason ordered. "Close your eyes and concentrate. It is time for us to commune with the other side."

"A séance?" Zach whispered to Ashley. "You didn't say we were going to have a séance!"

She whispered back. "I told you we speak to departed spirits."

Zach shook his head.

"What?" Ashley asked.

"Those aren't dead spirits."

"What makes you the expert?"

"I'm not. But the Bible says once we die we all go to face God."

"If they're not dead spirits, what are they?"

Zach swallowed, took a breath and answered. "Demons."

"Ashley? Zachary?" Although Jason's voice was quiet and smooth, his eyes flashed intensely. "You're not concentrating."

Zach's heart pounded in his chest. He knew what he should do, but with Ashley there, with all the kids standing around staring at him ...

Jason's eyes narrowed. "Is there a problem, Zach?"

Zach took a deep breath. And then another. Finally, with trembling legs, he rose to his feet.

Chapter Nine

Deception

Before Zach could speak, Jason closed his eyes and shouted. "Oh, spirit, we beseech you! We beseech you to speak! We beseech—"

Zach took another breath.

"We beseech you, speak!"

Finally, Zach answered. "This isn't right." But he could barely be heard.

"Spirit, we beseech you—"

"I said this isn't—"

Jason's head snapped back. Everyone gasped and the room fell strangely silent. Then, ever so quietly, Jason began to speak. But it wasn't his voice. It was someone, some*thing*, entirely different.

"I wisssh to sssspeak to Zzzachary."

Zach stiffened. All eyes in the room turned to him as people started to murmur.

"Sssilence!" the voice hissed. "Zzzachary. Do you hear me?"

Ashley looked up to Zach, "Answer him," she whispered. "He's calling you."

Zach turned to Jason. "Who ... who are you? What do you want?"

"I have a messsage from your mother."

Zach's heart skipped a beat. "What about my mother?"

"Your parentsss. They are trapped. Held sssome-where. Yesss?"

Zach gave no answer. Part of him was dying to know what the voice knew. But the other part knew the voice was a spirit. A demon. Memories rushed in. Memories of Bible stories where Jesus ran into just such creatures. And memories of the authority he had over them.

"You mussst hurry," the voice continued. "Ressscue them. Ressscue them before it isss too—"

Zach had enough. "Stop it!" he ordered.

"You mussst hurry and—"

"I command you to stop!"

Instantly, the voice fell silent.

Zach looked on, breathless and a little surprised.

Jason's mouth began to contort. Every so slowly he looked to Zach, his lips twisting into a snarl.

Zach took a shaky breath and continued. "I order you to—"

"Sssilencccce!" Jason roared. "You have no authority over me!"

Zach's mind raced. What happened? Maybe it was true. Maybe he didn't have authority. Maybe the demons didn't have to obey. But how could that be? Whenever Jesus ordered them in the Bible, they had to—

And then he had it. Of course! What was he thinking? It wasn't *Zach's* authority they had to obey. With the added knowledge, he took another breath and tried again. "By the authority of *Jesus Christ*, I order you to stop talking!"

Jason glared at him and opened his mouth. But instead of words, there was only a choking sound—like he was trying to speak, but couldn't.

Zach reached down for Ashley's hand. "Let's get out of here."

She looked up frightened, confused. "What have you done to him?!"

Zach turned back to Jason as the man continued to gurgle and choke. He wasn't sure how it worked, but he knew that it had. And that was all he needed to know. He looked back to Ashley. "Come on."

"You're hurting him!"

"I'm not—"

"You're not letting him talk!"

Zach tried to explain. "It's not me."

"You're ruining it!"

"Ash—"

"You're ruining everything!"

"Ashley . . ."

"Go!" Her voice cracked with emotion. "Get out of here!"

Zach looked back to Jason and then to the surrounding kids who glared at him. Then back to Ashley.

Her eyes flashed in hurt and anger. "I said go!"

As much as he wanted to help, it was clear she didn't want it.

"Go!" She was beginning to cry. "Get out of here!"

Finally, sadly, Zach turned and started toward the door.

●

Mom and Dad finished another song.

Originally, when they had first started, there was no difference. The situation was the same, the cell was the same, their fear was the same. But gradually, as they started the second or third song, they began to feel different. A type of peace settled over them. It was as if they sensed God was in charge. Everything else was exactly the same. The only thing that had changed was them.

And, at least for now, that was enough.

They'd barely finished the last song before they heard the rattling of keys.

"Mike!" Mom pressed against the wall, frightened.

The door creaked open, and a light flooded in. A figure stepped into the doorway. It was impossible to see his face because of the brightness behind him.

"Who, who are you?" Dad demanded. "What do you want?"

Without a word, the figure entered the cell and stooped down. He looked familiar, but Dad couldn't quite place him. "What do you want?" Dad repeated.

The man produced a key and quickly unlocked the chains to Dad's feet and hands. Silently, he moved to Mom and unlocked her chains.

"We're not going back to that monster!" Dad said. "There's no way, we're—"

"Your work here is finished," the man said quietly.

"Our ... *work*?" Dad asked.

The figure rose. "Your prayers have been answered."

"What do you mean?" Mom said.

The figure stepped out of the room and pointed. "Follow this hallway to the exit. You will find that the door is unlocked. One hundred fifty yards away, in the woods, you will discover your vehicle."

Dad rose to his feet. "I don't understand."

"Your prayers have been answered." With that, the figure turned and disappeared down the hall.

●

Cody scooped up the tomato in front of the computer. He looked it over and over, first one way, then another, searching for the slightest problem. There was none. The tomato was perfect. The test was a success.

"What did I tell you?" Willard gloated. "It just took a few minor adjustments. Now it's time for us to take the plunge."

"Not so fast," Cody said.

"Now what?"

"It's one thing for it to work with vegetables. What about animals?"

"Meaning?"

"Meaning we're animals, not vegetables. Meaning we have to make sure it's safe for animals."

"Oh, brother," Willard sighed.

"Better safe than sorry," Cody said.

"All right, hang on." Willard waddled out and returned a minute later. In his hand he held two cages. One contained a hamster, the other a parakeet. "Which one do you want to send?" he asked.

"How 'bout both?" Cody said.

"Both?"

"There'll be two of us. Let's send two of them."

"Why are you so picky?" Willard demanded.

"I'm not picky," Cody said, "I just got this thing about living."

"All right, all right," Willard sighed. "We'll do another test, just to keep you happy." He opened the phone booth and set both cages inside. Once again he pressed a series of numbers on the keyboard, shut the door, and waited as the sound and light show began.

First there was the:

GIRRR-GIRRR-GIRRR-ing

Next came the:

DING-DING-DING-ing

And, last but not least, came the:

KERUGACHA-KERUGACHA-KERUGACHA.

After the expected sparks, flashes, and the:

POP!

both animals appeared in front of the computer's speakers. It was another success.

Well, almost . . .

"How'd we do?" Willard asked, heading over to join Cody.

Cody stared at the two cages, blinking. The parakeet still had her parakeet body, only she no longer had wings. Worse than that, instead of her head, she now had the hamster's head. And the hamster? Not only did he have the parakeet's head, but he was also the proud owner of two parakeet wings.

"A little more tweaking?" Cody suggested.

Willard nodded. "A little more tweaking."

●

"There it is!" Monica shouted.

They had turned back again. And this time, to their right, was a diner and a small gas station. And parked directly beside the station was the kids' motor home!

Silas turned the van and brought it to a stop beside the RV.

"I don't see no lights inside," Bruno complained.

Monica answered, "They're obviously over in that diner."

"Are we gonna go in and grab 'em?" Bruno asked hopefully.

Monica shook her head. "Too many witnesses. We have to wait till they come out."

"And then we grab 'em!" Bruno giggled in glee.

"Yes my sweet, dumb pet. Then we grab them."

Chapter Ten

Tensions Build

"You're so judgmental!"

Ashley had come from Jason's to give Zach a good piece of her mind. Now they sat across from one another in the diner.

"Ashley, you know what was going on in there was evil. I felt it. You felt it."

"Just because it doesn't fit into your neat little world doesn't make it wrong."

"It's not my world, Ashley. It's God's. He's the one who makes the rules, and he's the one who says messing with spirits is wrong. Not only wrong, but dangerous."

"Stop it!" She covered her ears. "Will you just stop with the preaching!"

"I can't change the truth. Jason's bad news and—"

"Stop it!"

Those sitting closest to them turned and looked. It hurt Zach to see her so torn up, but he didn't know what else to do. Finally he reached across the table and took her hand. "I'm only trying to help—"

"Well, maybe you should stop trying."

"What?"

She pulled her hand away. "Maybe I'm not worth it. You ever think about that? Maybe Jason and his buddies are all I deserve."

"Ash—"

"You, your sister, and your weird little brother come breezing in with all your fancy God talk, and then you just up and leave."

"You're mad 'cause we're going?"

"No, I think you should go. And the sooner the better." She rose to her feet, tears filling her eyes.

"What are you saying?" he asked.

She took a deep breath and answered. "I'm saying good-bye, Zach. I don't want to see you. I don't want to hear from you. I don't want you ever to think about me again."

"How can you say that?"

She wiped her face and turned toward the back door.

"Ashley ..." He reached for her arm, but she shook it loose. She started for the door when Piper suddenly appeared from the kitchen. She was out of her uniform and holding Elijah's hand.

Ashley was in no mood for another confrontation, so she spun around and headed for the front door instead.

"Ashley," Zach called after her.

She walked faster.

"Ashley!"

She reached the front of the diner, threw open the door, and broke into a run.

Zach could only stare after her, speechless.

Piper arrived at the table and said, "Don't tell me you're just going to stand there."

He turned to her. "What else can I—"

"You really are clueless, aren't you?"

"What?"

"Go after her!"

"But she just said—"

Piper shook her head in disgust and looked down at Elijah. "Is every guy this ignorant about girls?"

Elijah grinned, shrugged, and then nodded.

She looked back to Zach, who remained standing, still puzzled.

"Go," she motioned him toward the door. "Go, go, go!"

And for once in his life, Zach took his little sister's advice.

●

"There's the oldest!" Monica pointed toward the diner as Zach raced out the door. "Follow him!"

Silas and Bruno leaped into action.

Well, actually Silas did the leaping. Bruno had a bit more trouble.

"Uh . . . I can't get my seatbelt undone."

Monica turned back to him and glared. "What?!"

"It's stuck or somethin'."

"No way," Silas said. He opened Bruno's door and reached for the buckle. "You probably just forgot how to use it."

"I'm not that stupid," Bruno pouted. "You showed me how this afternoon."

Silas gave the buckle a tug, but it wouldn't budge.

"See." Bruno brightened. "I told you."

"Fools!" Monica reached back to the buckle. "Do I have to do everything myself!?"

She gave the buckle a pull. Nothing. She pulled harder. Still nothing. Then she pulled with all of her might ... again and again and again, until the entire van started rocking back and forth.

"Uh, Monica ..."

"Not now, Bruno." She continued yanking and the van continued rocking.

"I think I'm going to get sick."

"Don't you dare," Monica warned.

"Okay," Bruno said. "Uh, Monica?"

"What now!?"

BLAAAAAAAAA!

●

Mom and Dad followed the hallway until they came to a sharp corner. Carefully, Dad peered around it. There was the exit fifteen feet away—a clear shot.

Well, except for the two men blocking the door.

Dad pulled back and whispered to Mom. "There are guards."

"How are we going to get past them?"

"I don't know. I—"

He was interrupted by a familiar voice. He peeked around the corner and saw the man who had unlocked their chains. He was talking with the guards smoothly, almost hypnotically.

Dad watched as the guards lowered their rifles. Their eyes were open but just a little glazed as they slowly turned and started down the hallway toward him.

He pulled back and flattened against the wall, motioning Mom to do the same.

She did, just as they rounded the corner.

Mom and Dad each held their breath, afraid to move a muscle.

But the trio continued right on past, so close the parents could have reached out and touched them. Yet for some reason the guards didn't see them. Instead they just kept walking by with that glassy look in their eyes.

Dad waited until they were a dozen feet away before he grabbed Mom's hand. "Come on," he whispered. "Let's go!"

They raced for the door and pushed it open. A shrill alarm started blasting as they ran out into the pitch-black woods. Behind them they heard shouting.

There was no turning back now.

●

Willard had run several more tests. Soon the parakeet and hamster began arriving exactly as they should—all body parts intact and on the right bodies.

That was the good news.

Unfortunately, there was some bad news.

"Okay, Cody, we're next."

Cody gave a nervous swallow. "Are you sure it's ready?"

"Yup. I've run every test I can run. And then some. We're all ready to go."

Cody looked at the phone booth, then to Willard, then to the hamster and parakeet, then back to the phone booth.

With nothing left to do, he gave another swallow.

●

"Ashley ... Ashley!" By the time Zach caught up to her, she was almost at Jason's porch.

She turned, tears streaming down her face. "Leave me alone," she cried. "Go back to your perfect little life and leave me alone!"

"Ashley, please ..." He grabbed her arm. "You don't belong here. Not with these people."

"Right," she sniffed. "I should go back to a drunk mom and a crazy stepdad."

"Yes. I mean no. I mean if you go back, there are people who can help you."

"Yeah, right."

"I'm serious. You don't have to do it on your own. And you sure don't have to be with people like Jason."

"But he accepts me," she choked out the words. "Just the way I am. And he says I'm special."

"You are special. You're God's kid.

"Puleease," she said with scorn.

"You are! And he'd do anything for you."

"Right, that's why he gave me a couple of loser parents."

Zach shook his head. "I don't have an answer for that. But I do know he gave you the most important thing he had."

"What's that?"

"His life. When he died on that cross."

Ashley snorted in disgust.

"I'm serious. When Jesus was up on that cross dying for all the wrong you and I did ... at that moment, he considered us way more important than his life. Think of that. God thought you were more valuable than his own life."

Ashley tried wiping away her tears, but they came faster. Even if she wanted to answer, she couldn't.

Unsure what to do, Zach pulled her into his arms. She didn't resist. As he held her, he felt her body tremble. She was sobbing. How long they stayed that way, he didn't know. But he did know when the door opened and light spilled on them from inside the house.

"Well, well, lookie here." Jason walked onto the porch. Some of the kids joined him. "It's the God squad."

Zach stepped forward. "It's over, Jason."

"And what is that?"

"Ashley's not staying with you any longer."

"Oh really," Jason sneered. "Is that true, my dear?"

Ashley hesitated.

"Is it?"

Finally she wiped her face and gave a little nod.

"Yes, well, we'll see about that." Turning to the kids on either side of him, he gave the order:

"Grab them!"

Chapter Eleven

Confrontation

Before Zach could move they were on him — Stump, X-Ray, and Big Red.

"Let go of him!" Ashley shouted. "Let — "

Someone hit the side of Zach's head and for a moment he started to lose consciousness — until he heard Ashley scream. They were attacking her too!

That was all he needed to stay awake and fight back.

He landed a powerful punch into Big Red's stomach, doubling him over.

One of Jason's thugs down. Two to go.

He caught a glimpse of Ashley being dragged up the porch steps by Stump. "No!" she screamed. "Let go of me!"

X-Ray, the tall, skinny kid, grabbed Zach's arms and

twisted them behind his back so he couldn't move them. But Zach could move his feet. He kicked his right foot back and slammed it into the kid's knee.

"Augh!" X-Ray cried.

But Zach wasn't done. Using the same foot, he scraped it down the boy's shin, hopefully taking off a layer of skin, and then stomped his heel on top of the kid's foot.

X-Ray let go and grabbed his foot. "AUGHHH!"

Two down.

Letting go of Ashley, Stump leaped on Zach's back and wrapped his arms around his throat. Zach put his right fist into his left hand and jerked his elbow into the kid's stomach.

"Oaff!"

Three down!

He turned toward Ashley just as Jason dragged her through the door. But Zach had no sooner taken a step toward her when his head exploded in pain. Suddenly his legs had no strength, and he dropped to his knees. He looked up and saw Big Red standing over him holding a board.

Zach fell forward, unable to stop himself. He was unconscious before he hit the ground.

●

The alarm continued to sound as Mom and Dad raced through the woods. The undergrowth grabbed their legs, and branches kept slapping their faces. But it was a small price to pay to get out of there. Now, if they only knew where they were going.

"I don't see a thing." Mom gasped for breath.

"He said the Jeep was just ahead!"

"But there's no road! Not even a trail!"

Back at the compound they heard the opening of a gate and the barking of dogs.

"We'll never make it!" Mom yelled.

The same thought shot through Dad's mind, but he pushed it aside. He had to be positive. He had to be brave. Not just for his wife, but also for the kids.

"What's that?" he asked.

"Where?"

"Just ahead, up on the ridge?"

They squinted into the dark. Maybe it was the Jeep, maybe it wasn't. There was only one way to find out.

"Let's go!" Dad shouted.

The raced up the hill, fighting through the brush and branches. Mom stumbled once, then again, nearly falling. But Dad was there to pull her to her feet.

"You okay?" he asked.

She nodded, but had to stop to catch her breath. So did Dad. They leaned over, their hands on their knees, breathing in the cold, sharp air. In the distance, the barking grew louder, closer.

He turned to her. "You ready?"

Still breathing too hard to answer, she nodded.

He grabbed her hand and they started back up the hill. In less than a minute they reached the top. But to their dismay, there was no Jeep. Instead, they discovered a rusted-out camping trailer. "Michael," his wife cried, "what do we do?"

"I don't know. The man said it was just up—"

"Look!" She pointed to a dirty window of the camper. Through the dirt, in clear, sharp lines, someone had drawn an arrow pointing to the right.

Dad followed it and—"There it is!" he shouted. He pointed to the Jeep parked less than fifty yards away. "Let's go!"

They sucked in another breath and resumed running.

●

"Are you ready?" Willard asked.

Cody stared at the phone booth. He wanted to nod, but he'd never been a big fan of suicide.

"I'll take that as a yes." Willard opened the door.

Reluctantly, Cody stepped in and Willard followed.

Suddenly, Cody's face was smooched up against the glass. Things had gotten very tight ... and it wasn't the teleporter's fault.

"Willard?"

"Yeah, Cody?"

"Maybe you better cut down on those cookies and chips."

"Wouldn't hurt," Willard agreed. With some effort he was able to move his hand up to the keyboard. With greater effort he raised the hand holding Piper's email. "Okay, stand by."

"Willard?"

"Yeah, Cody?"

"If we die, you're gonna live to regret it."

●

"Are you okay?" Zach whispered.

"Yeah," Ashley said. She was tied in a chair back-to-back with Zach. "I'm so sorry I got you into this."

He wasn't sure, but it sounded like she was crying again. "It's not your fault," he said. "You didn't know—"

"Silence!" Jason ordered.

"What are you going to do with us?" Zach demanded.

"It's not you I'm interested in."

Zach felt another cold chill. "Who ... who else is there?"

Jason's lips curled into a menacing grin. "I think we both know. And if my spirit guide is correct, he should be here any—"

There was a knock on the door.

Jason's grin grew bigger.

More knocking. "Zach?" Piper's voice called. "Zach, you in there?"

Zach's heart sank as Jason signaled for Big Red to open the door.

●

"What's wrong?" Cody shouted from inside the phone booth. "Nothing's happening!"

"I'll need to boost the power!"

"What?!"

"We're bigger than hamsters and parakeets. Hang on." Willard punched more numbers into the keyboard. "There that should do it. Hang on!"

Cody waited.

He waited some more.

Nothing.

More of nothing.

"Say, Willard?"

"Yeah, yeah, I know, I know." Willard opened the door and stepped out.

Cody sighed. It felt good to breathe again. "What are you doing?" he called.

"I'm going to grab an extension cord and plug us into another outlet. Don't worry, it'll only take a minute."

"Take your time," Cody said. "Take all the time you want."

"Zach!" Piper spotted her brother and raced into the room.

"Piper, no! It's a trap! They want—"

The door slammed shut, and Piper spun around to see X-Ray and Big Red behind her. She reached out for Elijah's hand, but for some reason the little guy seemed unafraid. In fact, was it her imagination, or had he started to hum?

"Shut that kid up!"

Piper twirled around to see a skinny man with long black hair and tattoos. She knew it had to be Jason.

X-Ray and Big Red started for Elijah. She stepped between them, but Big Red threw her to the side like a rag doll.

"Leave her alone!" Zach shouted.

"Bring the boy to me," Jason ordered.

X-Ray bent down to Elijah. The boy looked up at him and hummed even louder.

"I said, shut that kid—"

Suddenly, the door flew open, slamming into Big Red's head, knocking him across the room.

And there, standing in the doorway, were Monica and her two goons.

"It's him!" Monica pointed at Elijah. "Grab the child!"

Bruno and Silas entered, and Bruno scooped Elijah under his arm.

"What are you doing?!" Jason shouted.

"We're, uh, grabbing the boy," Bruno explained.

"You can't do that!" Jason yelled.

Bruno looked at Elijah who was still smiling and humming. "We can't?"

"We're on the same side, you twit. We both work for Shadow Man."

Monica frowned and then reached for her cell phone.

"What are you doing?" Silas asked.

"I'm checking with the boss."

Suddenly, Jason let out a bloodcurdling scream.

Everyone froze.

"Oaff!" Jason doubled over like he'd been punched in the gut. He tried to stand, but the same invisible force hit him again, even harder. He dropped to his knees, coughing.

The group traded fearful looks as he struggled to rise.

He made it back to his feet and stumbled to the closest chair where he collapsed. By now he was gasping and choking. He couldn't breathe.

"Please ..." he cried. "Please, no, I—" It was as if he was fighting some unknown force. And then, suddenly, he went limp.

Everything grew quiet. Deathly quiet.

Then, ever so slowly, Jason raised his head. Though his eyes were shut, his mouth had twisted into a strange, creepy smile. He began to speak. But, of course, it wasn't his voice. "Well done, my friendsss."

Silas turned back to Monica. "You won't be needing to check with the boss."

"Why's that?" she asked.

"He's already here."

Chapter Twelve

Showdown

Piper stared at Jason as the voice continued to speak. "Make hassste! Bring the child to my compound."

Monica took a half step toward Elijah. "Yes, sir!" She threw a glance to Zach and Piper. "What about the brother and sister?"

"My ordersss are the sssame."

"Sir?"

"Dissspossse of them!"

Unsure what to do, Piper bowed her head and began to silently pray. *Dear God, help us. Please protect us from —*

"Ssstop her!" the voice hissed.

"Her?" Monica asked. "Her who?"

"Her!"

Piper opened her eyes and stiffened. Jason was glaring directly at her. Actually, more like *through* her. She'd never felt such hatred. For a moment it made her forget what she was doing ... until she saw Zach. He had bowed his head and was also praying.

"Ssstop him!" the voice shouted.

Monica searched the room, trying to understand who Jason was talking about now.

But Piper knew. Encouraged by her brother, she bowed her head and continued praying—only this time, out loud. "Dear Lord. Protect us. Please help us to—"

"Ssstop!!"

Hearing Piper, Zach also began praying out loud. "Yes, Lord, help us. Jesus, we ask that—"

At the sound of Jesus' name, Jason's head flew back like he'd been hit. "AUGHHH!"

Both Piper and Zach looked up.

"Foolsss!" the voice shouted. "You dare challenge my power!?"

The table beside him started to shake. The brother and sister watched, speechless, as the table slowly lifted off the ground—an inch, then six inches, then an entire foot.

Piper's heart thumped in her chest. She was so frightened she forgot to pray.

Next, the glass ashtray lifted off the table. It hovered a moment, and then flew across the room, smashing into the wall directly behind her. Piper screamed. Come to think of it, one or two of the bad guys did too.

But the show wasn't over.

Jason began to laugh—softly at first, then louder and louder. As he did, doors around the house began opening and slamming. A mysterious wind came out of nowhere and, ever so slowly, Jason's chair lifted off the ground. His laugh turned into a mocking cackle as he raised his right hand and stretched it out towards Elijah.

Piper watched in horror as a swirling red glow appeared in Jason's palm. It grew brighter and brighter. Slowly it lifted off his hand and floated across the room toward Elijah. Piper wanted to scream, to yell at her brother to run. But she was so frightened no words would come.

The orb of light stopped just inches from Elijah's forehead. But, instead of fear, Elijah looked at it with fascination. It began to move around to the back of his head, then to the front again, circling him. Then again, faster. And again, even faster. And faster ... and faster.

But Elijah showed little concern. Instead, he started humming again. This time Piper recognized the song. It was an old-fashioned hymn.

"Ssstop ..."

A smile spread across Elijah's face. Slowly, he lifted his arms. He closed his eyes, tilted back his head, and to Piper's astonishment, the little guy began to sing.

"SSSTOP THAT!" the voice shouted.

Piper didn't understand the words to the hymn. They were foreign, like Latin or something. But she sure understood the impact they were having on Jason. He began squirming, tossing his head back and forth.

"SSSSTOP THAT SSSSINGING!!"

But Elijah didn't stop. Instead, he sang even louder. He was so happy that his face practically glowed. The red light that circled him faded, and then disappeared altogether.

"SSSSTOOOOPPP!"

Still grinning, still singing, Elijah finally turned to face Jason.

Instantly, Jason's chair crashed to the ground, shattering underneath him. The man cried out, but Elijah wasn't finished. He started walking toward him — still singing, still grinning.

"GET AWAY!" Jason scrambled to his knees. "GET AWAY FROM ME!"

Elijah stretched a hand toward him.

Jason scampered on his hands and knees to the far wall. "SSSSTOP HIM!"

But Elijah didn't stop

"SSSSTAY BACK!"

Elijah continued forward as Jason pressed against the wall, cowering. "SSSSTAY AWAY FROM ME!"

At last, the boy reached Jason. Elijah was still grinning, but singing softer now.

"SSSTAY BACK!"

Slowly, Elijah reached down to the man.

"SSSSTOP! DON'T TOUCH ME!"

But Elijah did touch him. And Jason screamed as though he'd been burned. "SSSSTOP IT! SSSSTOP IT! Sssssstooo …" Jason collapsed onto the floor, unconscious.

Elijah quit singing and looked down at the man with a sad sort of smile.

Everyone stared in absolute silence.

Well, almost everyone.

"Get him!" Monica shouted at her two goons.

But Silas and Bruno simply stared at her and blinked.

"I said get him!"

More blinking.

"Get him! Get him! Get—"

Elijah waved a hand in her direction, and she stopped shouting. It's hard to shout when you've fallen to the floor, unconscious.

"Hey!" Bruno cried in alarm. "What have you done to my Monica?" He started toward Elijah until the kid gave another wave and another body hit the floor.

Finally, he turned to Silas.

The man raised his hands. "Listen, I don't want no trouble." He started backing up. "Just let me go our way and—"

Elijah gave one last wave and, you guessed it, one last goon hit the deck.

And Jason's guys? They were busy falling over each other while running out of the room as fast as their feet could carry them!

●

Mom and Dad scrambled up the ridge toward the Jeep.

The dogs sounded closer. A lot closer.

They arrived and flung open the doors, causing the car alarm to chime.

"The keys are still here!" Mom cried.

"Thank you, Lord," Dad said as he scooted behind the wheel. "Thank you."

●

Ashley, Piper, Zach, and Elijah raced down the porch steps and toward the diner.

"Hurry!" Zach yelled. "Before they wake up!"

"What went on back there?" Ashley shouted. "Does he do that often?"

Piper glanced to Elijah and shook her head. "Never. But with him it's always a surprise."

"Talk about power."

"It's not his," Zach explained. "As far as we can tell, it all comes from—"

"I know, I know," Ashley interrupted, "God, right?"

"He's got more power than a million of those goofballs," Zach said. He looked at her and added, "And more love. Way more."

Piper threw a look to Ashley. She was nodding and thinking. Definitely thinking.

They reached the parking lot and the RV. Zach yanked open the door and was the first to enter when suddenly there was a blinding flash inside.

"What happened?" Piper shouted.

"It's your laptop!" Zach yelled.

"My laptop?"

"Well, not really your laptop. More like what came out of it."

"Hi, guys," a familiar voice said.

Piper stuck her head inside and couldn't believe her eyes. "Willard? Cody? What are you doing here?"

"You wouldn't believe us if we told you," Cody said. He was checking his arms and legs like he was glad they were all there.

"It doesn't matter!" Piper raced up the steps and threw her arms around him. "I'm just glad you're here!"

The only person more surprised than Cody was Piper. She immediately stepped back and cleared her throat. "What I mean is ..." She glanced down, obviously embarrassed. "It's good to, uh, see you again." She stole a glance back up at Cody. The guy almost seemed to be glowing. As a matter of fact, that's exactly what he was doing!

"Uh-oh," Willard said. He was glowing too. Not only glowing, but starting to short out. One minute he was there, then he'd blink out, then he was there again. "I guess ... I ... still don't ... have ... enough ... power."

"What's going on?" Piper asked in alarm.

The blinking grew faster as Cody tried to explain. " ... another ... Willard's ... stupid ... inventions."

"Oh, no," Piper groaned.

"Oh, yes," Willard shrugged.

And then, with another poof of light, they were suddenly gone.

"Nice of them to drop by," Zach smirked as he climbed behind the RV's steering wheel.

"Those were your . . . friends?" Ashley asked.

"It's another long story," Zach said. "But we'll see them again, 'specially if Piper gets her way."

Piper glanced down, feeling her ears heat up.

"Get in." Zach motioned for Ashley to come inside.

"But, I—"

"We'll take you home."

She took a tentative step into the motor home. "But that's, that's all the way back in L.A."

"Zach," Piper reminded him. "Mom and Dad are still in trouble. We gotta help them."

"She's right," Ashley said. "I can't put you out."

"Well, you sure can't stay here," Zach said. "Not with those creeps."

"I know, but—"

She was interrupted by the honking of a horn behind them. And more honking. And more. She poked her head outside and Piper joined her.

It was Gus the mechanic—sitting in his beat-up tow truck. "Will you kids move that bucket of bolts?!" he shouted from the window. "I gotta get this here fellow to Los Angeles and get back 'fore daybreak."

"Los Angeles?" Piper called, exchanging glances with Ashley. "That's a long way."

The old-timer jerked his thumb toward the passenger who was starting to climb into his truck. "He's paying me good money for it."

Piper looked over and was surprised to see the passenger was the gray-haired man Elijah had been studying the Bible with earlier.

The man smiled and explained. "Gus, here, says he won't have my car fixed for another two weeks, and I need to be in El Monte first thing tomorrow."

"El Monte?" Ashley asked in surprise.

He nodded. "I'm helping a youth pastor down there who works with families in crises—"

"*I* live in El Monte," Ashley said.

"Really?" the man exclaimed. "That's some coincidence."

Piper and Ashley exchanged a second pair of glances.

Ashley turned back to him. "Listen, you don't happen to have room for one more, do you?"

The man glanced into the truck and then called back. "Sure ... if you don't mind it being a little cramped."

"No," Ashley said, "I don't mind. I don't mind at all!"

As she spoke, Piper slowly turned to Elijah who sat in the motor home, humming away. Then she threw a look over to Zach, who was obviously thinking what she was thinking.

●

Mom and Dad clamored into the Jeep. As Dad fired it up, Mom rummaged in the back.

"Here's the computer!" she exclaimed. "Can you believe it?! They even left our computer!"

"Great!" Dad pulled the Jeep onto the gravel road. "Send the kids an email. Make sure they're okay and tell them there's a little town called Bensonville on Highway 14. Let's meet up there."

"Terrific!" Mom said. She turned on the laptop and started to type.

●

Zach stood outside the motor home. It was harder saying good-bye to Ashley than he thought. "You'll keep in touch?" he asked.

She nodded, her eyes already filling with tears.

"C'mon, boy," the mechanic shouted from the tow truck behind them. "Let's go!"

"He's right!" Piper called from inside the motor home. "We gotta hurry."

"Right." He turned back to Ashley. "I think things are going to work out."

Again Ashley nodded.

He cleared his throat. "Well, all right, then." Unsure what to do, he turned toward the RV.

"Zach?" Ashley's voice was clogged with emotion.

He turned back.

"Thanks."

"No problem." He felt his own throat tightening up.

"And what you said about God ... and all that stuff?"

"Yeah?"

"I'm going to give it some serious thought. I mean, *real* serious."

"Cool," Zach smiled. Suddenly his own eyes started to burn.

"Zach!" Piper called.

"Well ... we'll see you then."

"Yeah," she croaked. "We'll see you."

Before he knew it, he reached down and gave her a little kiss on the forehead. Nothing mushy or romantic. Just a way of saying that he cared for her. Cared a lot.

She looked up and smiled as tears spilled down her cheeks. And then, without a word, she turned and dashed toward the waiting tow truck.

Once again, the mechanic honked his horn.

"Come on, Zach!" Piper called. "They'll be here any minute. Move it!"

"All right, all right." He turned, gave his eyes a quick swipe, and stepped into the RV.

Piper sat in the passenger seat, working her laptop. "I got news from Mom and Dad!"

"Where are they?" Zach asked as he climbed behind the wheel.

"They're safe. They got away."

"All right!"

"They want us to meet them in a town called Bensonville on Highway 14."

"Perfect." He reached down and turned on the ignition. "Bensonville, here we come!"

"What do you think about that, Elijah?" Piper turned to her little brother. "We're going to see Mom and Dad!"

Zach glanced into the mirror, expecting to see one happy little kid. Instead, Elijah sat in the back with a deep frown on his face. A very deep frown.

And that made Zach nervous—real nervous.

●

Mom and Dad continued down the deserted mountain road. Although exhausted from the ordeal, they were incredibly excited. In just a few hours they would be reunited with their children. And that thrilled them.

They might not have been quite so thrilled if they realized that underneath their Jeep was a small metal box with an antenna ... and a blinking red light.

●

Inside a black truck another red light blinked. On its roof a large antenna swept back and forth.

Two burly guards climbed inside. A third opened the rear door of the vehicle and waited as Shadow Man emerged from the building. Despite the lights around the compound, his face remained in darkness as he walked towards the truck.

"Are you sure this is necessary?" the guard asked as Shadow Man arrived. "We can find them and bring them to you."

"I mussst come along," Shadow Man hissed. "The boy isss too powerful to control from afar. I mussst be near to sssubdue and control him."

"Yes, sir."

He climbed into the rear of the truck, which had been specially outfitted to handle his large form. The guard shut the doors, and the vehicle slowly pulled away. As it passed through the gate, Shadow Man called to the driver. "Do you have a reading?"

"Yes sir. They're on the highway, 1.7 miles ahead."

"Good," the Shadow Man grinned. "Ssstay far behind them. We don't want them to know we're following until they meet up with their children."

"Yes, sir," the driver answered.

"Then we will sssee who hasss the *real* power. Yesss, we will," he chuckled to himself. "Yesss, we will ..."

Trapped
by Shadows

For John Fornof
a man of God who knows about fighting the good fight.

Therefore put on the full armor of God, so that when the
day of evil comes, you may be able to stand your ground,
and after you have done everything, to stand.

—Ephesians 6:13

Chapter One

Pursuit

Thirteen minutes before midnight, three vehicles from three different directions sped toward a single destination, their occupants all focused on a single goal.

●

From the north, a mud-splattered Jeep Cherokee raced through the night. Dad concentrated harder as he tightened his grip on the wheel. His headlights caught a sign: Speed Limit 55. It slid from sight as the Jeep whipped around another curve.

"Mike!" his wife warned, her knuckles white as she clutched the dashboard.

"If we get pulled over, I'll explain our kids are in danger," said Dad, his mouth in a hard line as he stared ahead.

●

From the south, a sleek black Hummer roared down the highway. Its dashboard was lit up with indicators like the cockpit of a fighter jet: digital readouts, GPS map, radar screen, infrared monitor, and a flashing red light from the tracking device that had been attached to the underside of the mud-splattered Jeep, now only a few short miles away.

The glow from the dash lit the driver's face. He glanced into his rearview mirror, caring not so much what was on the road behind him so much as what was in the seat behind him — a dark presence that soaked up all the light around it.

Shadow Man.

●

And from the west, lumbering along as fast as it could, was an old beat-up RV camper. Its worn engine coughed and choked, puffing blue smoke out of its tailpipe.

Inside, sixteen-year-old Zach held the steering wheel with one hand while stuffing his mouth with the other — a Super Extreme Nuclear Burrito, featuring Flaming Fire Fajita Chicken. And forget the wimpy hot or extra hot sauce. Not for Zach. He'd gone for Taco Wonderland's newest sauce, the kind they advertised as *Danger: Explosive!*

Behind him, in the back of the RV, sat his thirteen-year-old sister, Piper. As the ultra-responsible one of the group (someone had to be), she was taking care of their six-year-old brother, Elijah.

"All right," she said, carefully tapping out some raisins into the little boy's hand, "you can have eight now and eight more when we get there."

Elijah, who hardly ever spoke, looked up at her with his big brown eyes and smiled—his way of saying thank you.

She smiled back. "Don't worry, it won't be long before we see Mom and Dad again. I promise."

Elijah nodded and laid his head on her arm. Piper tenderly stroked his hair, hoping she was right. Without her mom there, the job of caring for the little guy fell into her hands. Which was okay. She loved Elijah. He could be so sweet and caring ... when he wasn't being so weird. Honestly, she'd never met anybody like him. Sometimes it was like he knew what was going to happen before it happened. Sometimes when he visited sick people, they were suddenly well. And sometimes when the family really, absolutely needed something to happen, she'd see his little lips moving in prayer, and, just like that, it happened. Not all the time. But just enough to make things a little freaky.

And speaking of freaky, there was her older brother, Zach—it wasn't just his eating habits that were adventurous. It was everything he did. From seeing how fast a skateboard could go if you attached rocket motors to it (answer: ninety-three miles an hour before he crashed into a tree, flew through the air, and landed in someone's kiddie pool), to seeing how many bottles of ketchup you could drink before your hurl (answer: one and a half), to talking his little sister (as in Piper) into sticking her tongue on the frozen monkey bars in the middle of winter to see what would happen (answer: a visit by the paramedics who had to pour hot water on her tongue to unfreeze it from the bars). Good ol' Zach. That's why she had to keep an eye on him all the time. Like now, when she looked up front and spotted him biting into his burrito. Like now, when his eyeballs bulged and his dark hair—which usually looked like it was styled by a fourteen-speed blender stuck on Super Chop—seemed to stand on end.

She could tell he wanted to say something. She could also tell that his mouth was on fire. Which explains why the only word that came out was:

"AAAAAAAAAAAAAAH!"

"What's wrong?" Piper shouted. Then she saw the wrapper on the floor and understood. "Nuclear burrito?"

Zach nodded, waving air into his mouth, which caused the RV to swerve from side to side.

Piper sprang for the RV's sink. She turned the water on full blast and yanked up the sprayer, pulling the long hose to the driver's seat.

The RV bounced onto the road's shoulder as Zach slammed on the brakes, finally bringing the vehicle to a skidding stop.

"Open your mouth!" she yelled.

He obeyed.

She aimed for the screaming hole in Zach's face and pressed the sprayer.

The water hit its mark, and Zach's mouth sizzled like a frying pan dumped in cold water.

●

Meanwhile, in the Jeep, all Dad could think of was getting to his children before the other side did. He'd seen the evil their leader could do and he didn't like it. Not one bit. He wasn't sure if those dark powers came from this world or from somewhere else. Either way, the children had to be protected.

In the Hummer, the driver focused on the tracker beam and the GPS map. This time there would be no mistakes.

And in the RV, Zach's mouth continued to smolder.

Chapter Two

The Plot Sickens

There was a fourth vehicle: a dark green van sitting on the shoulder of the highway.

Inside, Monica Specter's shaggy red hair shone in the mirror light. She was busy applying another layer of bright red lipstick and shimmering, electric-green eye shadow. Granted, sometimes in the bright sunlight all that makeup made her look a little bit like a clown. But in this dimmer light she looked more like a ... well, all right, she still looked like a clown.

And don't even ask about her clothes. More often than not, it looked like somebody had just stitched a bunch of bright beach towels and bedspreads together and thrown them on her. It's not that she didn't have any fashion sense. It's just that ... well, all right, she didn't have fashion sense either.

Bottom line: The same charm school that taught her all those delicate, lady-like manners (and she didn't have any) taught her the same delicate, lady-like ways of choosing her clothing and wearing her makeup.

Bottom, bottom line: Monica was a real piece of work. Unfortunately, her partners weren't much better:

First, there was Bruno, a very large man with a very small brain.

Right on cue, she heard a cry of joy from the backseat. Bruno had breathed on the glass beside him and fogged it up. He drew a smiley face with his finger ... to join an entire family of smiley faces he'd drawn across the window. "Wanna see me do it again?"

Then there was Silas, a pointy-nosed, pointy-chinned, pointy-everything guy with bloodshot eyes and big, droopy bags under them the size of hammocks.

"Not again ..." Silas sighed. "I don't ever want to see another smiley face in my life. Do you understand?"

Bruno paused in deep thought. "So ... you want me to draw little frowny faces, instead?"

Silas turned away and moaned.

"Will you two grow up?" Monica snarled from the front seat. (Snarling was one of her specialties.)

"I'm not the one who needs to grow up," Silas argued. "He is." He thrust a pointy thumb in the direction of his partner.

"No sir," Bruno said. "You are!"

"No, you are!"

"Liar, liar, pants on—"

"Knock it off!" Monica shouted. "You're acting like big, fat, stupid morons!"

Bruno sucked in his gut. "I'm not fat."

Monica could only stare. They had been sitting here on the side of the road for hours, waiting for the kids'

RV to rumble past. And they were definitely going stir-crazy.

But Monica was as determined as she was nasty. This time she would not fail. Shadow Man wanted the little boy. He never said why, but there was something very, very valuable about him. And she would deliver him. She had to. This was her chance to finally prove her worthiness.

She glanced at her two partners sulking in the back-seat. They'd been assigned to her since the beginning— a skinny little weasel and a brainless baboon. They had bungled every assignment she'd been given.

But this time, it would be different.

Headlights suddenly appeared in the mirror.

"Duck!" she called back to them. "Duck!"

Bruno's face brightened. "You want me to draw a duck?"

"Duck! Duck!" she cried.

"Goose!" Bruno shouted back in glee.

"No, you moron," Silas scooted down in the seat. "She means *get down!*"

Silas yanked him down in the seat just as the RV swooshed by, rocking the van in its wake. Once it had passed, Monica rose and turned on the ignition. The van's engine roared to life. This time, the kid would be hers.

●

To anyone else, the run-down garage was packed with yesterday's junk. The sagging shelves bulged with old televisions, radios, and out-of-date computers. But to the inventor's eye, these old gadgets and circuit boards were the building blocks of imagination.

Willard, a pudgy genius with curly hair, punched in

numbers on his laptop. His reluctant assistant, Cody, watched with concern.

It was getting late, and they had to hurry.

"One more calculation ..." Willard punched a key on the laptop keyboard with the flair of a concert pianist hitting the last note of a great concerto, "... and the program has now reached terminal status!"

Cody, who was definitely smart but not Willard-smart, turned to him and, in his most intelligent voice, asked, "Huh?"

"We're done!"

"Why didn't you just say 'we're done'?"

"I am a man of science," replied Willard, closing the laptop with a flourish.

"No, you're a guy who uses big words."

"Oh," Willard nodded knowingly. "You mean a *logophile*. Or a *logogogue*. Or possibly a *logomachist*. Or—"

"Willard?"

"Yes, Cody?"

"Be quiet."

Willard grinned as the laptop's lights flickered greenly. "I will gladly desist, my friend."

Cody started to answer, then stopped. Willard had always been smart. But lately he'd been testing his vocabulary ... and Cody's patience. A lot of people get their exercise by working out with weights. Willard worked out with words. Not that Cody blamed him. At school everyone made fun of him. Maybe this was his new way of fighting back.

Willard yanked out the cables that snaked from his laptop to four tennis shoes on the floor. At the back of each shoe was a little box with an antenna and some ports for wires. These were *not* your regular, everyday tennis shoes. Really, nothing was regular and everyday with Willard.

Cody continued watching. "You still haven't told me how these are going to help Piper and her family."

"It will momentarily become clear," Willard said. "And you shall have nothing further to worry about."

Cody sighed, running his fingers through his hair. He'd heard that before. "That's what worries me."

"Here." Willard handed him two leg harnesses. "Put these on. They will assist in the stabilization process."

As Cody grabbed the leg harnesses, he thought back to some other not-so-successful-inventions Willard had recently created. Little things, like ...

The Solar-Powered Toaster that exploded into a fireball. Not bad, if you liked your toast well done.

The Computer-Guided Eyebrow Plucker. Unfortunately, it didn't stop with the eyebrows — as the first hundred bald, angry customers proved.

The Turbo-Charged Pickle Jar Lid Opener. A great success, except for the twenty-seven kosher dills still embedded in Cody's kitchen ceiling.

"Hurry!" Willard called over his shoulder. "We must dispatch ourselves with expedience!"

"Do what with who?" Cody asked, looking up at his friend.

"We gotta go!"

●

The map light illuminated Mom's finger as she traced the winding road on the atlas. "Just one more mile," she murmured. Her voice was both hopeful and anxious.

"All right, sweetheart," Dad said as they shot through the thick woods. He tried to sound reassuring, but inside his fear continued to grow. *What if we don't get to the kids before they do?*

He glanced to his wife and thought back to the beginning.

●

Mom had been pregnant with their third child, Elijah. She had just left the florist's with a giant bouquet of daisies for her sister's birthday. As she walked—more like waddled—toward the car, a bearded old man with a tattered jacket stepped in front of her, bringing her to an abrupt stop.

He spoke quietly, almost in reverence. "Your son will work miracles."

She blinked, more than a little surprised. How had he known she was going to have a boy?

He continued. "The Scriptures speak of him."

"Who?" she asked, hoping to slip inside the car and get away from the crazy man—not an easy feat when one is holding a bouquet of flowers.

"Your son."

She stared at him a moment, then nodded slowly, uneasily, as she opened the car door and got inside. She locked the car and put the key in the ignition. She glanced back at the man, but when she turned he had vanished. The old man was nowhere to be seen.

Unfortunately, that was only the beginning of the strangeness. It soon got stranger.

Just after Elijah was born, Mom and Dad began to notice little things. Like how their baby laughed and cooed as if he saw something above his crib ... when there was nothing there at all.

Or the time he was in preschool and his teacher ran out of snacks ... or thought she did. No one could explain how, when she kept reaching into the graham cracker box, she never ran out of graham crackers—not until the last child was served. Amazing. Well, to everyone but Mom and Dad.

That was the good weird. But there was also the bad ...

More and more, they got the sense that people were watching them. Sometimes it was a dark blue car that followed them at a distance when they pushed the baby stroller down the street. At other times it was a tall, skinny man in overalls who always seemed to be trimming hedges or sweeping a sidewalk when they went outside.

Then came the fateful Saturday morning when the strange old man appeared once again—but this time on their doorstep.

Spotting him through the window, Mom called upstairs to Dad. "Mike! That man from the florist—it's him! He's here!"

Dad bounded down the stairs and threw open the door to confront him. But the old man said only three words:

"You must leave."

"Guess again," Dad said. "I don't know who you are or what's going on, but you're the one who has to leave."

The man shook his head. "No. You must go. For the boy's safety—and your own."

Dad snorted in disgust and started to shut the door when the old man raised his voice. "Please ... there is an organization."

Dad hesitated.

The old man continued. "They are watching your son to see if he is the one of whom the Scriptures speak. Once they are sure, they will move in."

Dad frowned. "Organization?"

"They are empowered by a dark and sinister force, and they will show no mercy when they come for him."

Dad bristled. "That's enough. If you don't leave right now, I'm calling the police. Do you understand?"

The old man remained. "You've seen his gifts."

"I don't know what you're talking about."

"You've seen his powers. You've seen—"

Without a word Dad slammed the door.

"I'm not sure if you should have done that," Mom said.

"The guy's a loony!" Dad replied angrily. He turned, checking through the door's peephole.

Nobody was there.

That was when they decided to pack up the kids and move ... the first time.

But no matter how they tried to hide Elijah's special gifts, the little guy would do something that caused people to start talking ... and asking questions.

Then, just a few days ago, a red-headed woman and two men with guns showed up at the house. Mom and Dad tried to act as decoys to draw them away, giving their children a chance to escape to safety, but the plan backfired. Instead, the parents were kidnapped and taken to a mysterious compound where they first encountered ...

Shadow Man.

They had escaped. It was a miracle from God— there was no doubt about that.

But Shadow Man wasn't about to give up—there was no doubt about that either.

Chapter Three

Arrest

"We're going to *fly?!*" Cody's voice cracked. It hadn't done that since he was thirteen, but raw fear can do that to a guy. "*AGAIN?*"

"No," Willard chuckled, "we're not going to fly."

"Whew, that's good."

"Technically, we will simply be resisting gravity."

Somehow, that didn't make Cody feel much better.

"We must locate Piper's parents," Willard said as he slipped into his antigravity tennis shoes. "We must inform them of the tracking device my equipment has discovered under their car. This is the only way to warn them."

"If we survive," Cody said, giving the shoes a doubtful look.

Willard ignored him. "I've triangulated their last email transmission with their cell phone call. But we must proceed there quickly before we lose them."

Cody was silent, frowning down at the tops of his tennis shoes.

"Look, I know what you're thinking," Willard said. "You're recalling the time my Remote-Controlled Pencil Sharpener flew out the window, crashed into the power station, and shorted out the entire town for a week."

"Actually," Cody said, "I forgot that one."

"Then perhaps it was my Inviso-Bug Spray which I brought to summer camp that made us both invisible."

"Actually," Cody corrected, "it just made our clothes invisible."

"Ah, yes." Willard nodded. "That was rather embarrassing. However, I promise you there will be no such occurrences on this occasion."

"Don't you think we should at least test them?" Cody asked.

"Under normal circumstances, yes, you would be correct. A positive outcome of a trial run is crucial before the operation of any new device."

"Good!"

"However, we have no time."

"Bad!"

"I assure you, all my data indicates these shoes will perform perfectly."

Cody gave him a look. He knew Willard wanted to help. He also knew that not a single invention of his had ever worked ... well, had ever worked the way he'd planned for it to work. Still, Willard was right. The family was in trouble, and they had no time to waste. So, with a heavy sigh (and a prayer that someone somewhere would someday find their bodies) Cody slipped into the shoes and laced them up tightly.

Willard reached for the control panel strapped to his wrist and hit a flashing red button. "Hopefully, we won't have any problems. Hold on."

"What do you mean, *hopefully*?" Cody's voice cracked again. "And what do you mean, *hold on*?"

"I mean...

WHOOOAAAAAAAH!"

Suddenly Willard shot up and hovered in the air. For that matter, so did...

"WHOOOAAAAAAAH!"

... Cody.

There was only one minor problem.

"We're upside down!" Cody shouted, dangling from his feet. He kicked and spun around in the air as he tried to right himself.

"Yes, I am aware of that fact, however ..."

"However what?"

"We have no time for repairs! We must depart now!"

Before Cody could protest, Willard pushed a little joystick on his control panel, and they took off. Still upside down. And still shouting.

"WHOOOAAAAAAAH!!"

●

Mom and Dad pulled to a stop at the agreed-upon location: the parking lot of the Desert Sands Motor Lodge. They sat quietly in the Jeep, holding each other's hands, waiting for their children. Dad tried to relax, nervously drumming his free fingers on the dashboard, while Mom peered anxiously into the night.

"Mike!" she suddenly shouted.

He sat up and looked through the window, just in

time to spot a pair of headlights coming up the high-way. They belonged to the RV.

"It's them!"

●

Piper, peering out the window of the RV, gave a start. Her heart leapt as she cried out. "There they are!"

"I see them!" Zach exclaimed. He pressed down on the accelerator, urging the old vehicle forward.

Piper spun around and, in her excitement, gave Elijah a hug. The family would be together again at last. Maybe now things would finally get back to normal. No more kidnappings. No more escapes. Soon they'd be back home in the family room, munching popcorn, and watching the latest DVD.

The motor home pulled up beside the Jeep, and the doors to both vehicles flew open. Zach, Piper, and Elijah spilled out of the RV, while Mom and Dad raced out of the Jeep. Before they knew it, everyone was wrapped in one giant bear hug.

"Okay, okay," Zach gasped. "I can't breathe, give me some air."

Piper was enduring her own brand of suffocating, but the love felt too good to complain.

Finally they broke up, Mom wiping her eyes with the sleeve of her jacket. "Are you kids all okay?"

"We're fine," Piper said, blinking back her own tears. "What about you guys?"

"Couldn't be better," Mom laughed and threw her arms around them again for more hugs and suffocation.

"Whew," Dad waved his hand in front of his nose. "Son, what's that smell?"

Piper rolled her eyes. "Nuclear Burrito breath."

Elijah giggled as the family joked and hugged and

teased. After all this time, they were together. How long they stood in the parking lot like that, nobody knows. But eventually, they split apart and headed back to the vehicles. Mom and the kids would ride in the Jeep, while Dad would follow behind in the RV.

It was time to go home.

●

Zach slid into the front seat beside Mom as she started up the Jeep and pulled onto the road. Elijah sat with Piper in the back. He snuggled against her and quickly fell asleep.

"I've got a ton of questions," Zach said.

"Me too," Piper added.

"Me three," Mom exclaimed.

"Okay," Zach said. "It was kinda weird when we came home from school and there's the vacuum cleaner in the middle of the floor—"

"Along with all the clothes from the dryer," Piper added, "and the dirty dishes piled up in the sink."

"Yeah," Zach said, "it was like you guys got raptured or something."

Mom nodded. "Okay, let me tell you what happened. I was watching the news on television when—" Her eyes caught something in the rearview mirror.

"What's wrong?" Zach asked.

Piper turned and saw Dad flashing his high beams at them. "Mom?"

"I see," Mom said. She had also seen the bright blue lights of a police car flashing behind Dad.

"Oh, no," she groaned.

"What?" Zach asked.

"Your father is getting pulled over."

Chapter Four

The Trap

Back in the RV, Dad had spotted the police car and signaled Mom. He pulled onto the gravel shoulder and was relieved to see his wife doing the same up ahead.

He watched in his mirror as the police officer approached, the blue light on top of his car still flashing. The officer's flashlight beam poked around inside the RV until it finally arrived at Dad's side. He tapped on the glass and motioned Dad to roll down his window.

"May I see your license please?"

"Certainly," Dad said as he reached into his back pocket and pulled out his wallet. He opened it, produced his license, and handed it to the officer.

The man took it, shined his flashlight on the picture, and then on Dad.

Squinting in the bright light, Dad asked, "Is there a problem, Officer?"

Without answering the question, the man ordered gruffly, "Step out of the vehicle, sir."

Dad opened the door and obeyed. "Is this really necessary? I don't think I was speeding. Maybe if you just told me—"

The officer cut him off. "Come around to the rear of the vehicle."

Again, Dad did as he was told.

"Put your hands behind your back."

"Officer, what's going on?"

"Put your hands behind your back."

Dad shrugged and obeyed. That's when he felt and heard the metallic *click* of handcuffs.

"You're under arrest."

"What?!"

The officer said nothing. Dad looked ahead to the Jeep, where another officer was ordering Mom and the children outside.

●

Piper could tell her mother was confused and more than a little angry. "I don't understand," she was saying to the officer. "What do you mean, we're under arrest?"

"Please remain quiet and put your hands behind your back."

"Mom," Piper said, "what's going—"

"Please, put your hands behind your back."

"Mom?"

Reluctantly, Mom obeyed. Immediately her hands were cuffed.

Elijah tugged on Piper's shirt, and she glanced down

to see his worried expression. "It's going to be all right," she said.

But the look in his eyes said he knew better.

Zach knew better too. "You're no cop!" he said.

"Put your hands behind your back and keep quiet."

"You cannot arrest my children! We have done nothing wrong!" Mom cried out in protest, straining against the handcuffs.

"Real cops don't act like this," Zach insisted. "And real cops don't drive Hummers."

Piper whirled back around to the police car and squinted. He was right. It *wasn't* a police car! It was hard to see, with the RV lights between them, but in the darkness she could just make out the shape of a Humvee.

"It's a trick!" Piper yelled. "Mom, it's a trap!"

Before anyone could respond, Elijah suddenly took off.

"Hey!" The officer lunged for him, but the little guy was too quick. He dodged the man and ran toward Dad and the RV.

In the confusion, Zach broke free and raced into the darkness of the woods.

"You! Stop! Get back here!"

Piper tried to follow but she only managed a step or two before the officer spun around and grabbed her from behind.

"Let go of me!" she yelled.

"You're staying right—"

"Let go of me!

He produced another pair of handcuffs and before she knew what was happening he was cuffing her, too. "You're staying here!" he ordered. Then he spun around and took off after Elijah.

"Run, Eli!" Piper shouted. "Run!"

She could tell the RV's lights had blinded her little brother as he held up his hands, shielding his eyes from their brightness. Only then did she see the shadowy form standing in front of those lights.

"Elijah, look out!"

But she was too late. He ran straight into the folds of a large black cloak that quickly wrapped itself around his tiny body.

Mom saw it too and gasped:

"Shadow Man!"

●

Elijah sat in the back of the speeding Hummer, trying not to cry. Beside him was the dark, mysterious man of shadows. Up ahead, one so-called officer was driving the RV. The other was driving the Jeep.

And far behind them, handcuffed and left alongside the road were Mom, Dad, and Piper.

The man of shadows pressed the intercom button and spoke to the driver. "There isss a river on the other ssside of thisss tunnel," he hissed. "Tell the driversss to leave the other cars where they are and join usss."

"Yes sir," the driver answered and reached for his two-way radio.

Out the window Elijah caught a glimpse of someone standing next to the road. Someone who looked just like the old man who had explained the Bible verses to him back at the restaurant ... and exactly like the homeless man who had helped them escape back in Los Angeles.

The little guy closed his eyes and silently began to pray.

Suddenly, the driver slammed on his brakes and they skidded, barely missing the Jeep and RV which were stopped just ahead.

"What isss thisss?" Shadow Man growled.

Elijah opened his eyes and saw that the road ahead had been blocked by a van—the same dark green van that had been following them ever since Los Angeles. A moment later, the woman with flaming red hair and her two assistants tumbled out and raced toward the RV.

Angrily, Shadow Man opened his own door and stepped out, "What are you doing?"

In the confusion, Elijah hoped to escape. He reached for the door and opened it gently. But immediately an alarm began to beep.

"Hey!" the driver looked in the mirror. "What are you—"

Elijah hopped out and was about to make a run for it, but the driver was too quick. He leaped from the car and grabbed the boy. Elijah put up a fight, squirming and twisting, but it did no good. Within seconds the driver had tossed him back into the car and slammed the door.

As the driver slipped back behind the wheel, Elijah reached for the door handle, hoping to try again. But the driver spotted him and hit the auto lock. It came down with a soft *click*.

He grinned sinisterly at Elijah through the mirror. The boy slumped into the seat, unsure what to do. He watched as the driver spoke into his two-way radio.

"What's happening up there?" the man asked.

A gruff voice answered. "It's Monica and her two goons!"

"Oh no," the driver groaned.

"She didn't know we got the kid. Thought she'd try to nab him from the RV."

The driver shook his head. "Idiots."

Elijah looked back out his window and was happy to

see the old man again. He stood at the edge of the woods and gave the slightest nod to the boy. Immediately, the lock to the door clicked up.

The driver was too busy talking into the radio to notice. "What's Shadow Man gonna do to her?" he asked.

Elijah reached for the door handle.

"I dunno," the gruff voice replied. "But I sure wouldn't want to be in her shoes."

In one quick move, Elijah yanked open the door and leaped out.

"Hey!" the driver shouted. But he was too late. Elijah was already dashing into the dark forest.

Chapter Five

On the Run

Piper wanted to be strong. She stood on the side of the road, trying to stop the tears from coming, but she couldn't. And with her hands cuffed behind her back, she couldn't wipe them away either.

How could things get any worse? Not only was she handcuffed, but so were Mom and Dad. Plus her little brother had been kidnapped, and Zach was missing. Plus they were on a road so remote she doubted that they'd see any cars for the next hour ... or day ... or year.

"Maybe we should figure out where the nearest town is," Dad suggested, "and start walking to it."

"What if Zach tries to come back here?" Mom asked.

Dad sighed. She was right, of course, but he found it almost impossible to wait around when his youngest child was in such great danger.

"Are you okay, sweetheart?"

Piper looked over to see her mother watching her. "Yeah," she sniffed, then glanced away. "I'm fine." But she knew she wasn't. And she knew Mom knew.

"We can't let ourselves get discouraged." Piper could hear the thickness in her mother's voice. She knew she was talking as much to herself as to her. "We're going to be all right. God's looking out for us."

Piper blew the hair out of her eyes and breathed out slowly in a long, quiet sigh. If this was God's version of looking out for them, she'd hate to see what would happen if he didn't. It wasn't that she doubted God. She knew he existed and all. But if he was supposed to be so loving, why had he let all this hard stuff happen to them? Why didn't he just—

"Shhh," Dad motioned them to get down. "There's something in the woods."

Piper turned to look behind them. It was true, something was moving in the bushes!

Dad eased himself protectively in front of Mom and Piper. Not that he could do much with his hands cuffed behind his back.

The rustling came closer.

"What is it?" Mom whispered. "A bear?"

Dad motioned them to crouch closer to the ground. They did so, still peering into the darkness.

It was fifteen feet away.

"Should we run?" Piper whispered.

Dad shook his head.

It kept coming. It was just ten feet away now . . .

Now Piper could make out a shape in the shadows. It was big and dark—

Eight more feet.

Almost the size of a man.

Piper watched, refusing to look away. If she was going to die, she wanted to know how. She wanted to see it coming and face it down.

Seven feet.

It was nearly on top of them. For the briefest second she caught a glimpse of what might be a face.

Six feet.

Suddenly, it opened what must have been its mouth and let out the world's biggest...

BELCH!

This was immediately followed by a terrible stench. A stench that could only come from a ...

"Nuclear Burrito!" Piper cried.

"Hey, everybody!" Zach grinned.

Dad could only shake his head. "Zachary ..."

Before he could continue, Zach stepped aside. "Look what I found!" And there, behind him, stood little Elijah, smiling his biggest smile.

●

The family walked the twisting mountain road for nearly half an hour before they stumbled upon their vehicles. Above them, up on the hillside, Shadow Man's thugs were searching the forest, the beams of their flashlights crisscrossing back and forth.

"What's going on?" Zach whispered.

"They're searching for Eli," Dad answered.

"What do we do?"

Dad motioned them back behind some boulders. Once there, they worked out a plan. Piper listened, trying to concentrate, but it was hard to pay attention with the handcuffs cutting deeper and deeper into her wrists.

Finally, the plan was set.

Since Zach had no handcuffs, he went first. He dashed across the road to the Jeep, keeping as low as possible. Once he arrived, he quietly opened the back door. Leaving it open, he crossed around to the driver's side, opened that door, and slid in behind the wheel, where he ducked out of sight.

Now it was Elijah's turn.

He ran across the road and dove through the back door Zach had left open.

Next came Piper. It was hard for her to climb into the car with the handcuffs holding her arms behind her back. Zach and Elijah pulled, and she twisted and squirmed until she finally made it inside.

Then it was Mom's turn.

And finally Dad, who took some extra pulling.

Once everyone was inside, Elijah quietly pulled the door shut.

"Okay, Zach," Dad whispered. "Go for it!"

Zach turned on the ignition, and the Jeep roared to life.

In the woods, the flashlights stopped moving. They all turned and merged into one giant beam ... pointed at the Jeep.

Zach hit the gas. The tires spun, spitting gravel, and the family took off.

Piper looked over her shoulder to see the flashlights bouncing to the cars. It would take a couple minutes before they arrived and started after the family, but she knew they would soon be coming.

Zach pressed the accelerator, picking up speed.

"Be careful, Son," Dad warned. "These curves are sharp."

Zach nodded and slowed slightly. For a moment silence filled the car. But Piper had too many questions for it to last long.

"Um, Dad?"

"Yes."

"Now's probably not a good time to ask, but ..."

"Go ahead," he said. "Ask away."

"Okay. I'm wondering, I mean, if it's not too much bother, could you tell us, you know—*what's going on?*" She didn't mean to yell, it just sort of came out that way.

Mom and Dad traded looks. Dad arched an eyebrow. Mom hesitated, and then gave a little nod. Dad returned it and began:

"We can't tell you everything, because those thugs want the same information. The less you know, the safer you'll all be. But we can tell you this much." He took a breath. "Your brother is ... well, he's special."

"Thanks!" Zach called from behind the wheel.

"Not you," Piper said.

"You're special too," Dad chuckled, and then he grew serious. "It's just, well, there's a lot more to Elijah than you realize."

Piper looked over to her little brother who was curled up in Mom's lap, his eyes already closed. It wasn't a big surprise. Lots of times when everybody was nervous, he was completely relaxed. Other times when everyone was relaxed, he was really nervous.

Mom looked at Elijah and continued the explanation. "We knew something was up, even when he was a baby."

"Like what?" Zach asked.

"Oh, just little things."

"Such as?"

Once again Mom traded looks with Dad.

"I don't think you're ready for that information," Dad said. "Not just yet."

Zach grunted his disapproval from the driver's seat.

"We'll tell you when it's time," Mom said. "But for now, the important thing to know is that Elijah is special. And that there are others—an organization of others—who also know it."

"That's why they want him? Because he's special?" Zach asked.

"Yes."

"But there's something else."

Piper turned to Dad, waiting for more.

He hesitated just a moment before continuing. "We're in a battle. We've been in one for a while, but now it's getting worse."

Zach motioned over his shoulder. "You mean with those goons back there."

Dad shook his head. "It's more than that. It's a spiritual battle."

"Like the devil and stuff?" Piper asked.

Dad nodded. "Yes."

She felt goose bumps rise and crawl across her arms as a shiver went through her body.

Zach had a different response. "Cool!"

Piper cleared her throat. "That sounds kind of, you know ... scary."

Dad shook his head. "It doesn't have to be. Remember, as Christians, we have power over the enemy."

Piper did remember, but it didn't make her any more relaxed.

"That's the war we're fighting," Dad said. "And that's the war we're going to win."

Piper looked from her mother to her father. She was grateful for their faith. And she had little doubt that they had enough to succeed.

She just wasn't sure she did.

She looked out the window in time to see a jagged fork of lightning cut through the darkness. A moment later, the thunder followed, pounding and rolling through the sky.

●

Meanwhile, in the Hummer, Shadow Man was in no hurry to catch up with the family. The tracker attached to the bottom of the Jeep would always tell him where they were. No matter what they tried or what they did, the family would never be able to get away.

Never.

Chapter Six

The Crash

Zach glanced into the rearview mirror. He knew the bad guys weren't far behind. Up above, the sky flashed with bright, jagged forks of lightning. Thunder rumbled as Dad continued his discussion on spiritual warfare.

"Remember when you were all kids?" Dad said. "How I made you memorize Ephesians 6 from the Bible?"

"How could we forget," Zach groaned. "You had us say it like a billion times."

"Do you still remember it?" Dad asked.

Piper spoke up from the back: *"For our struggle is not against flesh and blood, but against the rulers ..."*

Reluctantly, Zach join in, *"... against the authorities, against the powers of this dark world and against the spiritual forces of evil in the heavenly realms."*

Dad nodded. "And the next verse?"

Zach frowned, but Piper continued:

"Therefore put on the full armor of God, so that when the day of evil comes, you may be able to stand your ground."

"Very good," Dad smiled. "I guess you were listening after all."

Mom spoke up. "And do you remember the weapons God gives us to fight with?"

"That one's easy," Zach said. *"The sword of the spirit, which is the word of God."*

"And the shield of faith," Piper added.

"And prayer," Zach added. "It's not on the list, but we've seen it do some major damage." He glanced in the mirror and spotted his sister.

"And don't forget worship," Piper said. "Like singing to God and stuff."

Mom agreed. "The devil really hates that. Remember how we used to sing, Jesus loves me, this I know?" As the family nodded, all remembering, the radio suddenly crackled to life.

"Come in, Dawkins family. Dawkins family, can you hear me?"

Everyone froze ... until Zach broke out laughing.

"What is that?" Mom asked.

"Not *what*," Zach grinned. "*Who*. It's Willard, good ol' Willard."

"On our radio?" Piper asked.

Dad motioned out the window. "Look at that!"

Two shapes were flying about a dozen feet above the car and to the right.

"It's Willard and Cody!" Zach exclaimed. At least he thought it was. It was kinda hard to tell with them hanging upside down and all. It was even harder to tell when Willard zigged and zagged, just missing a billboard.

Unfortunately, Cody wasn't quite so lucky. He zagged when he should of zigged and busted through the billboard.

"Oh, no!" Piper pressed against her window and watched the aerial acrobatics.

Now they were bouncing up and down like jet-propelled pogo sticks.

This time it was Cody's voice they heard over the radio. But he didn't do much talking. In fact, it was just one word. Still, you could definitely tell he wasn't thrilled about what was happening:

"WIL-IL-IL-IL-IL-IL-LARD-ARD-ARD-ARD-ARD..."

A moment later and Willard's voice came back on the radio: *"Dawkins family, listen up. There is a transmitting device planted on your Jeep. You are being tracked and must—"*

Lightning lit up the sky around them, and static filled the radio.

"Are they all right?" Mom gasped.

Dad leaned forward to look up through the windshield and search the sky.

So did Zach, which explains why he didn't see the sharp bend in the road just before the bridge.

"Look out!" Dad shouted.

But he was too late. The Jeep shot off the side of the road, and suddenly they were airborne. Mom and Piper screamed as the car sailed through the air, heading straight for the river.

"Hang on!" Dad yelled.

The nose of the car dropped, and Zach braced himself as the river raced toward them.

"Everybody hang—"

They slammed into the water. Zach's seat belt dug

into his chest as airbags exploded all around. The Jeep righted itself and floated as icy cold water poured in through the floorboards. Everyone was shouting and screaming.

Zach tried to open his door but couldn't. His mind raced, remembering something he'd heard—how if a car goes under water, the outside pressure keeps the doors shut.

"Roll down your windows!" he yelled.

"That's crazy!" Piper shouted. "We don't want to let in more water!

"He's right!" Dad shouted. "Do it!"

Elijah obeyed. He reached past Piper and cranked down the window as fast as he could. That's when the horror hit Zach. His mother, father, and sister were all handcuffed! They'd never be able to swim out! He'd have to save them all.

The river rose to their laps and continued filling the car.

Zach reached into the water, found the seat belt and unbuckled himself. He bent and squirmed until his head and shoulders were out the window, then he pulled himself the rest of the way.

"Zach!" Dad shouted. He turned to see his father struggling to open his own window. "Grab Piper!"

Zach nodded, panting heavily, and swam back to Piper's side. The water was up to her chest now. She'd managed to get her head through the window and was pushing against the seat with her legs, but with her hands cuffed behind her back, she could go no further.

"Zach, help me!" she cried, her eyes full of panic.

He grabbed her shoulders and pulled. She yelped as her stomach scraped across the window until she was finally out. But there was still no way to swim with her hands cuffed.

He wrapped his arm around her waist. Together they kicked and swam against the icy current. More than once they went under, but they kept fighting back up, choking and coughing until, at last, Zach's feet hit the river bottom. Then Piper's. They sloshed and stumbled toward the bank until they arrived and collapsed onto the muddy shore.

But where were the others?

Zach spun around to look. The Jeep had sunk almost to its roof. Without thinking, he dove back into the river and swam toward it.

Gasping for air, he finally arrived. Elijah was helping Mom out. Dad had managed to open his window, but he was too big to make it through the opening and the door was jammed!

Zach took a gulp of air and dove under water to reenter the Jeep through his side. His father's face was up against the ceiling, gulping breaths from the shrinking pocket of air. Zach tucked in his legs and spun around until his feet landed against Dad's door. He kicked it once, twice, three times before it finally gave way and opened.

With lungs burning for air, he pushed out through his window and resurfaced, taking in deep, gulping breaths. He turned and spotted Dad outside the car frantically kicking his feet to stay above the water.

"HANG ON!" he shouted. He swam around the car and grabbed the back of Dad's shirt. Together, they kicked and swam toward shore, where they finally arrived, exhausted.

"Elijah!" Mom cried.

They turned to see Mom had also arrived—obviously

with the help of Elijah. But the little guy was nowhere to be found.

"The current!" she cried. "It carried him away!" She staggered to her feet, searching. "He was here and then ... Elijah!"

Zach rose to his knees, also looking, also shouting. "ELIJAH! ELIJAH!"

And then he spotted him. On the *other* side. The outline of a man was reaching down and pulling him out of the water.

Joy filled Zach. They'd made it! Despite the crash, despite everyone nearly losing their life, they were all safe and sound!

Well, not quite.

Because Dad had also spotted Elijah. And instead of shouting or cheering, he gasped a single word—a name that chilled Zach even more than the icy water.

"Shadow Man ..."

Chapter Seven

Going Down

Mom, Dad, Zach, and Piper stood on the beach, dripping and panting, staring in disbelief at the far shore.

Should they try to find a town and tell the police? Or should they head back to Shadow Man's headquarters and rescue Elijah?

Not that it made any difference. They were so lost they didn't know which direction to go anyway ... until they heard a very familiar voice screaming overhead:

"WATCH OUT!"

Actually, two very familiar voices...

"*YOU* WATCH OUT!"

"I THOUGHT YOU KNEW HOW TO STEER THESE THINGS!"

Piper peered up into the night just in time to see two bodies ...

"AAAAAUGH!"

"WHOAAAAA!"

... drop from the sky and ...

Ker-*SPLASH!*

Ker-*SPLUNK!*

... fall into the river in front of them.

Willard and Cody surfaced, coughing and sputtering as they made their way toward the riverbank.

"Don't worry, he says," Cody was shaking his head. "*Trust me*, he says, *I'll find them*, he says."

"Well I did, didn't I?" Willard argued.

"And nearly got us killed!"

"Honestly," Willard pushed the dripping hair out of his eyes, "sometimes you can be so picky."

Piper smiled in spite of herself. Even though everything had gone wrong, it was good seeing them. Especially Cody. It's not that she liked him or anything. She just liked being around him ... even if his presence did make her a thousand times more klutzy.

"Are you two all right?" Dad asked.

"Couldn't be better," Willard answered. "Just great."

To which Cody, digging water out of his ear, replied, "This is obviously a new definition of *great*." He spotted Piper and gave her a little nod. She nodded back, suddenly finding it difficult to breathe.

Zach motioned to the sky. "Did you see any towns from up there?"

Willard shook his head. "Not for at least fifty miles."

"Well," Dad sighed. "I guess that rules out the police."

"What about a fortress?" Mom asked. "Big and long, made out of rock—almost like a castle."

"Yeah," Cody said, "we saw that."

Willard agreed. "I estimate some twenty miles back down that winding road."

"Or," Cody motioned behind them, "a couple miles straight through those woods."

Piper and her family traded looks. They had their answer.

"What about those handcuffs?" Willard said.

"Any suggestions?" Dad asked.

Willard dug into his pants. "Perhaps this combination picklock/bottle opener I always carry will be of some assistance."

Again Piper and her family traded looks. Willard could be a pain, but sometimes, like now, the pain was definitely worth it.

●

Ninety long minutes later they were crouched down in the woods, just outside Shadow Man's headquarters.

"There's nobody here," Zach said.

And he was right. As far as Piper could tell there were no lights, no movement, no nothing. She blew the hair out of her eyes in frustration. They'd just waded through dark and spooky woods with only Willard's and Cody's flashlights. They just risked being eaten by bears or who knew what, received a gazillion mosquito bites, and been scratched by every branch and rock in their path only to discover that nobody was home.

"I wouldn't bet on that," Dad said. "It's a big place. Maybe they've got him hidden somewhere."

"So are we going in to find him?" Zach asked.

Dad hesitated a moment, then nodded. "You and I will sneak in." He turned to the others. "The rest of you stay here where it's safe. If we find anybody, we'll—"

Mom interrupted, "No, I don't think so."

He came to a stop. "What's that?"

Mom thrust out her chin the way she always did when she got stubborn. "If you're going in, I'm going in."

"Judy," Dad said, "you know how dangerous it is. You know what Shadow Man can—"

"He's my baby!" she blurted out. Then, recovering, she took a breath and repeated, "If you're going in, I'm going in. I'm not staying here without you—not when my Elijah is in there."

"Me too," Piper said as she stepped forward.

"And you may count us in," Willard added.

Dad shook his head. "No. Absolutely not. It's too—"

"Dad . . ." Piper interrupted, "he's my brother."

"And our friend," Cody added. "We didn't come all this way just to stand around and be afraid."

For a long moment, Dad stood looking at the group. It was obvious he was outnumbered and no one would change their mind. He heaved a heavy sigh, "All right, then."

Piper's heart pounded. She was excited and terrified at the same time.

"Where do we start?" Zach asked.

"Your mother and I escaped from that door over there." Dad pointed to the far end of the building. "With any luck it's still unlocked."

"What about surveillance cameras?" Willard asked.

"That's a chance we'll have to take. Just stay low . . . and hope for the best."

Everybody nodded.

"All right, then," Dad said. "I'll go first. If the coast is clear I'll signal you. Any questions?"

There were none.

"Okay, then." He crouched low, took a breath, and started off.

Once he arrived, he pressed flat against the wall and pushed open the door to look inside. A moment later he turned back to the group and motioned them to follow.

Zach took off, followed by Mom, Cody, and Willard. Piper brought up the rear—not because she was scared, but because it's hard running crouched over, especially when you're busy praying for your life.

Dad held the door as they entered. It was a cold, stone hallway, much like a castle. Up ahead, the hallway split into a *T*, and a dozen yards beyond that it split again.

"We'll break up into groups of two," Dad whispered. "Check every room. And be careful!"

They agreed and, for the briefest second, Piper wasn't sure who to go with until ...

"Hey, Piper."

She turned to see Cody.

"You're with me, okay?"

If her heart was pounding before, it was doing cartwheels now. Not only cartwheels, but jumping jacks, back flips, and ... well, you get the picture. Fortunately she was able to swallow back most of the emotion and come up with a squeaky little, "Sure."

Cody grabbed her hand and they took the hallway to the left. Ten feet ahead was the first door. When they arrived, Cody tested the knob. He turned it and pushed it open.

Looking inside, Piper shivered. It was dark and completely empty, except for the squeaking of mice scurrying out of sight.

Cody turned on his flashlight and took a step inside. "I wonder what this place used to be."

Piper followed, inching her way into the room. To the right of the doorway, she noticed a switch. But instead of a normal up and down switch, this one was round. Curious, she gave it a little twist.

"AUGH!" Cody yelled as the floor tilted.

Piper leaped back into the hallway, but the floor tipped so quickly that Cody, who was further inside, didn't have a chance. He lost his balance and fell, clawing at the wood floor as he slipped toward the far wall and the darkness appearing below it.

"Cody!"

The floor continued tilting, growing steeper and steeper.

"Hang on!" she cried. She dropped to her hands and knees. Careful to stay in the hallway, she reached as far as she could into the room. "Take my hand!"

He reached out, but they just missed.

Piper stretched further, clinging to the door post with one hand as she leaned into the tilting room.

Cody dug in, half-scrambling, half-leaping, until their hands touched. Piper grabbed hold and held on tightly as he pulled himself up the floor and finally into the hallway, where he collapsed.

"Are you okay?" she gasped.

"Yeah," he said, trying to catch his breath. "Thanks."

"Look!" she pointed.

By now the floor was completely vertical, straight up and down ... and still it turned.

They watched in amazement as the flipside of the floor appeared ... complete with a stainless steel desk, black leather chair, and a six-foot floor lamp. In front of it rested a black leather sofa. Piper guessed the furniture had been screwed into the floor to keep it from falling when it was upside down. But, strangest of all, in the center of the room was a weird glass chamber shaped like the bud of a flower—big enough for somebody to stand inside.

Dad called out from down the hall, "Are you guys all right?"

Piper turned to see Mom and Dad running to them. Zach and Willard were right behind. They'd obviously heard her cries.

"Yeah," she said, "we're okay."

Suddenly Mom came to a stop and gasped. Dad reached out to steady her.

"What?" Piper asked.

"It's where we were interrogated," Dad said. He stepped around the kids and with a breath for courage, entered the room. "It's Shadow Man's office."

Never one to be afraid (or think before he leapt) Zach followed Dad inside. He spotted the round switch and reached for it. "Hm, I wonder what this—"

"Zach!" Piper shouted.

But she was too late. He turned it, and once again the floor tilted . . . the other way!

Now it was Dad's turn to shout, "AUGH!"

"Turn it back!" Piper yelled, "Turn the switch the other way!"

But Zach was too busy leaping out of the room to hear.

Piper reached past him. Keeping her feet in the hall, she stretched around the wall to the switch and cranked it hard in the opposite direction.

A good idea . . . except she turned it too far and the floor reversed direction . . . throwing Dad in the air like a pancake.

"AAAUGH!!"

The floor kept turning, and by the time he landed, it was so steep he slid into the desk.

"AAAAAUUGHH!"

He clutched the desk legs for all he was worth as the floor finished flipping, and he completely disappeared.

"Dad!" Zach yelled.

"What happened!?" Mom cried. "What did you do with your father!?"

Piper fumbled with the switch, turning it back the opposite direction until, once again, the floor flipped to reveal the high-tech office ... and Dad, hanging onto the desk.

He looked over to Piper as he tried catching his breath. He did his best not to yell, but she could tell he was pretty upset: "DON'T YOU EVER ... (*pant, pant*) ... TOUCH THAT ... (*gasp, gasp*) ... SWITCH AGAIN!"

Piper nodded hard, making it clear she understood.

"Quite fascinating," Willard said. He stuck his head inside the office and spotted another button on the opposite side of the door. "However, I wonder what this one—"

"Don't!" Piper cried. But she was too late.

"—does."

Dad braced himself for another ride, but absolutely nothing happened ... well, except for the panel on the wall behind the desk suddenly sliding open.

"Cool," Zach said as he reentered the room and strolled toward it. "I wonder where it goes."

Dad rose to his feet and joined him.

"Be careful, you two," Mom called.

They moved closer.

With rising curiosity, Willard and Cody took a tentative step into the office. So did Piper.

"What do you see?" Mom called to Dad.

"It looks like some sort of elevator." Dad stepped into it.

Zach joined him.

"An elevator?" Mom asked. Against her better judgment, she also stepped into the office.

"Hey," Zach said, reaching to a switch inside the elevator. "Here's another one of those round—

"DON'T—"

"—knobs." He gave it a twist. Once again the floor tilted toward the elevator, giving everyone a chance to ...

"AUUGHHH!"

... as they tumbled, bounced, and rolled their way toward the open elevator. One after another they landed inside.

"Ooof!"

"Oaaf!"

"Your elbow's in my ear!"

"Sorry!"

... until they were one giant mound of people. And before they could untangle themselves, the panel door *swiiished* shut and the elevator dropped.

Chapter Eight

The Cave

Piper thought the screaming and falling would never end. But finally the elevator stopped, and the panel door slid open to reveal a cold, dark cave. It might have been a relief, except she hated cold, dark caves even worse than out-of-control, falling elevators.

Dad was the first to step out. When he was sure it was safe, he motioned the others to follow.

One by one they filed out.

"Be sure to keep our buddy system," he said. "There're lots of tunnels branching off, and we don't want anyone getting lost down here."

Dad and Mom led the way, followed by Zach and Willard. Piper and Cody brought up the rear. As they made their way forward, Piper began to feel a strange uneasiness—almost as if someone—or some*thing*—was watching them.

And then she heard it. A scraping sound. Behind them.

Was it her imagination? It must have been.

They continued walking until—there it was again. And again.

Almost like footsteps. And they were getting closer!

Mustering all of her courage, she stole a quick look over her shoulder. That's when she saw what looked like a flash of red fire and two black shadows coming toward them!

She screamed. Dad shouted something, but Piper didn't stick around to hear. Seized with panic, she began running. Not forward—there were too many people in the way. Instead, she darted into the first passageway she found and ran for her life.

She only looked over her shoulder once. But that was enough to miss seeing the giant hole in front of her. The giant hole that she tripped, stumbled, and fell into . . . screaming all the way.

●

Mom wasn't sure how far she'd run when Dad pulled them into a small nook of one of the tunnels. Zach and Willard were nowhere to be seen. Neither were Piper or Cody. Everyone had taken off in different directions.

Well, almost everyone.

It seemed they were still being followed by the red fire and two dark figures, which soon became visible as the woman with fiery hair and her two goons.

"Nice work!" the redhead shrieked. "He sent us back to find them, and now they're gone!"

"Sorry, can we leave now?" the biggest one asked.

"You're nothing but an overgrown chicken!"

"Sorry, can we leave now?"

"I agree with Bruno," the skinny one said. "This place really creeps me out."

"So can we leave now?"

"Quiet!" the redhead bellowed.

As the yelling drew closer, Dad reached into his pocket.

"What are you doing?" Mom whispered.

"If we stay here, they're bound to find us."

"So . . ."

"So I'll scare them off."

"With what?"

He proudly pulled out a pocket breath sprayer. "This!"

Mom blinked, wondering if there was a chance he'd lost his mind.

He explained. "When I give you the signal, shine that flashlight on me."

Now she was sure he'd lost his mind. "What?"

The shouting voices were almost there. Without further explanation, Dad wrapped his hand around the breath spray, stepped forward, and shouted, "Stop!" His voice echoed through the cave.

The woman and her goons stumbled to a stop.

Dad nodded to Mom, who reluctantly turned on the flashlight. It cast a giant shadow of him against the wall. And, as he held the breath spray toward them with his index finger pointed out, it looked like a very big man holding a very big gun.

"Stay where you are!" he shouted in his deepest voice. "Don't make me use this!"

It must have done the trick. The goons leapt back, spun around, and ran away as fast as they could.

Mom could only stare.

When the coast was clear, Dad turned to her and smiled. "So what did you think?"

Mom shook her head. "Amazing."

"Thanks," he said, and then gave his mouth a good spritz of spearmint breath spray.

●

Piper woke up to a pounding headache. She wasn't sure how long she'd been unconscious, but the hard cave floor—complete with rocks jabbing into her back—told her she wasn't exactly dead . . . at least not yet. Then there was the darkness. It made no difference if her eyes were open or closed—the blackness was complete, and she couldn't see anything around her.

Then she heard the sounds. Whisperings. Quiet, like the wind blowing through leaves.

A chill rippled across her shoulders.

The whisperings grew louder—eerie and haunting as they echoed against the cave walls.

She reached into the darkness for her flashlight. It had to be there, somewhere.

By now the whisperings were so close she could almost hear words.

She scrapped a rock with her knee, and the whispering stopped—just a few feet away.

Where was that flashlight?! Where had she dropped it?

She could hear breathing now. Quiet, and very close.

At last she felt the flashlight. She grabbed it, making sure it pointed the right direction. Her fingers searched for the on/off switch. There it was.

The breathing was practically on top of her.

She took a silent breath of her own. It was now or

never. She let go a bloodcurdling scream while snapping on the blazing light.

Three pairs of boys' eyes widened like saucers. The pair with the glasses rolled up into their head and fell out of sight ... as Willard hit the ground with a dull *THUD*.

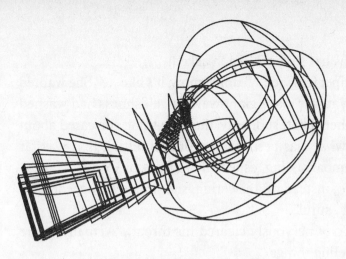

Chapter Nine

Darkness Tightens Its Grip

"Willard!" Cody dropped to his knees and knelt over his friend. "Willard, wake up!" He reached down and slapped his face.

Willard's eyes popped open. "OW!" He immediately slapped Cody back.

Zach had left their side to check on Piper. "You okay?"

"Yeah," she said in a shaky voice. "Thanks for finding me. Where are Mom and Dad?"

"They're next on our list," Zach said as he helped her to her feet.

But she had barely stood before she felt it. "Whoa ... what's that?"

The guys exchanged glances.

"What's what?" Zach asked.

Piper frowned. "I don't know, it's like . . ." She wanted to say it was like a giant wave of selfishness had washed over her. That, suddenly, the only thing she cared about was what was best for her. But admitting that was far too embarrassing, especially in front of Cody.

So, instead of answering, she simply shrugged, "I'm not . . . sure."

Cody nervously cleared his throat. "Actually, we're all feeling things."

Willard added, "And the further we proceed into this cave, the stronger those emotions become."

Piper gave a shudder. The selfish part of her wanted to run away, to let the others find her parents, to let them save her little brother. She had her own life to live. Why should she care? But she fought against the feelings, refusing to give in.

"So, which way?" Cody asked.

"That's an ignorant question," Willard snapped. "We press on, of course."

The rudeness surprised Piper. That wasn't like Willard at all.

He continued. "We are already aware of what is behind us. We are unaware of what lies ahead." Without waiting for the others to agree, he started forward.

"I'm—I'm not sure that's such a good idea," Cody said. His voice sounded unsure, almost like he was afraid.

"Why not?" Willard demanded.

"Because"—Cody glanced from side to side—"because . . ."

Willard rolled his eyes. "Out with it, we don't have the entire day."

Piper came to his rescue. "Because we should pray first."

Now it was Zach's turn to show contempt. "Oh, brother."

Piper turned to him in surprise. Zach had never felt that way about prayer before.

"If you want to hang back and get all religious on us, go ahead," Zach scorned. "But the rest of us are going."

"Get all religious?" Piper frowned. "Zach, what's wrong?"

"Will you please cease this mindless communication?" Willard ordered. "We will proceed, and we will proceed now!"

Piper turned from Zach to Willard, equally as surprised. Before she could answer, Willard shook his head in contempt and started off. Zach followed.

But Cody glanced nervously around, refusing to move.

"Let's go, Cody," Zach called over his shoulder.

"I, uh ..." Cody coughed. "I think I'll stay behind. You know, to protect Piper and all."

But it was a lie. Piper could see it in his eyes. If anything, it was the other way around—he was hoping she would protect him. How strange. She'd always known Cody to be brave and courageous.

What was going on?

●

It was time to report to Shadow Man. Monica was grateful her cell phone didn't work underground. She was even more grateful that she had to leave the caves to call in her report. It's not that she didn't like the caves ... she was just terrified by them. Or at least where they led to.

Actually, not *where* they led to, but *who* they led to.

By the time they caught the elevator and went back upstairs, they were all pretty jittery. Of course Bruno was the worst. The big lug was shaking hard.

"Are w-w-we th-th-there yet?"

"Yes, Bruno," Silas sighed. "You can open your eyes now."

"Great. Can I go to the bathroom?"

"As soon as I call Shadow Man." Monica punched in his number on her phone. "He's still in the Hummer with the kid. And with any luck, he's still in a good mood."

Silas frowned. "I didn't know he had good moods."

"Don't be ridiculous," Monica snapped. "Of course he has good moods."

"Really," Silas asked, "like when?"

"Remember that day there was a big earthquake in California and a major hurricane in Florida and all those tornadoes in Kansas? And when that giant typhoon hit Asia?"

Silas nodded. "You're right. I think he might actually have smiled that day. Well, at least a smirk."

Finally the phone on the other end picked up and a voice demanded, "Ssspeak to me ..."

"I'm, I'm sorry to disturb you, sir," Monica stammered.

"Your very presssenccce dissssturbsss me."

"Yes, well, thank you ... I mean, I'm sorry ... I mean—"

"Sssilenccce!"

Monica gave a nervous swallow. Come to think of it, so did Silas and Bruno.

"Have you found them?" the voice demanded.

"It's just as you suspected," Monica said. "They've

returned to the compound in search of the boy. They found the elevator and are heading down into the abyss."

"The absysss?" She could almost hear him smiling on the other end. "Excccellent. The massster will deal with them ssswiftly."

Monica gave a sigh of relief. "Then you won't be needing us to go down there, will you, sir?"

The three smiled anxiously at each other, giving a confident thumbs-up over a job well done, until Shadow Man answered:

"You mussst return and retrieve the bodiesss."

"But—"

"GO!" The command blasted through the phone with such force that the speaker crackled.

Their smiles wilted as Monica stared at her phone. "Well . . . I guess we have our orders."

"We're n-n-not going back d-d-down there," Bruno said.

"Of course we are," she scolded. "As soon as you go to the bathroom, we're heading into the abyss."

"Ah, actually . . ." Silas coughed slightly. "The bathroom part won't be necessary."

"Why not?" Monica demanded.

Instead of answering, he nodded at the growing puddle at Bruno's feet.

●

Mom and Dad wandered through one tunnel after another, shouting. "Piper! Zach!"

But there was no answer. Just their returning echoes.

"We'll never find them," Mom said, doing her best to hide the trembling in her voice.

But Dad heard it. He put his arm around her and said, "We will, dear. I promise you, we will."

"First we lose Elijah." She sniffed. "Now Piper and Zach ..."

"We'll find them," he said. "God has not taken us this far to abandon us now. We'll find them."

She looked down and then nodded.

Dad gave her another hug and, once again, they started calling, "Piper ... Zach ..."

•

Zach and Willard followed the cave deeper and deeper. Willard had demanded that he take the lead, and the further they went, the bossier he got.

Things were even worse for Zach. It was as if all his faith was being sucked away. And the deeper they went, the worse it got, until he no longer trusted God for anything.

Finally, unable to help himself, he blurted out: "We're gonna die. I know it!"

Willard glanced over his shoulder and sneered. "What?"

"God's left us here, and we're all going to die!"

"Shut your trap, Dawkins!"

But Zach couldn't stop. " 'Left us here?' What am I saying? I'm not even sure he exists!"

"Who? What are you talking about?"

"God! I don't know what's happening, but—"

"Look, *I'm* in control here!" Willard barked. "Not God."

"But—"

Willard spun around, raising his flashlight over Zach's head. "You shut up, or it's gonna be lights out for you, got it?"

•

Even though she was far away, Piper heard the sound of Willard's shouting echo through the cave.

"Cody?" She turned to see him huddled against the side wall, wide-eyed and frightened. "Something's going on here. Our thoughts, our feelings—they're getting out of control."

Cody nodded.

"And it's getting worse." She paused, listening to the shouting. "Especially for Zach and Willard."

"What can we do?" Cody's voice was shaking.

For the briefest second, Piper wanted to throw up her hands and tell him to forget it. What did she care? Let them fight their own battles. The same with little Elijah. Then, suddenly, out of the blue, she remembered what Dad had said in the car:

"We're in a battle . . . a spiritual battle."

And she vividly remembered one of the weapons they were to use in that battle.

"Cody." She moved toward him. "There is something we can do."

He looked to her, waiting for more.

"We can pray."

"What?"

"We're not fighting against anything we can see. We're fighting something spiritual. And the only way we can win a spiritual battle is to fight it spiritually."

His eyes were wide as he looked at her. "How . . . how do we do that?"

She kneeled down. "Take my hand. Let's start praying hard. Real hard."

●

Still holding the flashlight, Willard shouted into Zach's face. "Now get in front of me so I can keep an eye on you!"

"What's wrong with us?" Zach asked. "I don't understand what's happening."

"Now!"

Of course Zach could easily have taken Willard with one hand tied behind his back. Make that two hands. Make that two hands and one foot. But he was worried about the guy. And since God could no longer be trusted to help, it was up to him to do whatever he could. Reluctantly, he took the lead, his faith fading with every step he took.

Together, the boys plunged deeper and deeper into the cave — until suddenly they ran out of steps.

Without warning, the path fell out from under their feet, and the boys tumbled down into darkness. But this fall wasn't like before, when they had all fallen into the elevator. No, this fall seemed to go on . . .

"Aughhhhhhhhhhh!"

. . . forever.

Chapter Ten

The Sword

Zach's cry echoed so loudly through the cave that Piper stopped her prayer. Which was too bad, because the more she prayed, the less selfish she felt and the braver Cody seemed to become. But, even now, when she looked up at him, she saw that same cold fear starting to return to his face.

"What, what do we do?" he stammered.

Of course she was also fighting her own emotions. After all, she wasn't the one who got them into this mess. Wasn't it better just to turn and run away, to save her skin, to look out for herself?

But even as these thoughts filled her mind, she knew they were wrong, and she quickly resumed praying. "Dear God, help me, help us ..." As she continued, Cody rose to his feet. He swallowed nervously and spoke.

"We've got to ... we've got to go down there and help them."

The words surprised her almost as much as they did him.

"Come on." He reached out his hand. She took it, and they started forward. But they'd only taken a few steps before he started to shake.

"Is it getting bad again?" she asked.

He nodded. "The deeper we go ... the worse I feel."

"Me too."

"It's like something is trying to control my emotions."

Piper nodded. "And if it's doing that to us up here ..." she looked down the tunnel, "imagine what it's doing to Willard and Zach."

Cody gave another shudder.

Piper gripped his hand tighter. "Let's keep praying. Don't pay attention to what you're feeling and just keep walking and praying."

Cody nodded, and they continued.

●

Elijah wasn't sure how long Shadow Man had been gone. They'd been parked along the side of the road for quite a while when the Hummer's door opened and the dark presence slipped into the seat beside him.

"I brought you sssomething," he hissed.

From the sleeves of his cloak, he produced a small cage. Inside was a shiny blue butterfly that flitted back and forth.

Elijah's eyes lit up as he watched.

"You like butterfliesss?" Shadow Man asked.

Elijah gave a shy nod.

Shadow Man lowered his voice. "Do you want to sssset it free?"

Elijah nodded more enthusiastically.

Shadow Man held the cage before Elijah. At its front was a small door. "Go ahead," he whispered gently. "Open it."

Elijah reached out and unlatched the little door. Carefully, he slipped his hand inside the cage and held out his finger. The butterfly darted back and forth and then, as if knowing Elijah was there to help, it landed softly on his finger.

Elijah smiled as he gently pulled his hand from the cage.

The bright blue wings almost glowed while the butterfly opened and closed them, as if to share its beauty, as if to thank Elijah.

A tiny giggle of joy escaped from the little boy, until Shadow Man's hand appeared and, in one quick movement, crushed the insect.

Elijah's smile turned to horror as Shadow Man tossed the dead butterfly to Elijah's feet. It twitched its wings once, twice, and then stopped moving altogether.

Elijah's big brown eyes welled with tears.

"You loved that little butterfly, didn't you?" Shadow Man hissed.

Elijah nodded. Tears spilled onto his cheeks.

"Remember, I have the power to crush everything you love—jussst like that. Do you undersssstand?"

Elijah stared at him.

Shadow Man leaned closer. "Do you undersssstand?"

Ever so slowly, Elijah began to nod.

"Yesss. Good. Very good." He reached to the Hummer's door and opened it. "I ssshall return in a few minutesss." He stepped outside and leaned back into the truck. "Think about what I have sssaid, Elijah Dawkinsss. Think very hard." With that, he closed the door and disappeared into the dark forest.

Elijah stared down at the butterfly on the floor. Cautiously, he reached down and scooped up the dead creature. He held it in his hands and closed his eyes, silently moving his lips in prayer.

Several moments passed before he looked back into his hands with hopeful expectation.

The butterfly remained dead.

Biting his bottom lip, Elijah placed the creature on the seat beside him. He pulled himself into a little ball, closed his eyes, and began to cry quietly.

He did not see the butterfly move its wing.

●

"Look!" Mom said. "Footprints."

Dad kneeled down to examine the cave's floor. He was already breathing faster in excitement. But only for a moment.

Mom saw his shoulders droop. "What's wrong?" she asked. "They're tracks. Fresh footprints."

"Yes," Dad said, slowly rising. "But they're ours. We've been traveling in circles."

It was Mom's turn to wilt. "Oh, Mike ..."

He took her in his arms as she fought back the sobs. "It's okay," he said. "We can't give up. God will do his part. Our part is to believe and keep going."

She nodded and wiped her eyes, doing her best to be brave.

They turned and looked ahead. Directly in front of them were the openings to three tunnels. Without saying a word, they both knew what the other was thinking.

Yes, it was their job to believe and keep going ... but keep going which way?

●

As Piper and Cody continued deeper into the cave, Piper began whispering the verses her father had mentioned in the car.

"For we wrestle not against flesh and blood ..."

As she whispered them, her thoughts of selfishness again started to fade.

"But against principalities, against powers, against the rulers of the darkness of this world ..."

"What are you doing?" Cody asked.

"Bible verses," Piper said.

"Bible verses?"

"Yeah." Remembering more of her parents' conversation, she added, "It's one of our weapons. In fact, the Bible says it's our *sword*."

"Sword?"

She nodded. "The sword of the Spirit."

"I don't get it."

"Me neither," Piper admitted. "But remember the devil took Jesus to the mountain to tempt him?"

"Sort of."

"They didn't use guns or bombs or any of that. Their only weapon was the Bible."

"What's that got to do with us?"

She shrugged. "I don't know, but if it's good enough for Jesus ..."

Cody finished her thought, "... then it's good enough for us. What other verses do you know?"

Piper thought a moment, then recited another:

"I have given you authority to trample on snakes and scorpions and to overcome all the power of the enemy."

"I like that one. Say it again."

"I have given you authority to trample on snakes and scorpions and to overcome the power of the enemy."

"Again."

She did. And each time she said it, she felt a little better. And by the strength returning to Cody's eyes, she could tell he was feeling better too.

Until the darkness passed over them. Not a shadow. But a darkness.

Cody shuddered. "Did you see that?"

Piper nodded. "I wish I hadn't."

It passed again.

She pointed her flashlight to the ceiling, to the walls. Nothing.

At least nothing she could see. It was more of a sensation. A presence.

"There!" Cody pointed behind her.

She spun around. Again, there was nothing—nothing she could see. But her pounding heart told her something entirely different.

So did the scream she heard in the distance.

●

Dad turned to the left tunnel. "Did you hear that?"

Mom pointed toward it. "It came from that one, there!"

Dad nodded and took her hand. "Let's go!"

Together, they raced into it.

The ground was uneven, and both of them tripped more than once. But every time Mom started to fall, Dad was there to pull her back up. And whenever Dad slipped and lost his balance, Mom was there to help. Together, they went deeper and deeper into the tunnel.

But after several minutes it seemed like they were getting nowhere fast.

"Wait a minute," Dad said, "wait a minute."

They slowed to a stop and caught their breath. They paused to listen but heard nothing. There were no more sounds.

"Are you feeling what I'm feeling?" Dad asked.

Mom hesitated, then nodded. "All creepy and cold?"

"Yeah."

"Like when they kept us prisoners in that cell or dungeon or wherever that awful man was holding us?"

Again Dad nodded. "Exactly."

"What do you think it is?"

Dad shook his head. "I'm not sure. But when we were in the cell, do you remember what we did? It not only made us feel better, but it helped us get out."

Mom looked at him. "Do you think that will work?"

He gave no answer.

"Here," Mom repeated, "do you think that would work here?"

"I think whatever we were battling there is the same evil we're dealing with here."

Mom started to nod. "All right, then, let's give it a shot."

Dad agreed and once again they took each other's hand and continued down the tunnel. Only this time they did more than run. This time they tried something else as well.

Chapter Eleven

The Pit

The scream belonged to Zach—that much she knew. Piper raced through the cave, shouting his name until she ran out of cave . . . well, at least cave floor. Suddenly, it dropped before her, revealing a giant cavern stretching far below.

Fortunately, she dug in and was able to stop.

Unfortunately, Cody didn't, which explains why he slammed into her from behind.

"Cody!" She started to fall, but he reached out and grabbed her, pulling her in and holding her close.

Once they'd caught their balance and realized they were hugging, they immediately let go.

"Uh, sorry," he coughed.

"That's uh, that's okay," she stammered.

They looked back to the cavern and inched their way over to the edge. They were standing atop a giant, fifty-foot cliff. Piper shined her flashlight back and forth until she discovered ... down at the bottom ...

"Zach!"

But her brother didn't hear. He was too busy swinging his arms and covering his head—all the time shouting, "No, no! Get away! No!"

She tried again. "Zachary!"

He continued waving his arms like he was fighting off an unseen attacker. But what was it? And where was Willard?

Then she saw it. A misty smoke. It was pouring out of a cave at the far end of the cavern. It blew out of the opening toward Zach and encircled him, swirling slowly around his body. But it wasn't mist. Not entirely. Because the longer she stared, the more she caught glimpses of something else. Wings. Tiny black wings.

"Zach!" she yelled. "Zach, can you hear me?"

At last he looked up and saw his sister. He cried her name as relief flooded his face. "Piper!"

"What is that stuff?"

"I don't know!" He continued slapping and batting the air. "It's all around! They're everywhere!"

Whatever they were, they weren't good. Piper could tell by the cold chill wrapping around her shoulders and the giant knot in her stomach.

"Zach, something's not right!"

"You think?" Zach replied, still swatting at the shadows.

"We've got to pray!" she shouted. "You've got to join me and Cody in prayer!"

Zach didn't answer. In the shadows, Piper could just make out the frown clouding his handsome feature.

"Zach?"

"Prayer didn't work for Elijah," he said, just barely loud enough for her to hear.

Piper was silent, not knowing how to answer.

"If all that God stuff works, why is he still missing?" Zach continued. "And Mom and Dad—why did they get kidnapped in the first place?"

It was Piper's turn to frown. This didn't sound like Zach at all.

"Why are we here? Why are we lost? Why are—"

"I don't know!" Piper interrupted. "But I know you're being attacked, and I know we've got to pray."

"Pray?" Zach shouted. "To whom?"

"What do you mean, *to whom*? To God!"

"Yeah, right," he scorned. "We don't even know he exists."

Piper couldn't believe her ears ... or her eyes.

For even as he spoke, the shadows surrounding him grew darker and thicker. More and more solid.

More and more powerful.

●

Deep in the caves, Monica slowed and held up her hand for everyone to stop—which, of course, meant Silas banged into her, which, of course, meant Bruno banged into both of them.

After completing her mandatory glare at them, she whispered, "Do you hear that?"

Everyone grew quiet and strained to listen. It was faint, but there was no missing the quiet sound:

knock-knock-knock
knock-knock-knock

"It sounds like a code," Silas said.

"Maybe someone's trapped," Monica exclaimed.

"Maybe it's a monster!" Bruno cried.

knock-knock-knock

knock-knock-knock

"It's louder," Monica said.

"Or closer," Silas whispered.

"We're all gonna die!" Bruno cried.

Monica turned to him and let out a weary sigh. "Bruno ..."

"We're all gonna die and get eaten!"

"Bruno!"

"Or get eaten, then die! Or get eaten, then die, then—"

"Bruno, put a sock in it."

He stopped and looked at her with hurt in his eyes.

Seething in disgust, she shook her head and pointed at his legs.

"What?" he asked.

"It's your knees."

The big fellow looked down to see his knees banging together spastically.

knock-knock-knock

knock-knock-knock

"Oh." Monica blinked in disbelief and turned to continue down the tunnel. Honestly, five more minutes of this and she was really going to lose it.

●

Elijah woke as the Hummer's door opened.

Shadow Man entered. "Ssso, have you given thought to what I have sssaid?"

Elijah simply looked at him.

The dark form moved closer. "Do you not grow weary of people thinking you are a misssfit, sssome sssort of freak?"

Elijah was surprised at how easily his thoughts had been read. Truth be told, there were days when he wished he were, well, *normal*.

A flicker of a smile crossed Shadow Man's face. He scooted closer and lowered his voice. "You have powersss that no one around you understandsss. Not your friendsss, not your family. How lonely you mussst feel."

Elijah glanced away. He could feel himself being drawn into the man's powers.

A clawlike hand reached out and turned Elijah's face back to him. "But I underssstand. I underssstand you have powersss greater than even you are aware. And if you will join forcesss with my master, there isss nothing we cannot accomplisssh together."

Elijah tried turning his head, but Shadow Man held it firmly. "Propheciesss can be changed. You need not oppossse usss. Combine your powersss with mine. Join me in ssserving the master, and together we can defeat the enemy."

Elijah tried closing his eyes, to push the thoughts away. But the man's words slithered into his brain. They made such sense. Why fight? It would be so much easier to simply deny God and to give in.

Chapter Twelve

The Battle Rages

"Zach, you've got to pray!"

But her brother didn't answer. He didn't even look up.

"Zachary!"

The blackness continued pouring out of the cave and surrounding him — so thick that he could no longer see her. Or hear.

"Zachary!"

She gasped as more of the blackness began taking shape. Besides the wings, she now caught glimpses of faces. But not human faces. More like the creepy, inhuman faces of gargoyles on old cathedrals.

She looked back down to the cave. Was it her imagination or could she see eyes deep inside it? A pair of them. Red and glowing.

She gave an involuntary shudder.

She turned around to Cody. He was pressed against the wall, cowering with his old fear. She could tell that it had returned.

Piper closed her eyes. She just wanted to leave—get away from all this pain and despair. It would be so easy to turn away and leave all of this darkness. None of it was her fault. She hadn't caused any of these problems. It didn't make sense to stay here and suffer.

Stop it! she ordered herself. *This isn't right! I will not give in!* But talking to herself wasn't the solution, and she knew it. So, once again, she closed her eyes and began to pray.

Dear Jesus, I need your help. We've prayed. We've quoted your Word. But there's another weapon. What was it? What did Mom and Dad say? What—

Suddenly, singing filled the air.

Jesus loves me, this I know . . .

Her parents! She spun around. They were approaching. And they were singing!

For the Bible tells me so.

She raced toward them. "Mom! Dad!"

They fell into an embrace as tears filled her eyes. It felt so good to be in their arms, she could stay there forever.

No! She caught herself. It was another form of selfishness. Her brother needed her help, and he needed it now.

She pulled away, motioning to the cavern. "It's Zach! He's down there in some sort of pit. And there are these awful, evil things attacking him and—"

"We know," Dad said. "We could feel something was going on."

"That's why we started singing," Mom explained. "That's why we started worshiping."

"Well, don't stop!" Piper grabbed both of their hands and pulled them toward the cliff. "Whatever you do, don't stop!"

When Mom saw her son surrounded by the evil blackness she cried out, "Zach! Zachary!"

"He can't hear you!" Piper said. "Those things are stopping him."

"What can we do?"

"It's a battle," Piper said. "Just like you taught us. A spiritual battle. I've been praying, I've been quoting Scripture but I forgot to—"

"Worship," Dad completed her thought. "We have to keep singing."

"Right," Piper nodded, "We have to keep worshiping and singing!"

Mom looked down to Zach. She was at a loss for words.

But not Dad. Taking a deep breath, he started singing again:

Jesus loves me this I know. . .

Piper joined in.

For the Bible tells me so.

Mom turned back to them. They nodded for her to join in. And slowly, haltingly, she did:

Little ones to him belong.

We are weak, but he is strong.

Piper paused a moment. Was it her imagination or were those faint screams coming from the cavern? She peered down at the darkness surrounding Zach. The misty faces seemed to be twisting as if in pain, as if something were hurting them. Not only hurting them, but making them grow fainter.

Dad must have seen it too, because he shouted, "Louder. Sing louder!"

And they did:

Yes, Jesus loves me,

Yes, Jesus loves me . . .

The screams grew worse, the cloud thinner.

Suddenly, the air crackled with a roar or a voice or a thought . . . it was hard to tell which. But Piper knew exactly where it came from. She looked down into the black tunnel. The red eyes glowed with rage as the sound roared in her ears:

"YOU HAVE NO AUTHORITY HERE! THIS IS MY DOMAIN!"

"Keep singing," Dad shouted. "Keep singing!"

Yes, Jesus loves me,

The Bible tells me so.

"Again!" Dad shouted. "Again!"

And so they repeated the song, singing with more and more confidence, watching as the blackness around Zach's head grew fainter and fainter.

●

"Join usss," Shadow Man repeated as Elijah continued looking deep into his eyes. He tried looking away but could not help himself.

"No more battlesss. No more fighting. The massster will give you all that you desssire."

Shadow Man had him. It was all over, and Elijah knew it.

Until . . . ever so faintly, he began to hear singing. At first it was barely discernable. But it grew louder and louder. Soon, a tiny smile appeared on his lips.

"What?" Shadow Man demanded. "What are you thinking?"

And then, softly, Elijah began to hum.

"Ssstop that."

The humming grew stronger.

"Ssstop that thisss inssstant!"

Finally, Elijah joined in the song:

Jesus loves me, this I know ...

●

Piper was the first to see him ... the old man they had run across so many times since they'd begun their journey. He stood on a ledge across the cavern from them. How he got there, she had no idea. His eyes caught hers and seemed to twinkle.

There was a flash of light, and suddenly he held a giant broadsword. But not a sword of steel. This was a sword of words. The very words she and Cody had quoted from the Bible. She could actually see them, right there in the shiny blade of light.

The remaining creatures that circled Zach must have seen them too, because they began shrieking and howling. Then, as if desperate, they rose from Zach and raced toward the man. He swung his sword, effortlessly swatting them away. The creatures screamed as they sailed across the cavern and slammed into the wall, finally sliding to the ground.

The next arrived, and the man swung again, repeating the process ... with the same results.

And then the next ... and the next ...

They came faster and he swung faster until everything was a blur ... the swarming mists of darkness racing at him, the glowing blur of the sword swatting them aside.

"Dear God ..."

Piper looked over to her father, who had once again begun to pray.

"We take authority over this darkness, in the name of Jesus."

At the sound of the name, the man with the sword looked up. For a moment, he seemed to smile. Then, suddenly, he leapt into the air, floating toward the cavern floor. For the briefest of seconds Piper thought she saw wings, but she couldn't be certain.

As he landed, the few dark mists still surrounding Zach pulled away.

"Cody!" Dad motioned to the boy who was still curled up against the wall. "Join us."

Cody hesitated.

"We're not the ones who have to be afraid. Come on!"

He rose to his feet, cautiously glancing from side to side. Finally, he moved to join them as Dad reached out for Piper's and Mom's hands. They were forming a circle. A prayer circle.

But they were one short.

"Zach!" Dad shouted.

Piper looked down into the cavern. The clouds had left Zach and were retreating back to the cave where the red eyes glowed. Already, she could see a difference in her brother's face. It was clearer. Brighter.

"Zach!" Dad repeated.

Zach looked up, for the first time hearing his father's voice. "Dad!"

"We're going to pray. Join us."

"I don't think there's a way to climb up there."

"You don't have to; just pray where you are!"

"Got it!" he shouted.

Piper couldn't tell if Zach could see the man with the sword or not. But she could. And she watched with amazement as he started toward the clouds of blackness that had retreated to the cave's entrance. Their little mouths snarled and snapped as he continued his approach.

"Dear Lord." Dad's voice echoed against the stone walls with authority. "We order the enemy to leave. In your name we command him to go and —"

As Dad continued praying, the man raised his sword. He began swinging it into the clouds. Screams of pain and howls of agony filled the cavern as he continued forward, driving them into the tunnel.

Dad squeezed Piper's hand, and she looked at him. "Don't get distracted," he said. "Our job is to pray."

She nodded and lowered her head. He continued to pray as the creatures continued to scream.

●

"What's that shrieking sound?" Silas asked.

"Ghosts?" Bruno trembled.

"Demons!" Monica shuddered.

"Us getting out of here?" Silas cried.

"YES!" all three screamed as they turned and raced back to the elevator.

●

The screaming slowly faded into faint echoes, which finally ended altogether.

Piper opened her eyes and peeked down into the cavern. The clouds of blackness had disappeared. She knew they had escaped deeper into the cave along with the glowing red eyes. She also knew they were defeated.

At least for now.

And the man with the sword?

He'd also disappeared. Big surprise. But she knew they would see him again. At least when he was needed.

In the silence, she heard someone crying, whimpering. Zach heard it too. She watched as her brother slowly walked over behind a boulder and found Willard curled up in a ball, sobbing.

Zach gently put his hand on the boy's shoulder. "It's okay, Willard," he said. "It's over. It's all over."

Epilogue

Now that his mind was clear, it didn't take Zach long to start searching for footholds and begin climbing up the steep cliff. Of course he did plenty of slipping and sliding, but eventually he reached the top and joined his family.

It was a little harder for Willard (actually, a lot harder), which was why everybody tied their shirts and coats together to make a type of rope with a sling to pull him up.

Of course there were more than enough hugs to go around, and Mom cried. To be honest, Zach felt his own eyes burning a little, though he was careful to keep it hidden from everyone. After all, he did have his reputation to keep up.

Eventually, they turned and started out of the cave. It was still just as cold and dark, but definitely not as scary. They traveled for what seemed forever but finally, after a few wrong turns, they found themselves at the elevator. The good news was it still worked and the doors opened for them. The better news was it carried them back up to the creepy office. The best news was they were able to quickly get out of the office and back outside.

"Weird," Zach said as they looked around. "There's still nobody here."

"There was." Willard pointed to some fresh tire tracks. "But they must have left. And by these skid marks, I'd say they were in a major hurry."

Piper smiled. It was nice to hear Willard talking normally again. Granted, he could be kind of odd sometimes. Okay, lots of times. But, let's face it, that oddness was part of what made him so fun.

She turned to her parents and asked, "So what do we do?"

Dad gave a heavy sigh. "I guess we head back through the woods to the RV."

"And then?" Zach asked.

"And then we find Elijah. Come on." He started forward.

But he'd only taken a couple steps before Zach called, "Dad?"

His father stopped. "Yes, son."

"Shouldn't we, you know, like pray or something?" .

Dad broke into a smile. "You're right," he chuckled. "You're absolutely right." He turned and headed back to the group. "So ... do you want to lead us?"

"Sounds good to me," Zach said.

Piper couldn't believe her ears. Zach wanting to pray? Amazing.

Then again, maybe it wasn't so amazing. After all, everyone seemed to have gone through some positive changes. Who knows, maybe even Zach was changed a little for the better. All right, *very* little. But, hey, a little change was better than no change.

Once again the family gathered for prayer

"You okay?" Piper asked as Cody joined her side. "You haven't said a word since we left the cavern."

He shrugged. "Guess I'm kind of embarrassed. I mean, nobody likes cowards."

Piper's heart melted a little for him. "It wasn't just you, Cody." She pointed to herself. "Nobody likes self-centered brats either." Then motioning to Willard she added, "Or know-it-all bullies or," she motioned to Zach, "big-time doubters."

"Yeah, but still . . ." He dropped off, unsure how to answer.

"We've all got weaknesses," she said. "Whatever was down there was just trying to use them against us. But the important thing is, we discovered how to fight back, how to beat it." She stopped. But when she stole a peek at Cody, she was grateful to see him nodding as if she actually made sense.

"Okay," Zach said, "everybody grab a hand."

Without a word, Cody reached out to take her hand. Suddenly she forgot what she was embarrassed about.

Zach continued. "We're going to pray that we beat these bad guys once and for all."

Cody squeezed her hand a little tighter. She returned it.

"And we're going to pray that we find my little brother."

Everyone nodded. Then the group bowed their heads and began.

•

Elijah heard the flutter of something pass his ears. He opened his eyes to see the butterfly circling his head. He wasn't sure how long he'd been asleep, or how long he had been traveling with Shadow Man. All he knew was that he had needed the rest. Another battle was about to begin, and it would call for all of his strength.

Funny thing about battles. It seemed like every one pushed them to their limits. And just when they were sure they couldn't go another step, they somehow found the strength to take it. And then take another. It was almost like someone was giving them extra strength. Like someone was training them, making them stronger and stronger.

Elijah smiled quietly. Because he knew who that Someone was. And he knew that that Someone would never let them slip through his fingers. Because he loved them. Loved them more than they would ever know.

The butterfly made one last circle before landing on Elijah's shoulder.

The boy smiled just a little bigger and then he started to hum. It was another song of worship.

The
Chamber of Lies

For Doc Hensley
A teacher committed to truth

Consider it pure joy, my brothers, whenever you face trials
of many kinds, because you know that the testing of
your faith develops perseverance. Perseverance
must finish its work so that you may be mature and
complete, not lacking anything.

James 1:2–4

Chapter One

To the Rescue

"That's impossible!"

Willard looked up from the computer in the back of the rattling RV. "What is?" he asked.

"How can Elijah send us a message?" Thirteen-year-old Piper blew the hair out of her eyes. "He doesn't even know how to turn on a computer." She scowled back at the message on the monitor.

Don't try to save me!

Shadow Man has weapons you don't understand.

Elijah

Willard, Piper's geeky inventor friend, shoved up his glasses with his chubby sausage-like fingers. (Willard liked to eat more than your typical guy—actually, more than your typical *two* guys). "Run it past me again. Who exactly is this Shadow guy?"

"*WHO* isn't the right word," Piper said.

"More like *WHAT*," Zach, her sixteen-year-old brother, exclaimed. "We heard him speak back at Ashley's."

"Heard?" Willard asked, shoving his glasses up his face again.

"It's a long story, but believe me, the dude is not someone you want to mess with."

"Everything all right back there?" Dad called from the driver's seat of the RV.

He and Mom sat up front as they drove through the twisting mountain road. The past few days had been rough on them. First, they'd had to leave the kids behind while they acted as decoys for the bad guys. Then they'd been kidnapped. Then they'd lost little Elijah. Then they'd wandered deep into mysterious caves and a cavern filled with strange supernatural beings. Definitely not good times. In fact, on the fun scale of 1–10 they were somewhere below 0.

But at least they had Piper and Zach, and their two friends, Willard and Cody. Together, the four kids sat at the back table.

"Don't worry about us," Zach called up to his parents. "Everything's cool." He shot a look to Piper, telling her to keep quiet about the message on the computer screen. She couldn't have agreed more. After all that Mom and Dad had been through, they didn't need to worry about strange new weapons.

Suddenly, Dad hit the brakes and everyone flew forward.

Piper screamed and nearly hit her head on a cupboard, but Cody reached out and caught her in his arms. As the RV shuddered to a stop, he looked down at her and asked, "Are you okay?" His eyes were worried.

Piper gazed into his incredible blue eyes and half-croaked, "Yeah." She always half-croaked when she looked into his eyes. But it wasn't just his eyes. Everything about him made her a little unsteady on her feet (and a little fluttery in her heart).

Zach called up to Dad. "What's going on?"

"Looks like a detour," Dad said.

A sheriff approached the side door of the RV. Zach rose and opened it for him.

The man stuck his head inside. "Afternoon, folks."

Piper caught her breath. He looked exactly like the homeless person who had helped them in the streets of L.A. . . . and the customer who had helped them in the mountain restaurant . . . and the angel who had fought for them in the cavern.

Piper stole a look to Zach. The way his mouth hung open, she knew he'd noticed it too.

"Is there a problem, Officer?" Dad asked.

The man nodded. "Highway is out. You'll have to turn around."

"But—"

"There's a dirt road about a mile back. It'll take you to where you're going."

Mom frowned. "How do you know where we're—"

"And be careful," he interrupted. "You folks still have plenty of dangers ahead. But you'll be okay. You've got plenty of folks looking out for you."

It was Dad's turn to frown. "I don't understand. 'Plenty of folks?' "

"That's our job," the officer smiled. "To look after the good guys." With that, he stepped back outside . . .

but not before catching Piper's eye and giving her a quick wink.

Piper could only stare. Who was this man? She moved to the window for a better view. But by the time she arrived, he was gone.

●

"They are coming thisss way."

Monica Specter stared across the picnic table to Shadow Man. Looking at the massive bulk of darkness always gave her the creeps. Actually, looking at him didn't give her the creeps, not being able to see him did. Well, at least not *all* of him. There was something strange about the way the man always sucked up light — even in the brightest day.

"Want me to hurt them?" Bruno, her brainless assistant, asked. He sat on the bench beside her. To make his point, he reached into his coat for his gun. A thoughtful gesture, if it hadn't been for the soda can sitting on the table beside him.

The soda can that he knocked over with his elbow.

The soda can that dumped its fizzy contents all over Monica's lap.

She leapt to her feet, wiping the soda away. "You idiot!"

"I'm sorry," he said. For a moment he looked puzzled, wondering if he should help her or use his gun to shoot the offending can.

Shadow Man saved him the trouble. With a wave of his arm, he sent Bruno's gun flying out of his hand and into the side of Monica's parked van. It gave an ominous *THUD,* then fell to the ground.

"Your weaponsss are of no ussse," he hissed. "Not in thisss battle."

Monica glanced nervously at her two assistants: Bruno, who was as big as he was stupid, and Silas, who was as skinny as, well, as Bruno was stupid. The three of them had spent many days tracking down Elijah. And now, with the help of Shadow Man, they had finally captured him.

But instead of looking scared, the six-year-old sat on a nearby rock, humming happily to himself. Talk about strange.

Stranger still, Monica had never heard Elijah speak. In fact, she was beginning to wonder if he even knew how.

A low rumble filled the air. A vehicle was coming up the dirt road that they'd parked alongside.

"Is that them?" Silas asked.

Shadow Man grinned. "Yesss. They've come for the boy."

"Shouldn't we do something?" Monica screeched. (She didn't mean to screech; it was just her normal voice). "At least get the brat out of sight?"

Shadow Man turned to look at her. At least she thought he was looking at her. It was hard to tell with his eyes always in shadows.

"After the accccident, I ssshall take care of the child. You three will ssstay behind and sssearch for sssurvivorsss."

"Accident?" Bruno said. "I don't see no accident."

"You will." Shadow Man smiled and for the briefest moment Monica thought she saw teeth ... or was it fangs? "You will."

The rumbling grew louder.

Shadow Man turned to Elijah. "Boy. To the vehicle."

Monica watched as Elijah rose and turned toward Shadow Man's enormous Hummer. The child's legs began walking, but they seemed to move against his will. He tried to stop, but one stiff step followed another until he arrived at the truck.

The driver, a huge bald man who stood guard, opened the back door.

Monica cleared her throat nervously. "Shouldn't we hide too? We're right next to the road, so they're bound to see us."

"There isss no need. The crasssh ssshall prevent it."

"But I don't see no crash," Bruno insisted.

"Watch and be amazzzed …"

Chapter Two

The Crash

"Dad," Zach called from the back of the RV, "if this is a detour, how come we don't see any other cars? Or detour signs?"

"He's right," Mom agreed. "I've got a weird feeling about this."

Willard motioned to the computer monitor. "Check it out."

Zach looked down and saw the letters to another message appearing on the screen:

Deer coming from right.

Tell Dad to look out his window!

"Dad," Zach called. "Look to your right."

"What?"

"To your right! Look to your right. Now!"

Dad turned just in time to see four deer appear at the side of the road and dart in front of the RV. He cranked the wheel hard, veering to the left, barely missing them but sending the RV into a squealing skid.

●

Shadow Man watched with displeasure as the RV slid across the road, just missing the deer.

He turned to the Hummer and shouted at Elijah, "And you think that will ssstop me?!"

He raised his arm toward the cliff looming to the right over the roadway. Several giant boulders came loose and began to fall, bouncing toward the RV.

●

Zach was too busy fighting to keep his balance in the swerving RV to notice another message forming on the computer screen:

Rocks! Look out!

The first boulder slammed into the vehicle's side. The force was so powerful that it ripped the steering wheel out of Dad's hands. He grabbed it and fought to regain control of the vehicle. For a moment it looked like he had it, but then the second boulder hit. And then the third. And the fourth. The RV was batted around like a ping-pong ball as rocks continued to hit it.

"Hang on!" Dad shouted.

Dishes fell from the cupboard, crashing to the floor. Everyone was yelling. Zach stumbled, tried to catch himself, and was thrown down.

But only for a second.

Before he realized what was happening, he was thrown into the left wall of the RV — then the roof.

They were rolling!

Bodies flew past him, legs kicking, people screaming. Glass exploded around him. There was more yelling as he hit the opposite wall, then finally the floor again.

Well, not actually the floor. More like Willard.

"Oaff!"

Zach landed on top of him, grateful for all the junk food and extra doughnuts the chubby kid had eaten, cushioning his fall.

"Sorry, Willard."

"That's ... okay ..." the kid groaned.

Zach scrambled back to his feet. He looked around to see if anyone was hurt. And then he saw Dad slumped over the wheel, blood trickling down the back of his head.

That's when he panicked. "Dad!"

●

Monica watched with amazement as the RV finished rolling and landed back on its wheels, filling the air with dust and smoke.

"Well, don't jussst ssstand there," Shadow Man hissed.

She turned to see the massive bulk of a man stepping into his Hummer.

"Go! Take care of the othersss!"

Monica wasn't exactly sure what he meant by "taking care of," but she could make a good guess. She motioned to Silas and Bruno to follow her toward the RV, then pointed to Bruno's weapon lying next to her van where Shadow Man had flung it. "Don't forget your gun!"

As Piper staggered to her feet, she could hear Zach coughing and shouting, "Dad, are you all right?"

She called out to her mother. "Mom, you okay?"

"Yes. It's just my leg. It's pinned against the dash, but I'm all right. How's everybody back there?"

Zach was crawling toward the front as Piper glanced to Cody and Willard. They were also rising to their feet. Cody was wincing, holding his right arm, but everyone else seemed okay.

"We're fine!" Piper shouted back.

She glanced around the RV. The kids may have been fine, but the place was a mess—dishes thrown out of the cupboard, everything tossed around and dumped on the floor. It was as bad as Zach's room.

Well, not quite, but close enough.

"How's Dad?" she called.

"He's unconscious!" Zach shouted.

Piper sucked in her breath.

"It's the TV," Mom cried. "It fell off the shelf and hit the back of his head! Mike? Michael?"

Zach was kneeling beside him. "Dad, can you hear me?"

Piper's heart pounded as she moved forward to join them.

"Dad?"

She heard a groan and saw him move his head.

"He's coming around," Mom said. "Mike, can you hear me? Michael, can—"

She was interrupted by the voice of a woman approaching from outside. "Anybody alive in there?"

Piper frowned. She'd heard that voice somewhere. More than once. But where? A second voice joined it.

"Want me to blow off the door?"

"Not yet, you idiot!" the woman screeched. "Try opening it first!"

"Oh, yeah." The man gave a nervous laugh. "Why didn't I think of that?"

Piper had her answer. There was no mistaking the rudeness of the woman—or the lack of intelligence of her assistant. And because of their missing manners (and brain cells), these were not people Piper wanted to meet again. Ever.

Zach must have recognized the voices too. "Dad," he said, "Dad, can you turn on the engine? Dad, can you get us out of here?"

But of course Dad couldn't. He was too busy just trying to open his eyes.

"Anybody in there?" The woman's voice was much closer. Any second now she'd open the door.

"Here," Zach said to his father, "let me scoot you over."

"What are you doing?" Mom asked.

He shifted Dad far enough to ease behind the wheel. He turned on the ignition. The motor ground away, but nothing happened. He tried again.

"Zach ..."

He tried a third time, and the engine finally turned over. It wasn't happy about it, but at least it was running. And just in time.

Suddenly, the side door was yanked open, revealing a woman with flaming red hair. Beside her stood the biggest of her assistants. But they only stood there a second before Zach dropped the RV into gear, punched the accelerator, and took off.

"ZACH!" everyone shouted.

Well, everyone but the red-haired woman and her goon. It's hard to shout when you're busy leaping out of an RV doorway so your head doesn't get ripped off.

●

Shadow Man stared out his Hummer's window watching Monica and her bungling assistant start chasing after the RV. Despite dozens of dents, scratches, and broken windows, it still ran. This surprised Shadow Man and for a moment he didn't understand how it was possible.

Unless . . .

He stole a look at Elijah, who was seated at the back. Was this more of the boy's trickery? He knew the child had powers, but this?

Shadow Man couldn't be sure. All he knew was that the little brat was humming again. He hated it when the boy did that. He could make him stop, of course. But then the child would simply find some other way of trusting and thanking—of praising—the Enemy.

The Enemy. That was the whole reason Shadow Man was in this mess in the first place. The Enemy had finally started his preparation to bring about the end of days. And for some unknown reason he had chosen little Elijah as one of his most important tools in bringing about that end.

Shadow Man's lips curled into a tiny smile. Well, let the Enemy choose whom he would. And let the boy hum away, because very soon the child would turn his back on the Enemy. Very soon Shadow Man would bring Elijah over to his side of the battle, to where the real power lay.

All it would take was a little time in The Chamber. A little time to show the child the wonders and glories that would be his if he would deny the Enemy and follow Shadow Man's master.

Chapter Three

Decoy

"Where are they?" Zach shouted over the sputtering RV. He checked the cracked side mirrors for any sign of Monica or her assistant. "I don't see them!"

Cody called from the back window. "They've turned around. They're running back to their van!"

"Zach, slow down!" Mom cried.

"I will in just a second."

"We'll never get away!" Piper shouted. "Not in this thing. What do we do?"

"Hang on, I've got a plan."

"That's what I'm afraid of," she groaned. Piper always groaned when her big brother had a plan. Mostly because it was impossible to forget some of his more famous plans ...

Like his plan to become a billionaire by selling bottles of air. Not fancy stuff like hospital oxygen bottles or anything like that. Just plain ol' air. "They do it with water," he reasoned. "So why not do it with air?"

Then there was his weight loss plan that involved eating ground up toe nail clippings mixed with slug slime. Actually, the eating wasn't too bad, it was the throwing up that wasn't so popular. In fact, the only bottle he ever sold was to Piper (which was how she knew about the throwing up).

His latest plan involved building an indoor swimming pool by shoving a hose under her bedroom door, taping up all the cracks around it, and turning on the water. (If she hadn't opened her window, she would have drowned). Good ol' Zach.

Fortunately, this plan worked just a little better. Well, sort of ...

They rounded the bend and Zach pulled over to the side of the road, bringing the RV to a shuddering stop.

"What ..." Dad coughed, "what are you doing?" He was still pretty out of it, but at least he could talk.

"We're going to lure them away from you guys," Zach said. "Away from the RV."

"What?" Mom asked.

"That will give you time to call 911 and get an ambulance up here for you and Dad."

"I'll be okay," Dad said, doing his best to sound all right but failing miserably.

"Yeah, right," Zach answered. He motioned for Piper, Willard, and Cody to head out the side door. "That van will be here any second. Come on, let's go!"

Normally, Piper would have put up a fuss. It made no difference whether it was a good plan or a bad plan. As the younger sister, she had to complain; it was an unspoken law. But at the moment, causing a diversion actually seemed like a pretty good idea—even if it was Zach's.

She stepped outside through the door. Willard and Cody followed.

Zach stayed inside just a second longer to talk to his parents. "Both of you keep your heads down so they can't see you. I'll lock this thing up. Once we're safe, we'll circle back around to make sure you've been picked up."

"Don't worry about us," Mom said. "I'll phone 911 and we'll be okay. But you be careful."

"Right—"

"I'm serious, Zachary . . . be careful."

"Got it. I love you, Mom."

"I love you, too."

With that, Zach stepped out of the RV and locked the door—just as Monica and her van squealed around the corner.

By now Piper was standing at the edge of the woods. "Let's go," she motioned to her brother. "Come on, come on!"

"Not yet." Instead of joining her, Zach actually took a step closer to the road.

"What are you doing?!" she cried.

The van lurched and skidded to a stop fifty feet away.

"Zach!"

"Not yet."

The doors flew open and the red-haired woman and her two assistants piled out, both pointing guns.

"Zach!" Piper hissed.

"I want to make sure they see us."

The biggest goon was the first to fire, hitting a tree ten feet above Piper's head.

"They see us!" she cried.

"Good point!" Zach turned and sprinted toward her. The second goon fired. This shot came a lot closer.

"Yes, they definitely see us!"

Zach, Piper, Willard, and Cody raced into the woods and disappeared. With any luck, the bad guys would follow.

●

"In here!" Shadow Man ordered. "Bring the boy into my officccce, and put him into The Chamber."

The bodyguard brought Elijah into Shadow Man's dark, wood-paneled office. At its very center sat a glass-enclosed case. The case was shaped like the bud of a flower and was only large enough for one person to stand inside.

As soon as Elijah saw it, his eyes widened.

Shadow Man gave a slow smile. The child could not possibly know what awaited him, but he obviously sensed the danger.

"Hold him!" Shadow Man ordered. "Don't let him go!"

The bodyguard gripped Elijah's arms tighter as he stooped down and shoved the boy into The Chamber.

Shadow Man could have used his powers to force the child inside, but those powers had been draining ever since they'd been away from the Compound. That's why they'd doubled back to return to his base of operation. Shadow Man drew his energy from the Compound. Actually, it was the cavern underneath the Compound. The cavern where the Supreme Master dwelled.

"Now leave usss," Shadow Man ordered.

The bodyguard nodded and stepped past Shadow Man, keeping his eyes on the ground since he was never allowed to look at him. As the servant exited into the hallway, Shadow Man gave one final command.

"Ssshut the door."

The guard obeyed, slamming the door with a foreboding ... *BOOM*!

For a long moment Shadow Man remained motionless, staring at the boy. Hard to believe such a simple child would one day—one day soon—cause so much trouble. Still, children grow up. And since the Enemy's prophecies always came true, there was much to fear from this one.

He knew Elijah could not be killed. The Enemy would forbid it. He could not even be hurt. That was another promise the Enemy made to those who served him.

But the boy could be turned.

Not by force; it would have to be the child's own decision. But if Shadow Man could persuade Elijah to change his allegiance ... well now, that was another story.

And that was what The Chamber was all about.

Shadow Man approached the wall of the glass pod.

The boy was watching his every move—but not in fear. And it was this lack of fear that outraged Shadow Man. The Enemy's servants always seemed to serve him with such joy, even love. Shadow Man always served *his* master with cold, gut-twisting fear.

"Ssso, tell me, Elijah," he hissed. "Thisss God you follow." He was careful never to speak the Enemy's name. Speaking his name brought unbearable pain and drained Shadow Man of his power. "Don't you find it odd that he promisssesss to protect and defend you, yet your family isss conssstantly under attack?"

Elijah just stared at him through the glass.

"Haven't you ever imagined what your life would be like if you didn't follow thisss ssso called God of love? Haven't you ever imagined how much more fun you would have living like othersss? Being your own bosss? Doing whatever you like, whenever you want? You could finally be free. *Really* free."

Elijah started to smile.

Shadow Man fought back his irritation. The brat wouldn't be smiling for long.

He moved to a nearby pedestal. On top of it rested a strange sort of keyboard. "Imagination isss a powerful thing, young Elijah." He reached for the keys. "Just imagine what life would be like without your God. Better yet, imagine what my Massster could provide you. Unlimited fame. Unlimited popularity. Imagine being loved and adored by all who sssee you. He can give that to you. That and ssso much more."

The boy simply blinked.

"Are we having a hard time imagining that?"

Again, there was no answer.

Shadow Man reached for the keyboard. "Allow me to assissst you." His fingers flew across the keyboard. As they did, The Chamber grew brighter and brighter. A circular tube at the top began to pulsate: orange, red, green ... orange, red, green ... orange, red, green...

A strange look came over the child's eyes. They no longer blinked; they no longer moved.

Instead, they glazed over as the boy began to see the glorious future that could someday be his ...

●

Bruno had been the first to enter the woods, followed by Monica, and finally Silas, who brought up the rear. They'd been going in this order for several minutes, and it seemed a fine idea.

K-THWACK!

Well, except for the branches.

K-THWACK! K-THWACK!

The ones that Bruno kept letting fly back and hitting Monica's—

K-THWACK! K-THWACK! K-THWACK!

—face.

Unable to take any more, she finally shrieked, "Bruno!"

He came to a stop and turned. "Huh?"

Trembling with rage, she pointed to the thin red scratches covering her cheeks and forehead.

"What happened to your face, Monica?" he asked. "It's all red and puffy."

She clenched her jaw, ready to explode.

"Are you allergic to something?"

Knowing she was about to blow a vessel, Silas stepped in and explained. "Yes, Bruno, she is allergic to something."

"What's that?"

"You!"

Bruno frowned. His bottom lip trembled. Then, just as he was about to break into a good cry, Silas noticed something on the ground.

"Look." He pointed to the footprints in the mud they'd been tracking. "They've split up. One set goes to the left, the other to the right."

"Oh no, what do we do?" Bruno cried. "They've outsmarted us!"

"Bruno."

"They've outfoxed us!"

"Bruno!"

"They've out—"

"BRUNO!"

The big man stopped.

Silas threw a glance to Monica. She was still trembling. That blood vessel could go any second, so he again explained. "There's three of us, right?

"Right."

"So we'll split up."

"Split up?"

"That's right."

Bruno's face brightened. "Oh, you mean one and a half of us will take the left path and one and a half of us will take the right?"

Silas glanced at Monica again.

She was feeling no better.

"Yeah," he said. "Something like that. But I've got a better plan. Why don't you head down the path to the right, and Monica and me, we'll take this one to the left."

"So we don't got to cut one of us in half?"

"Yeah," Silas nodded. "So we don't got to cut one of us in half."

"Cool," Bruno nodded. "I like that way lots better."

●

Zach had been the one to think of splitting up. That way if one group got caught, the other could still get away to help Mom and Dad—and Elijah.

Of course, his little sister, Piper, did her usual fretting and worrying, but eventually she agreed to follow the path to the right with Cody, while Zach and Willard went to the left.

That had been forty-five minutes ago, plenty of time for the ambulance to arrive and take Mom and Dad to the hospital. So now, according to Zach's plan, both his group and Piper's were circling back to the RV.

Everything was going perfectly ...

Except for the gun that was suddenly pointed in Zach's face.

"Hold it right there."

Zach froze. It's hard to keep walking with a gun shoved in your face.

He wasn't sure how, but the skinny guy and red-haired woman had traveled through the brush and cut them off here on the trail.

"Now," the skinny guy said, "turn around nice and slow."

Zach and Willard obeyed.

"Did you honestly think you'd get away?" the red-haired woman sneered.

"You only got half of us," Zach shot back. "The others did get away."

"I wouldn't be so sure of that," the skinny guy answered. "We have someone hot on their trail."

Zach looked past him to see a big man lumbering up the path toward them. "You mean him?" he asked.

The red-haired woman turned and screeched, "Bruno?!"

"Present," the big man panted as he approached.

"What are you doing here?!"

"I gotta question."

"A question?!"

"When Silas said to take the right path, did he mean my right or his right?"

"My right or his right?! *My right or his right?!—*"

Zach noticed the woman's face getting strangely red, the veins in her neck starting to bulge.

That's when the skinny guy took over. "Actually, they're the same."

Bruno shook his head. "Nope. Cause when you face me, your right is your left." He frowned. "Or is it my left is your right. No wait, a minute, I had this figured out a second ago. Your right is my—"

"Uh, Bruno?"

The big fellow looked to him, hopefully. "Yeah, Silas?"

The skinny guy took the big fellow's arm and turned him so they faced the same direction. "This is the path, correct?"

"Correct."

"And when we face the same direction, my right is exactly the same as your right. You see?" He tapped his right arm. "My right." He tapped the big guy's arm. "Your right. Exactly the same."

Bruno's face lit up like a kid who finally understood complex fractions. "That's ... amazing."

"I thought you'd appreciate it."

"You are so smart sometimes."

"Yes, well," he came to a stop. "What do you mean, 'sometimes?'"

But Bruno wasn't listening. He was too busy studying his arms. "Wow! Do other people know about this?"

"Just a few, Bruno. Just a few."

Silas turned back to Zach and Willard and sighed heavily. "Well, at least we've got you two."

"You want I should go after the others?" Bruno asked. "They'll be on my left, right?" He stopped and frowned.

Silas covered his eyes and looked to the ground.

The big guy continued. "Unless I turn the other way.

314

Then they'll be, don't tell me now, then they'll be on my …" He scratched his chin trying to figure it out.

Zach glanced toward the red-haired woman, who had dropped her head into her hands, slowly shaking it. Then, before she exploded or the big guy could share any more brain bruising insights, her cell phone rang.

She pulled it from her pocket and looked at the number.

"It's Shadow Man," she murmured nervously. Opening it, she answered in her most pleasant voice, which still sounded a lot like fingernails on a blackboard.

"Yes, sir?"

The voice on the other end was so loud she had to hold the phone away from her ear. "Did you find them?"

"Uh, well, that is …"

"It isss a sssimple quessstion. Are they in your possessssion?"

"Uh, we have the children. But the parents are—"

"The parentsss are on the way to the Johnsssonville Hossspital."

"The hospital?"

"My workersss there will handle them. But regarding the children … I have far greater planssss for them."

"The children?" Monica asked. "*BOTH* children?"

"Yesss. I want you to contact Reverend Festool. Bring him in for a little chat with them."

Monica swallowed. Everyone in the group swallowed.

"What about their friends?" she asked.

All eyes shot to Willard, who would also have swallowed if his mouth hadn't become as dry as the Sahara Desert.

"Leave them. They are of no usssse. I want only the brother and sssisssster."

"The brother *and* sister?" Monica repeated.

"Yesss. The others will be free to live their pitiful exissstence as they pleassse. But not the brother and sssisssster."

"Got it," Monica said. "We're heading back to the van ... with the brother *and* sister."

"Excccellent."

She slowly closed the phone.

"What do we do?" Silas asked. "We've only got the brother."

Monica glanced about the woods then sighed heavily. "Well, one is better than none. We'll keep lying and say we got both."

Silas gave her a look. "You know what will happen when he finds out."

"We'll cross that bridge when we come to it. Let's go." She started forward, giving Zach a push.

Silas motioned toward Willard. "What about Pillsbury Doughboy here?"

"Leave him," Monica called over her shoulder.

"But ..." Willard whined. "You just can't leave me. How am I going to find my way back? It's getting dark and cold. What if I catch the sniffles? You wouldn't want me to catch the—"

"Silence!" the woman shouted.

Willard grew quiet.

Then, turning on her most pleasant voice (more fingernails on the blackboard) she said, "I assure you, you will not have to worry about any of those matters."

"I won't?" Willard asked nervously.

"Certainly not. The wild bears in these woods will make certain you never have to worry about anything again."

Chapter Four

Temptation

"What do we have here?" the doctor asked.

"Car accident," the ambulance attendant said. "Up on Bern Road." He continued pushing Dad's gurney down the hospital hallway.

Dad tried to lean up on one elbow. "Really, guys, I'm okay. I just got a little bump on the back of the head."

"Right," the doctor nodded, "but those little bumps can be nasty." He turned to the attendant. "Get him into the ER."

"ER?" the attendant asked. "If he's just got a little—"

"Did you hear what I said?"

"Right, but—"

"What about his wife?" the doctor asked. "You radioed that his wife was also—"

"I'm just a little bruised," Mom called from where she stood in the doorway. "I got my leg caught under the dashboard, but I'm fine."

"What are you doing standing?" the doctor demanded. "Somebody get her a wheelchair!"

"I'm fine, really."

"I'll be the judge of that."

Mom protested, "No, really, I'm not—"

"Is everybody questioning my authority today?" the doctor demanded.

"I'm not questioning your—"

"Will somebody *please* get this woman a wheelchair?"

A nurse appeared from one of the rooms and scurried down the hall. "Yes, Doctor, right away."

●

"Shh." Cody motioned for Piper to press against the RV.

The voices approached from the other side. There was no mistaking who they belonged to or who they were talking with . . .

"You'll like Reverend Festool," Monica was saying. "He used to be one of you."

"What's that supposed to mean?" Zach asked.

"It means he also worked for the wrong side until Shadow Man turned him—just like he'll turn you."

"Ooo, you've got me quaking in my boots," Zach answered.

Piper had heard enough. She started around the RV to help her brother until Cody grabbed her arm.

"What are you doing?" he whispered.

"Zach needs our help."

"They've got guns, remember?"

Reluctantly, she stopped as the voices passed by the other side. They were so close she could actually hear them breathing as the gravel crunched under their feet. There was one other sound—the faint clang of metal, which she could barely hear.

"Remember the last time we got together?" Zach was saying. He sounded just as cocky and overconfident as always. At least that's how he was pretending to sound. "Seems that one didn't exactly turn out the way you guys wanted, did it?"

"This time things will be different," one of the men answered. "Now that we've taken care of that little brat brother of yours."

Piper caught her breath. They were talking about Elijah. But what did they mean, *"taken care of"*?

As the voices headed toward the woman's van and started to fade, Piper felt herself trembling. The thought of losing one brother was bad enough. But two? Her eyes began burning and she gave them a quick swipe. Cody must have seen it for suddenly he was wrapping a warm, comforting arm around her.

"It's okay," he whispered. "We'll get them."

She looked up at his face. She wanted to ask how, and when, but her throat was so thick with emotion that she couldn't speak.

●

Elijah wasn't sure how he wound up on the giant stage screaming into the microphone. To be honest, he hardly spoke to anyone. But now he was singing to them, to thousands of them.

And they were loving it.

As he looked into the blinding lights he saw them screaming, shouting, trying to reach up to the stage to touch him. *Him!* Little Elijah Dawkins. Elijah Dawkins the runt. Elijah Dawkins, the boy nobody paid attention to.

He looked over to see his lead guitarist leap into the air, sweat flying off his body, as he made his instrument scream like some tortured animal. Off to his left, a keyboard player's long wet hair whipped back and forth as his fingers raced across the keyboard. Behind him, the drummer pounded out an intoxicating rhythm that shook the entire auditorium.

Elijah leaned back into the microphone and shouted out the next lyrics.

Guys pounded their fists into the air to the rhythm of the beat.

Girls screamed, fainted, held out their hands to him.

They all sang the words along with him, idolizing him, wanting to be him.

It was heaven. Better than heaven. One hundred thousand fans adoring him.

Loving him.

He caught a glimpse of himself on the giant TV screen above the stage. No longer was he little Elijah trapped in his puny body. With his shirt off, he looked incredible. Sweat glistening off his chest and bulging biceps, streams running down the chiseled muscles of his stomach. No wonder they loved him.

He looked like a god.

He pulled his focus back to the fans who were reaching up to him, begging him for the slightest touch. How could he refuse such devotion? Without hesitation, he ran to the edge of the stage and leapt into the air. They would catch him, he knew it. They would do anything for him.

He landed on a hundred eager, outstretched hands, all grateful for the contact, all grateful to pass his body across the crowd, skimming their surface, like a surfer on the water.

So much adoration. So much love. So much worship.

And it was *all* for him.

●

Willard sat on a fallen log having a good old-fashioned pity party. Actually, he wasn't having the party yet. He was still working on the guest list, wondering which wild animal would be the first to eat him. It's not that Willard didn't like the wilderness. He just wasn't exactly an animal lover.

Some say it was because of the cute little puppy his parents bought him when he was four years old. The cute little puppy that loved to chew and tear up all Willard's favorite shoes ... especially when Willard was wearing them.

Others say it was from the ant farm that he slept with because he loved it so much ... until he accidentally rolled over and broke it. Actually, it wasn't the "breaking" that was difficult. It was the little critters crawling all over him as he slept that caused the problem—if you call six years of nightmares about being attacked by giant ants and five years of therapy a problem.

Finally, there was the incident of the sea gull landing on the patio bug zapper, spilling all the dead insects into his cup of chocolate milk. Unfortunately, nobody knew what happened until Willard started wondering why the chocolate milk had suddenly turned so crunchy.

All that to say, Willard was not thrilled with any type of wildlife, bug or animal, crawly or crunchy. This would explain why he practically leaped out of his skin when a voice called to him from behind:

"Hey there, young fella."

"AUGH!" He spun around to see an old hermit, complete with a scraggy beard, approaching.

"Sorry." The old man chuckled. "Didn't mean to frighten you."

"Who . . . who are you?"

"Who I am ain't important. But my problem is."

Willard checked out the old guy—plaid shirt, torn jeans, suspenders. He was so skinny a strong gust of wind would blow him over. Definitely not the kidnapper type. And definitely not a threat (unless he collected ants or had a bug zapper). Still, Willard wasn't going to take any chances. "What . . . what type of problem?" he asked.

The old man approached. "You know anything about computers?"

"Well, yeah, that's kinda like my specialty." Willard pushed up his glasses and gave an asthmatic cough, as if proving his point.

The hermit nodded. "Thing is, I got all this new-fangled computer equipment in my cabin over yonder and I don't know the first thing 'bout using it."

"You have computer equipment?" Willard asked. "Out here?"

The man nodded. "Figured it's about time I enter the twentieth century."

"Actually," Willard corrected, "we're in the twenty-first century now."

"The twenty-first century! When did that happen?"

"Awhile back."

"Shoot. See how fast time flies when you ain't payin' attention?"

Willard gave half a nod.

"So you think you can help me out?"

Willard didn't answer, but continued staring at him. Because, despite the man's age, his scraggly beard, and worn clothes, there was something strangely familiar about him.

"Come on, son, we ain't got all day. It's gonna get dark soon."

Willard frowned, still trying to decide. He knew what his folks said about hanging out with strangers. But this guy was so old and frail that he couldn't possibly be dangerous. And he was right, it was getting dark—and cold.

"How ... how far is your cabin?"

"Just over yonder a piece."

Willard continued to think.

The old man gave a sigh. "Well, listen, if you ever decide to make up your mind," he turned and started back up the path, "just let me know and I'll—"

"No, wait!" Willard interrupted.

The man turned back.

Willard tried to sound less panicky. "What I mean is, I think I can squeeze you into my schedule."

The old-timer broke into a grin that showed more gums than teeth. "Well, that would be real neighborly." He turned and limped back up the path. "We'd best get a move on."

Willard scrambled to catch up.

"With any luck maybe we'll get inside 'fore supper time."

"Supper time?" Willard asked. "I wasn't planning on eating dinner with you."

"Oh, not me, son," the old man chuckled. "The animals. With any luck, we'll get inside before they decide to have us for supper."

Willard nodded and picked up his pace.

"What are you doing to my husband?" Mom leapt from her wheelchair and started across the ER toward Dad.

"Grab her!" the doctor ordered.

The ambulance attendant reached out and caught Mom's arm, pulling her back to the chair. "Ma'am, you'll have to—"

"Let go of her!" Dad tried to rise from the gurney to help.

"Somebody hold him down!" the doctor yelled.

A big hulk of an intern pressed Dad's shoulders back onto the gurney.

"Get off me! Get—"

"Give me his arm!" the doctor yelled. "Hold it steady!"

The intern gripped Dad's arm and held it as the doctor prepared the hypodermic needle.

"Let go of me!" Mom yelled at the ambulance attendant. Then at the doctor. "What are you doing to him?!"

Dad continued to fight, but he was no match for the giant intern.

"What are you doing?!" Mom cried. "He doesn't need anything! He's just—"

The doctor inserted the needle into Dad's arm and emptied the syringe.

Mom went wild. "Mike, Mike ..."

It was all the attendant could do to hold her in the chair.

"Michael!" She watched in horror as Dad's eyelids began to droop.

"It's all right," he mumbled. His whole body began to relax. "Everything's all ..." He closed his eyes.

"Every ..." His jaw went slack and his head rolled to the side.

"Michael ...!"

But he no longer answered.

"What did you do?!" Mom yelled. "He didn't need that! It was just a bump on the head! What did you give him?!"

"Just a little something to help him sleep." The doctor reached for another syringe from a steel tray and crossed to her. "You seem a little tense as well, my dear."

"Tense! You just gave my husband a shot of who knows what! You bet I'm tense! And I'm mad! I'm real—"

"Yes," the doctor said, raising the syringe to the light and tapping out the air bubbles. "You must be going into shock from the accident." He came closer.

Mom grew cold. "What ... what are you doing?"

"I think you need something to help you relax."

"Relax! I don't need anything to relax!"

"Of course you do. Just listen to yourself—shouting, screaming, near hysteria." He glanced toward the ambulance attendant. "Hold her good and tight."

The attendant protested, "But Doctor—"

"Do as I say or get out."

"But—"

The doctor had enough. He motioned over to the big intern to come and help with Mom. The man understood and joined them. He grabbed her shoulders and pressed her firmly into the chair.

"Let go of me! LET GO!"

The doctor swabbed her left arm. "This won't hurt a bit. I give you my word."

"LET GO OF—"

The needle punctured her skin and Mom felt a slight burn. She watched in shock as the syringe emptied into her arm. Again she tried squirming, kicking. But her body began to feel strangely heavy.

"Let go of ..."

Like Dad, her lids began to droop.

"There we go," the doctor said as he removed the syringe.

She looked up to him, saw him smiling down at her, his face blurring.

"That's it, just relax. Close your eyes."

She tried to keep them open, but they were so heavy.

"It really does no good to resist. Just relax."

Maybe he was right. Maybe closing them for just a second would help. She did, then immediately forced them back open. Now, the entire room was a blur. To clear it, she closed her eyes again.

This time, however, she did not have enough strength to reopen them. Or to remember why she wanted to ...

Chapter Five

Dark Times

"What's this?" Cody bent to the ground and picked up the RV keys with his uninjured hand.

"I thought I heard Zach drop something," Piper said. "You think he did it on purpose?"

Cody headed for the door. "Well, we definitely have a way to rescue him."

"Right," Piper agreed as Cody shoved the key into the lock and it clicked open. "Now all we need to do is find them."

Cody pushed open the door, and they stepped into the RV. "It was a smart call getting an ambulance to pick up your folks," he said. "So was the idea of us splitting up and circling back."

Piper nodded. "Must be some kind of record."

"Record?"

"For Zach to be right two times in the same day."

For a second, Cody broke into that heartbreaker smile of his. Even now, even in this awful situation, Piper felt her stomach do a little flip-flop.

"Hey, check it out." Cody had made his way back to the table and the computer Willard had been using. "Looks like we got another message."

Piper joined him and read the monitor:

Guys, they got Zach.

IM me when you get this!

Willard

Cody frowned. "I thought Willard was with them."

Piper slid behind the computer. "All we did was hear voices. We never saw any faces."

She reached for the keyboard and began to type. At least she tried. But with Cody watching she felt self-conscious and made tons of mistakes. Why did he have to keep watching when she needed to concentrate?

Finally, she got it right:

This is Piper. Where are you?

A moment later the answer appeared:

In the woods with some old hermit guy and lots of very cool computer stuff.

"He's still in the woods?" Cody asked.

Piper typed:

You're right—they got Zach. Took him in their van.

We don't know where.

Almost immediately the answer came back:

This guy's got major state of the art stuff.

I can patch into satellites and search the roads.

They can't be far. Stand by.

Piper stared at the screen, then looked up to the driver's seat. Finally, she turned to Cody. "You think you can drive this thing?"

He held up his bad arm, wincing at the movement. "Not with this."

She blew the hair out of her eyes. "So even if we know where he is, we can't get to him."

"Why don't you drive?"

"I've never even driven a bumper car," she admitted.

"Then it's about time to learn."

She hesitated.

"Really, I can't drive like this," Cody said. "You're going to have to."

Piper wanted to fire off a snappy comeback, but it was hard to be clever when the little flip-flops in her stomach were tying it into one giant knot of fear.

●

Elijah looked out into the glaring lights and the mass of people shouting and screaming for his attention. The longer he looked, the deeper he saw into their hearts. And the deeper he saw, the more he realized the truth.

They weren't shouting and screaming for him—at least not on the inside. Something much greater was happening. Beyond the music. Beyond the concert. Deep inside their souls, a different screaming was going on. Not for him, but for something much more serious. They were searching to fill their emptiness. To fill that awful loneliness they felt when they were by themselves, when they were alone in the silence, when they wondered if anybody really cared.

That was what Elijah saw as he looked into their faces, as he saw deep into their souls.

And that was what broke his heart.

He looked around the stage. The guitarist was still strangling the guitar. The keyboard player was still ripping up the keys. And the drummer was still pounded his drums with a passion that worked the crowd into a frenzy.

But it no longer meant anything—at least to Elijah. Now he saw the people's real need. Their emptiness. He knew there was nothing wrong with entertaining them, but he had so much more to offer. Instead of an hour's noise to drown out their emptiness, he would someday offer the power to fill it.

Forever.

In just a few years, when he was grown, he would be telling them about someone who would fill their hearts to overflowing. Someone who loved and adored them. Someone who would completely satisfy their hunger.

Compared to that, all this strutting and screaming meant nothing.

Now, at last, he understood.

Shadow Man thought he was tempting Elijah with fame and glory, but the temptation was nothing compared to what Elijah knew he could be doing for people in the future if he stayed true to what God wanted. Compared to that, this concert was worthless. This fame and glory was empty. It was as if Shadow Man was trying to convince Elijah to eat rubbish instead of the incredible banquet that had been prepared for him.

As understanding flooded Elijah's mind, the concert

began to dissolve before his eyes. The music faded. The faces disappeared.

After a moment, he opened his eyes and found himself back inside The Chamber, all alone, staring out at Shadow Man. A very, very angry Shadow Man.

"Ssso, you think your powersss are greater than my Chamber, do you?"

Elijah was silent. He knew the truth, and that was all that mattered.

Shadow Man's fingers blurred across the control's keyboard as he typed in another new and tempting reality. "We ssshall sssee about that, young Elijah. For thisss is what you can be if you will deny your God and follow my Massster. Behold, and be amazzzed!"

Once again Elijah felt himself leaving the room. Once again he felt himself falling deep into his imagination.

The imagination of The Chamber ...

●

The dingy motel room smelled of old carpet and stale smoke. The only good thing about it was that Zach was bigger than the cockroaches ... well, most of them.

Monica and Silas had stepped out for a bite to eat. Bruno, the big guy, lay on the bed snoring up a storm. Just a few feet away, Zach sat at a rickety table sharing a pizza with Reverend Festool. He seemed a nice enough guy. Young, in good shape, funny. And the pizza he ordered, double-cheese with everything on it, wasn't half bad either.

"Let me get this straight," Festool said while chewing. "You and your folks think this little brother of yours is actually mentioned in the Bible?"

"Yeah, from what we can tell." Zach took a giant gulp of Coke and tried not to belch.

Festool laughed and shook his head as he reached for another slice of pizza. "That's too bad."

"Why's that?"

"Well, the Bible. I mean, let's face it." He took another bite. "We're talking about a book of fables that's thousands of years old. Don't tell me someone as smart as yourself buys into that stuff."

Zach lowered his cup. He'd been made fun of before for believing the Bible ... but not by a minister. "Don't you?" he asked.

Festool continued chewing. "Don't get me wrong, it's a great book, lots of good teaching ... but you don't actually believe all that stuff about people walking on water or raising folks from the dead."

Zach shrugged. "Why not? I mean, some things you just gotta believe cause of faith, right?"

Festool looked up from his pizza, a smear of grease shining on his chin. "Just like you believed in the tooth fairy?"

"That's completely different."

"How?"

"The Bible, well, it's the inspired word of God."

"Says who?"

"The Bible."

Festool broke out laughing.

Zach didn't.

Seeing the look on his face, Festool apologized. "I'm sorry. It's just, well, you're telling me the Bible is true because the Bible says it's true." He gave Zach a look. "Doesn't that strike you as just a little ... convenient?"

Zach felt his face start to redden.

Festool continued, an almost pitying look on his

face. "That's like me telling you I'm president of the United States. And when you ask me to prove it, I say the proof is because I just told you."

Zach fidgeted. He was liking this conversation less and less. Come to think of it, the pizza wasn't so hot either.

Festool leaned toward Zach. "Seriously, let me ask you: what proof do you have that the Bible is even vaguely accurate—other than the fact that it says so?"

Zach's mind raced, trying to come up with an answer. All his life he'd been taught to believe in the Bible. That was what his parents believed, what his Sunday School teachers taught, and what his youth pastor preached.

But where was their proof?

Did they just believe because they were taught to believe? And if that's all he had to go on, then maybe Festool was right. Maybe believing in the Bible was no different than believing in Santa Claus or the Easter Bunny ... or the tooth fairy.

Festool lowered his voice, sounding more gentle. "Don't feel bad, Zach. There's nothing wrong with believing in the Bible or Jesus or God. Lots of good, decent people believe—especially children."

He wiped his chin with his napkin and continued.

"But as an adult, well, maybe it's time for you to put away childish things and start thinking like a grown-up."

Zach opened his mouth to answer, but he had none to give.

The Reverend pushed back his chair and stood. "Listen, I have some matters to attend to in town. But I'll be back in a little while and we can continue our little discussion, okay?"

Zach stared at the table, barely hearing.

"Okay?"

He looked up to see the Reverend smiling down upon him. It was a kind smile. Gentle and understanding.

Ever so slightly, Zach began to nod. "Yeah. Sure."

Chapter Six

Wild Ride

"Look out!" Cody yelled, his hands clutching the armrests. "You're going the wrong way!"

Piper muttered angrily to herself. It wasn't her fault that Cody made her so nervous she'd shifted the RV into reverse instead of forward. Or that she'd pushed the gas instead of the brake.

"Stop! Left! Turn left!"

Or that when driving backwards her left was her right and her right was her—

"Look out!"

KERRRASH!

The good news? The RV finally came to a stop. The bad news was some poor tree had to sacrifice its life to make that possible.

Then, of course, there was the RV's back end. It probably wouldn't show from the roll Dad had given the RV earlier, but as a neat freak, Piper wasn't crazy about the giant dent she'd just put in it.

"I'm sorry ..." She dropped her head onto the steering wheel —

HOOOOONK!

— then bolted back up.

"No, no, that's okay," Cody said as he crawled off the floor and back to his feet. "You did just fine."

"You're just saying that," she sniffed, wiping a sleeve across her eyes.

"No, really," he said, testing his arm to see how many more places he'd broken it. "For your first time, I think you did great."

She turned to him. "Really?"

She knew he was lying when he tried to smile but couldn't quite pull it off. His lips turned up at the corners, but his eyes darted back and forth like a caged turkey on Thanksgiving morning.

"I guess ..." she sniffed and reached for the gear shift. "I guess I'd better try again."

The second sign that he was lying came when his voice got higher and cracked like a thirteen-year-old boy going through puberty.

"Wait just a second!" he croaked. Forcing himself to calm down, he continued. "You know, until we catch our breath."

Piper gave him a look.

He gave her a weak smile.

●

Zach sat at the table staring at the unfinished pizza. The words the Reverend had spoken earlier still haunted him and he didn't feel much like eating ... which was a first as far as he could remember.

There was a knock at the door, and a voice called out, "Housekeeping."

Bruno got up from watching a rerun of *The Brady Bunch* and opened the door. An aging, disheveled man stood in the hall beside a rollaway bed, "You order an extra cot?" he asked.

Bruno looked over to Silas, who was now asleep on the sofa, then to Monica, who was sprawled out on the bed. "Uh, I don't think so."

"How many you got in here?" the man asked.

Bruno scratched his head. "Just the three of us. Oh, and the boy at the table that we ain't supposed to tell nobody about."

The janitor nodded. "Ah, then it must be for him." He entered the room and rolled the bed toward the table.

Zach looked up numbly and watched. There was something strangely familiar about the man, but he couldn't place it. Bruno hobbled back to the TV to continue watching *The Brady Bunch* marathon as the janitor opened the cot for Zach.

There, lying in its center, was a cell phone.

"What's that?" Zack asked.

The janitor picked it up and frowned. "Must be left over from the last guest." He tossed it to Zach.

"Don't you want it?" Zach asked. "In case they come back to claim it?"

The janitor shook his head. "Nobody will come back for that."

"How do you know?"

"I know." He held Zach's eyes a moment, and suddenly Zach remembered. The man's eyes were the same as the sheriff's who had sent them on the detour.

The janitor glanced over to Monica, Silas, and Bruno, then back to Zach. He lowered his voice. "You won't be able to make any calls, but you may receive some interesting e-mails."

Zach's mouth dropped open. He had a thousand things to ask. Unfortunately, all that came out was, "But ..."

The old man headed for the door.

"But ... but ..."

He turned the knob and opened it.

"But ... but ... but ..."

He looked back and interrupted Zach's motorboat imitation. "Everything will be okay, son. You just keep trusting God, and everything will be all right." He gave a wink, stepped outside, and gently closed the door.

●

The computer equipment was incredible. Everything was top of the line. There were even a few extras that Willard hadn't known existed. He had no trouble tracking Monica and her thugs to a Motel 3 (they were too cheap for a Motel 6). Once he found the address he sent it to Piper and Cody.

Apparently, the two had been having a little trouble driving the RV (Piper refused to give details), but it sounded like everything was going better now.

Willard hoped so. He knew Piper could be the shy type and not talk a lot. He also knew she was crazy over his friend, Cody. Nothing obvious. Just little things like forgetting what she was saying when she looked at him. Becoming super clumsy. And always pushing her hair behind her ears or blowing it out of her eyes.

Of course, Cody never noticed any of that. There he was, the best-looking guy in the school. All the girls flirted with him to his face and sighed longingly behind his back—and yet he was totally clueless. Maybe that was one of the things they liked about him. He had no idea how cool he was.

But Willard didn't have that trouble. He knew exactly how *un*cool he was. No girl ever flirted with him to his face (unless you call making up excuses for running away "flirting,") and they *definitely* never sighed behind his back (unless it came with all their giggling and eye-rolling).

Why someone like Cody would ever hang out with someone like him was beyond reason. But they'd been friends ever since they were little kids. And that was another cool thing about Cody. He never forgot his friends.

Back at the cabin, Willard had barely finished sending out the information over the computer before the hermit opened the door and stepped inside.

"Where have you been?" Willard asked.

"Had a couple of loose ends to tie up. How's it goin' with you?"

"I just sent the address to Piper and Cody. They should—"

One of the computer screens flickered, and Willard turned to look at it. "What's going on?"

The old man hobbled to his side. "What?"

Willard stared at the screen. It was filled with all sorts of writing. It seemed to be mostly historical and archeological stuff. "How'd that get on there?" he asked.

The hermit leaned toward the screen. "Hmm ... What's that say at the bottom?"

Willard read the final sentence:

Please send by pressing *Enter*.

The old man reached past Willard and hit the key.

"What are you doing?" Willard asked.

The old guy shrugged. "It said to press *Enter*, so I figured we should press *Enter*."

"But you don't even know who it's from — or where it's going."

Again the hermit shrugged. "If there's one thing I learned about these newfangled computers, it's that when they want somethin', it's usually best not to argue with 'em."

Willard looked at the screen then let out a weary sigh. The old timer obviously didn't know what he was doing. Then again, most of the time, neither did Willard.

●

It was getting late. Maybe the Reverend wouldn't be coming back after all. At least that's what Zach hoped. Their last discussion really got him to thinking. And to doubting. Maybe the guy was right. Maybe you really couldn't trust the Bible was accurate. Just because he learned it in Sunday school didn't necessarily make it true. Or did it?

A few moments later he felt the cell phone vibrate in his pocket. He reached for it, glancing around the motel room to make sure everyone was watching *The Brady Brides Reunion* (Bruno sure liked his *Brady Bunch*). When he was sure the coast was clear, he pulled out the phone and read the subject on the screen:

"Some Arguments Proving the Accuracy of the Bible"

He scrolled down and read:

FACT

Jesus Christ believed the Scriptures and often quoted from them.

FACT

Archaeologists have used the Bible to discover over 200 ancient locations. Every few years another discovery is made that proves the absolute historical accuracy of Scripture.

Zach caught his breath. It was like the screen was answering the very questions Reverend Festool had raised. He scrolled down to read more:

FACT

Other historians who lived around the time of Christ also wrote about Jesus, supporting what was recorded in the Bible. In fact, there are so many historical writings about Christ outside of the Bible that it is possible to construct his entire life without ever going to the Bible.

Zach's heart pounded. There was more:

FACT

Here is an example from the famous Jewish historian named Josephus who lived back in the First Century. None of his writings are in the Bible.

"Now there was about this time Jesus, a wise man, if it be lawful to call him a man, for he was a doer of wonderful works, a teacher of such men as receive the truth with pleasure. He drew over to himself both many of the Jews and many of the Gentiles. He was the Christ and when Pilate, at the suggestion of the principal men among us, had condemned him to the cross, those that loved him at the first did not forsake him; for he appeared to them alive again on the third day; as the divine prophets had foretold these and

*ten thousand other wonderful things concerning him.
And the tribe of Christians so named from him are not
extinct at this day."*

Zach couldn't believe his eyes. He especially liked
the part about being called a "tribe of Christians." But
he had no sooner finished reading before there was a
knock on the door.

Monica rose from the sofa, crossed to the door and
gave her usual screeching, "Who is it?"

"Reverend Festool," came the reply.

She unlocked the door and opened it. Then, in her
ever-pleasant manner, she turned without a word and
headed back to watch TV.

The Reverend entered and nodded to Zach. "So,
have you given any more thought to what we were dis-
cussing earlier?"

"Yeah," Zach coughed slightly as he slipped the cell
phone into his pocket. "I sure have."

"Good," the Reverend pulled up a chair. "So tell me,
as a bright and intelligent young man, what conclusions
have you come to?" He gave his usual smile.

Zach pulled up his own chair. He took a deep
breath and began, somehow figuring Reverend Festool
wouldn't be smiling quite as big when he heard the
information Zach had to share with him.

Chapter Seven

To the Rescue Again — Sorta

Elijah felt the football snap into his little hands. Only they weren't so little anymore. Now they were a man's hands. A *big* man's hands.

He dropped back from the line of players, his muscular legs powerful and poised for action.

He was no longer wimpy little Elijah, the pip-squeak that everybody made fun of. Thanks to The Chamber he now towered six feet five inches high and had the body of a superstar athlete.

He glanced to the turf below and saw the Superbowl logo. He was the star quarterback playing the Superbowl!

The stadium was packed with cheering fans. But it wasn't the fans that thrilled him. He'd overcome wanting to be loved by the masses back at the concert. Instead, it was the power of his new, magnificent body.

He looked downfield and saw his receivers trying to break free from the defense, trying to open themselves up for a pass.

He glanced to the scoreboard: 14 to 14 with eight seconds left in the game.

This was the final play. It all depended on him.

Two giant linemen, 300 pounds each, broke through the line and charged toward him.

He looked back downfield. His teammates still weren't open.

There was only one choice.

Tucking the ball under his massive arm, the mighty Elijah pivoted to the right and broke toward the left, heading for the only opening he saw.

But that opening was immediately filled by another giant opponent who charged toward him. Still, he was no match for Elijah's speed and agility. Elijah faked to the right and continued to the left. The giant lunged and grabbed his jersey, but Elijah spun free and raced through the hole.

More arms reached for him, a pair grabbed at his legs, but he leaped away and continued running.

A tunnel formed ahead of him. His blockers were finally clearing a path.

His legs pumped as he sprinted forward. He would have to push his body to the very edge, but that was what it was for.

Another player came at him from the left. Elijah turned on the afterburners and jetted away like a rocket. Nothing could stop him!

The goalposts shimmered sixty yards ahead!

The tunnel narrowed. He picked up speed. There was no end to his power.

Fifty yards.

The crowd was on their feet roaring.

Forty yards.

Adrenaline pumped; his heart pounded.

Thirty yards.

The roar was deafening.

He could go on like this forever. What a fantastic body, what awesome power! He had never imagined this strength and power—and now it was all his!

●

The good news was that Piper had finally managed to shift the RV into forward. The bad news was, well, that Piper had finally shifted the RV into forward.

Minutes later, thanks to Willard's directions, they were heading down the mountain road to Motel 3 to rescue Zach. She wasn't exactly sure what they'd do once they found him. Or how to find Elijah. Or how to find her parents.

But, at the moment, none of that mattered, because right now she had other things on her mind, like ...

"LOOK OUT! TURN RIGHT!"

... staying alive.

She yanked the wheel to the right, pulling the RV back into her lane and out of the oncoming traffic with the approaching...

HONKKKK

... semi truck.

It was a good move.

What was *not* so good was when she turned too hard, which meant she not only swerved to her side of the road, but also beyond … toward the 800-foot drop-off directly in front of them.

"LEFT!" Cody shouted, grabbing at the wheel with his good arm. "TURN LEFT!"

"Left! Right! Make up your mind!" Piper yelled as she cranked the wheel hard to the left and barely missed the drop-off.

Unfortunately she cranked too hard, swerving back into the wrong lane, and right into the path of the school bus loaded with kids.

"AUGH!" Cody yelled.

"AUGH!" Piper replied.

"AUGHHHHHHHHHHH!" the kids agreed.

Once again Piper yanked the wheel, and once again she barely missed death, though the side mirror on the school bus wasn't so—

CRUNCH!

—lucky.

"How many more miles?" Piper asked, a note of desperation in her voice.

Cody didn't answer.

"How many more—?" She turned to him and stopped. She figured it was rude to interrupt someone whose eyes were closed and who was praying for his life.

Not that she blamed him. In fact, it made so much sense that she turned back to the road and tried it too. Not that she closed her eyes (though at this rate she wasn't sure how much difference it would make).

But she did start to pray.

●

Reverend Festool was pretty steamed when Zach gave him the answers that offered proof of the Bible's accuracy. But it didn't stop him. Instead, he came at Zach with a whole new argument.

"What about Jesus?"

"What do you mean?" Zach asked.

"So what if the Bible accurately recorded what he said and did. What if he was lying? What if he was just out to fool people?"

Zach looked at the Reverend. It was another good point. Even if the Bible did quote Jesus correctly and even if it did report his miracles ... what if he was just a liar? What if all Jesus' miracles were nothing but a bunch of magic tricks to fool people?

Before Zach could answer, he felt the cell phone in his pants pocket start to vibrate.

"Uh, excuse me." He rose from the table. "I need to use the bathroom for a sec."

"Take your time," the Reverend said. "And think about what I've been saying." He gave Zach a smile. "After all, these are very important questions."

●

The roar of the crowd filled Elijah's ears. Just a few more yards and he would cross the goal line and win the Superbowl!

He didn't know how much of his magnificent body was his imagination or how much of it had become real. But, even as he ran toward the end zone, he began to wonder how long it would last. How long would he be in such fabulous shape? Ten years? Twenty? Sure, that was a long time, but it wasn't forever.

Because everybody gets old. And everybody dies.

The goal line lay twenty yards ahead.

He remembered his grandfather, another great athlete, strong as an ox. He also remembered him dying last year as a shriveled old man. Then there was Elijah's father. Even he was starting to get old. It happened to everybody. As great as Elijah's body was, it wouldn't last forever. Nothing lasted forever.

Fifteen yards to go.

But that wasn't true. There *was* something that lasted forever. If he obeyed God, there were the people he would touch. The people he would lead to God. The people whose lives would be changed—forever.

Ten yards.

Sure, he could have the fantastic body now and get all the trophies and awards. But in a few years, who would remember? Or care? And after that? After he was dead? It's not like he could pack his fancy body and trophies into a coffin and take them to heaven.

Five yards.

But changed lives—those he *could* take to heaven. And if he obeyed, if he did what God wanted him to, there would be thousands of those lives.

Suddenly, the choice appeared very easy. A moment of greatness now, or an eternity of greatness later?

Elijah made up his mind. As he did, the roar of the crowd started to fade. He dug his cleats into the turf and veered to the right. Instead of crossing the goal line, he headed off the field. Only it was no longer a field. Now it was turning into a smooth floor.

The floor of The Chamber.

His powerful legs continued to drive his body toward the stadium's exit. Only it was no longer a stadium. Now it was becoming the glass case.

But he did not stop. He lowered his shoulder and slammed into the glass. It shattered and fell all around him.

"Look what you've done!" Shadow Man shouted. "Look what you've done!"

Elijah knew his body had never changed, that it was all in his imagination, in his mind ... but his body didn't know it, not yet. Still, thinking he was strong, he leapt from The Chamber and raced past Shadow Man toward the door. But before he even arrived, the big bodyguard appeared blocking his exit.

Or at least he tried.

Remembering his moves on the field, Elijah faked to the right, and the big man lunged for him. Then Elijah pivoted to the left, slipping past the man and sprinting down the hallway.

"Ssstop him!" Shadow Man screamed. "Don't let him get away!"

Elijah began wheezing, trying to catch his breath. Making fancy moves was one thing. But he was not the mighty man who could run forever. He was just the wimpy boy. Still, he would not stop. At the end of the hall, he saw a door and, beyond that, freedom.

"SSSTOP HIM!"

Elijah's lungs were on fire. His legs felt like rubber. The edges around his vision started to turn white. He was going to pass out.

Still he ran.

He stumbled into the door and opened it. Fresh night air struck his face. An alarm began to sound. Guard dogs barked.

Where should he run? What direction?

He paused, waiting for an impression, waiting to hear that still, small voice that so often directed him.

Into the woods.

He turned and staggered toward the forest.

"He gave us the wrong directions!" Piper shouted. "There's no way this road leads to any motel!"

Cody nodded and quickly typed into the computer:

Willard, where are we?

You told us the wrong way!

For the most part, Piper's driving had improved. Even in the early evening with her headlights on, she managed to stay on her side of the road. Most of the time. More importantly, she hadn't killed anyone—yet. If anybody needed proof that prayer really does work, she had it.

Now they were driving through the forest on a dirt road. There were more than enough dips—

SLAM.

"AUGH!"

—and pot holes.

"YIKES!"

But somehow the broken-down RV just kept going. The fact that Piper was able to avoid hitting any more trees also came in handy. The fact that a squirrel darted out in front of her, was not.

"HANG ON!" she shouted.

She yanked the wheel hard to the right and the RV did the usual skidding and sliding out of control while the kids inside did their usual screaming and shouting for their lives.

"AUUUUGH!"

But somehow Piper straightened them out and they kept going.

She looked to the rearview mirror and called back to Cody. "Any news from Willard?"

"Something's coming in!" he shouted up to her.

"What's he say?"

"Hang on!"

"Tell him it looks like he's got us heading back to Shadow Man's headquarters!"

"Oh, brother!"

Piper looked back into the mirror. "What?"

"We've lost the connection."

"Not now!"

Cody shook his head. "There's no signal."

Piper sighed and whispered under her breath. "God, what are you doing? Why aren't you helping us?"

"To the right!" Cody shouted. He pointed out the window into the darkness. "What's that in the field to our right?"

Piper glanced from the road to an approaching field. A person was running, stumbling in the moonlight. A little person.

"Elijah!" Cody shouted. "It's Elijah!"

Piper's heart skipped a beat.

Cody pressed his face against the cold glass. "Oh no!" he shouted.

"What?"

"There's a bunch of guys after him."

"Guys?" Piper asked.

"Yeah. And dogs!"

Without word, Piper cranked the wheel hard to the right. They bounced off the road and into the open field. Now they were heading straight for Elijah.

Chapter Eight

Pick up and Delivery

People never look their best when they're angry. Reverend Festool proved this with his red face and bulging eyeballs. "I have studied all of my life," he sputtered. "I have a PhD in theology. How do you, a mere child, know these things?"

Zach shrugged. "Guess I just did my homework. Oh, and did you also know that Jesus fulfilled over 300 prophecies about himself in the Bible? Some of them were written hundreds, even thousands, of years before he was even born."

The Reverend's face grew redder.

Earlier, when Zach was in the bathroom, he'd memorized the information that came in over his cell phone.

Now he was reciting it as quickly as he could, before he forgot.

"Those prophecies included everything from his birth in Bethlehem, to going to Egypt, to his healing people, to his death on the cross between two thieves, to his resurrection, and on and on."

"He could have manipulated those things," Festool said, "to fulfill those prophecies!"

Zach smiled. "Maybe. But the chances of one person fulfilling only the top eight prophecies about Jesus in the Bible are something like one in one hundred quadrillion."

"You're ... you're making that up."

"Nope. Those are the same odds you'd get if you covered the whole state of Texas with silver dollars two feet deep, painted one red, tossed it in the center, stirred up the pile, and gave a blind man one chance to pick out the red one."

"That's impossible!" Festool shouted. He was so worked up that he even managed to draw Monica and her thugs away from *The Brady Grandchildren Revisited*.

"You're right," Zach agreed. "That is impossible. Unless, of course, he really was who he said he was. Unless he really was God."

"No," Festool was on his feet. "He was a good teacher, I'll give you that, but he certainly wasn't God!"

"Wrong again. Jesus claimed to be God over and over. A good teacher wouldn't claim that. Maybe a con artist. Maybe a nut case. But no way would a good teacher claim to be God—unless, of course, he really was."

"This is ridiculous!" Festool sputtered. "I don't have to stand for this."

He turned and started toward the door.

"Where do you think you're going?" Monica shouted.

"I'll not be instructed by a mere boy." He opened the door.

Monica headed toward him. "Shadow Man gave you direct orders."

Festool came to a stop.

"You would dare defy him?"

"Well, no. I ... I ..."

"You have a job to do; I suggest you finish it."

"But—"

"Shadow Man is turning his brat of a brother at the Compound. Your orders are to turn this one. If you don't, there will be serious consequences."

Festool hesitated.

"And I think you know what I mean by *serious*."

The Reverend wilted. He turned and shuffled slowly back to the table. Fortunately, he was so distraught that he forgot to close the door, leaving it wide open. That was his big mistake.

And Zach's big break.

Zach leapt up and raced for the doorway. Monica lunged for him but grabbed only air as he ran outside into the night.

"After him!" Monica screeched.

Zach darted through the parking lot, looking for some way out. Unfortunately, the only way came in the form of a burly, tattooed biker standing a few yards from his monster bike, trying to impress a burly, tattooed woman.

Zach raced to the bike and hopped on.

"HEY!" Burly Guy shouted. "What are you doing with my bike!"

"Sorry!" Zach yelled as he hit start and the engine kicked over. "I'll bring it back, I promise!"

The good news was the biker was so heavy, it took him seven and a half seconds to lumber over to the bike.

The better news was Zach had the bike off its stand and the engine revved in five and a quarter seconds.

The bad news was the bike was a lot more powerful than Zach's motor scooter at home.

So powerful, and with such awesome acceleration, that Zach could barely control his wheelie and, of course, his hysterical screaming.

•

"Closer!" Cody shouted to Piper from the RV's open door. "I can't reach him! Closer!"

Piper kept a careful eye on the side mirror as she brought the moving RV beside her running brother. If they'd had time, she would have stopped. But the guards were quickly closing in and the two German shepherds were already at Elijah's heels, snapping away.

The RV leaped and bucked as it hit ruts and holes. More than once, the wheel nearly jerked out of Piper's hands. But she held on tight. This was her little brother they were trying to save, and nothing would make her let go.

"Closer!" Cody yelled.

The dogs were right there. She could hear their growls and snarls.

"Closer!"

Another series of bumps, but she held on.

"Closer … closer … GOT HIM!"

She glanced in the mirror and saw Cody pulling Elijah into the RV. She figured the weight was probably killing Cody's bad arm, but he didn't complain. She was surprised that she still heard snarling and growling until she saw that the dog had latched its jaws onto Elijah's pant leg and wouldn't let go, even if it meant being hauled on board with Elijah.

But the free ride didn't last long. Cody kicked the dog off and slammed the door on it. It took two or three slams before the dog finally let go. It fell to the ground with a few strangled yelps and then angry barking as the RV sped away.

"You all right?" Piper shouted back to Elijah

The boy nodded.

"Where to now?" Cody yelled.

"Zach and the motel!"

"Which way?"

"I'm not sure." Piper glanced back and saw that her little brother was pointing to the left. "Are you sure?" she called. "We're supposed to turn left?"

Elijah nodded. Without questioning, Piper threw the RV into a skidding, sharp turn—

"AUUGGHHH!"

—and they headed left.

●

"They're going back to Shadow Man's Compound!" Willard exclaimed as he and the old-timer watched the blip move across the map on the computer screen.

He reached for the keyboard and typed:

Don't go back to Shadow Man's headquarters!

But when he looked at the monitor, he saw that the word *Don't* was somehow missing.

Willard scowled and retyped the word. But the computer was jammed. No matter how many times he tried to type it, the word *Don't* just wouldn't appear.

"What's going on?" the old man asked.

"Your computer is frozen."

"Really?"

Willard kept trying to type the word but had no success.

"That's strange," the man said. And before Willard could stop him, he reached toward the *Enter* key

"No," Willard cried, "not that key. It'll send it!"

"What key? This one here?" the hermit asked as he hit the key and sent the message.

"Yeah," Willard sighed in defeat. "That one."

●

Zach had barely managed to get control of the motorcycle when the cell phone began vibrating in his back pocket. He reached in and dug it out. Keeping one eye on the road he read the tiny screen:

go back to Shadow Man's headquarters!

He frowned. It didn't make sense. If there was one place he didn't want to revisit, it was Shadow Man's Compound. Still, the instructions over the cell phone hadn't been wrong yet.

He slid the cell phone into his pocket and threw the bike into a sharp left, heading toward the Compound.

A moment later a pair of headlights bounced onto the road behind him. He glanced over his shoulder. It was Monica and her goons.

He revved the bike faster and roared down the dark road. But no matter how fast he went, the van stayed on his tail.

●

Piper peered out the windshield. She didn't believe her eyes. "What have you done?" she shouted back to her little brother.

"What's wrong?" Cody called.

"He's brought us back to the Compound!" she cried. "Elijah, what did you do?!"

The little guy gave no answer except for his usual satisfied grin.

Suddenly, Shadow Man's fortress loomed before them. Piper hit the brakes and slid the RV to a stop just a few yards from the front entrance.

The area was too small to turn around, so she threw the vehicle into reverse. It would have been a good idea, except for the Hummer that suddenly appeared behind them, blocking their path. She wasn't sure how much more abuse the old RV could take, but she had no choice.

She stomped on the gas, preparing to ram the Hummer.

But the RV didn't move. Not an inch. Instead, its wheels just spun in place.

"What's going on?" Cody shouted, his eyes wide and his face white with fear. "Are we stuck?"

She blew the hair out of her eyes and pressed the accelerator harder.

More spinning but no movement.

Her mind raced, trying to understand. There was no mud, no snow. Why couldn't they move?

Suddenly, the side door flew open. She twirled around and had her answer. Shadow Man stood before them, one arm raised toward the RV, holding it in place with his powers.

"Welcome, children," he sneered. "Ssso nice of you to return."

Piper turn to Elijah. The little guy didn't look frightened ... but he was no longer smiling.

●

Dad groaned and tried to move his head, but it seemed to weigh a ton. He forced his eyes open and saw the blur of a hospital room. With lots of effort, he finally rolled his head to the side and saw another bed.

And his wife.

"Juud ... ..." His tongue was so thick no words came. "Juuu ... ..." ..."

He heard a small beep on the other side of him and a nurse's voice. "Doctor, the husband is coming around."

There was another beep, and the doctor's voice answered through the intercom. "It's time for another dose. Give one to both of them."

"Yes, Doctor."

Dad tried to move, but his body felt like lead. He opened his mouth and forced out the word, "No ... "

"It's all right," the nurse said. "You'll be just fine."

"Nooo."

He saw the glint of a needle in the dim light. Desperately, he tried to move—not to save himself, but his wife.

"Steady now."

He felt the tiny burn of the needle.

"No ..."

"There we go."

Once again his eyes grew heavy. No matter how he tried, he could not keep them open. They closed, and the silence returned.

●

The Compound came into Zach's view. So did the Hummer and RV. He immediately hit the brakes. Unfortunately, Monica's van behind him wasn't quite as quick, which would explain the ...

SCREETCH!

followed by the

THUD!

of it slamming into the back of Zach's bike and throwing it forward.

Zach yelled as he hung onto the handlebars. He managed to steer clear of the Hummer but had to dump the bike in order to miss the RV. He came to a sliding stop at Shadow Man's feet.

Monica's van wasn't quite so lucky.

It slammed head-on into the rear of the Hummer. Of course, the Hummer was barely scratched, but the van didn't survive as well. Now it looked like a crunched accordion with steam rising from it.

Unfortunately, that didn't stop Monica from prying herself out of the metal accordion and screaming. "You moron! Who taught you to drive?"

"Nobody," Silas said as he stumbled out after her.

"Well, it shows! Where's Bruno?"

There was no answer. She turned back to the van. "Bruno?"

Finally, the big lug crawled out and tumbled to the ground.

Monica raced to him. "Bruno ... Bruno?"

The man was definitely dazed.

"BRUNO!"

He grinned foolishly at her. "That was fun, Mommy. Can we go on the ride again?"

"Silence!" Shadow Man demanded.

Bruno fell silent. So did everyone else.

"You will come with me," he ordered. "And bring the children." Leaning closer to Elijah, he hissed. "And you thought you dessstroyed my Chamber, did you?"

Elijah blinked.

"You did not dessstroy it, my little friend. You have only increasssed itsss range ... ssso everyone can enjoy itsss power!"

Chapter Nine

Testings

Piper sat tied to a chair along with Cody, Zach, and Elijah in Shadow Man's office. They were facing what Shadow Man called The Chamber. Well, it had been a chamber. Now it was a pile of shattered glass. The only part that remained was a circular tube where Piper guessed its ceiling had been. A circular tube that was pulsing orange, red, green ... orange, red, green ... orange, red, green...

Monica and her thugs had been told to wait in the hall. Now the kids were alone with Shadow Man, whose fingers flew over some sort of computer keyboard.

"You'll like thisss," he hissed. "You'll like it a lot."

Piper leaned over to her brother and whispered. "Got any more plans?"

"Yes," he whispered.

Piper's heart pounded. "Great," she said. "What are they?"

"I think we should escape."

Her hopes soared. "How?"

"I haven't worked out the details."

Her hopes crashed.

She looked back to Shadow Man as he hit a final key and the room exploded with light so intense that, for a moment, she was blinded.

As her eyes adjusted to the brightness, she saw that things had majorly changed.

For starters, Cody sat in an actor's chair holding a movie script. He wore top-of-the-line clothing, sunglasses, and had a smile that revealed dazzlingly perfect teeth. And on a scale of 1 to 10, his body was a definite 11. Around him stood a team of makeup ladies, hairstylists, and about a dozen girls all sighing and begging for his autograph.

Piper frowned and then spotted her brother. He was still his sloppy self (complete with hurricane haircut), but now he was decked out like some sort of multi-gazillionaire, with gold chain necklaces, bracelets, a diamond studded watch, and a silk suit with wads of money stuffed in the pockets. Pretty amazing.

But not as amazing as what both Zach and Cody stared at. Instead of paying attention to how they'd been transformed, they were both gawking at ...

Her!

At first she didn't understand, thinking something was wrong. But when she looked down at herself, she saw that *nothing* was wrong. Nothing at all! She no longer saw the scrawny, all-knees-and-elbows tomboy who hid under extra-large baggy sweatshirts. Now she had the looks and shape of a model—a supermodel. Tall and lean, with all the right curves in all the right places. No wonder they stared. She looked fantastic! And, as she swished her thick blonde hair to the side, she felt fantastic.

"Ssso," Shadow Man hissed. "You like?"

Zach was the first to speak. "Are you kidding?" Zach said, pulling out a thick wad of cash. "What's not to like?!"

Shadow Man grinned. "Yesss. Thisss and ssso much more will be yoursss as sssoon as your brother decidesss."

Piper turned to Elijah. Unlike the others, he was exactly as he had been. No fancy clothes. No fancy body. No fancy anything.

"What's wrong?" she asked her little brother. "Why haven't you changed?"

Shadow Man answered for him. "Your brother isss a ssstuborn one. He refusssesss all that I offer."

Piper frowned, not understanding.

"Yet that will change," Shadow Man said. He reached back to the keyboard, and once again his fingers flew. When he'd finished, he looked up grinning. "Yesss, that will change very sssoon."

With a flourish, he hit the final key and more light flooded the room—light so bright that Piper had to cover her eyes. When she finally removed her hands, she gasped.

Now they all stood on a giant stage the size of a football field and at least fifty feet high. Below them, stretched out as far as she could see, were people. Thousands of them, no, millions. They were all looking up and chanting her name: "Piper … Piper … Piper …"

She immediately glanced down to make sure she still had her incredible body. And, of course, she did.

Cody and Zach were across the stage, checking themselves out, equally as pleased.

But where was Elijah? Where had he—

And then she saw him. At the very center of the stage, sitting on a throne.

To his right, Shadow Man sat on another, grinning and laughing.

Piper glided toward them, as graceful as any runway model, while thousands of adoring fans continued calling her name.

"What's going on?" she shouted.

Shadow Man didn't hear. He was too busy yelling to Elijah. "Thisss can all be yoursss! You can help me rule the world! Together we will ssshare all itsss power and glory!"

But Elijah seemed totally unimpressed.

Shadow Man leaned forward. "What about your brother and sssisssster? You would deprive them of such joy?"

Elijah hesitated.

Shadow Man nodded. "That'sss right. If you won't do it for yoursssself, then do it for them."

Elijah swallowed, then looked out over the crowd as their chanting grew louder.

"All you need do isss sssubmit, and they will be given thisss. Thisss and ssso much more."

Piper wasn't sure what Shadow Man meant, but she couldn't imagine her little brother turning all this down. How could he? Everything was so incredible! And if he wasn't interested, then it was true, he should at least think about her and Zach.

Still, Elijah hesitated. He turned toward Zach, who was eating up the money and worship like a starving man gobbling up food. And, speaking of food, there were at least a dozen tables surrounding him, all filled with his favorite meals: chips, pizza, chips, steak, chips, ice cream, and more chips.

It was true, Zach loved to eat. He loved in-between-meal snacks, and in-between in-between snacks, and in-between, in-between, in-between ... well, you get the idea. This was the happiest Piper had ever seen him. All that food plus the fame plus the money. For him, it was a dream come true. To be honest, it was also a dream come true for her.

Yet Elijah still hesitated. What was wrong with him?

The boy turned back to his sister. She motioned to her fantastic body, to the millions of people loving and adoring her, to everything that surrounded them. He wouldn't deny them this, surely.

But instead of nodding in agreement, a deep sadness filled Elijah's eyes. She didn't understand. How could he be sad when all this could be theirs? Unless ...

She turned to Shadow Man. "Is this some sort of trick?" she shouted. "Another one of your lies?"

"No, my dear. I ssswear by all that isss unholy, what you sssee before you isss truth."

"What's the catch?" she shouted.

"There isss no catch. If your brother followsss the Massster, thisss isss the truth of your future."

Suddenly, a voice thundered.

"Truth?"

Piper spun back to Elijah. She knew it was his voice, but it was a thousand times more powerful. Weirder still, when he spoke, his mouth didn't move.

"You call this truth?"

For a moment, Shadow Man seemed surprised. But he quickly recovered. "Yesss, if you follow the Massster."

"No. This is only part of the truth."

It took Piper a moment to find her own voice. "What?" she squeaked. "What do you mean?"

"Here is the *complete* truth."

Instantly, Piper found herself inside a magnificent palace. Handsome men and beautiful women were waiting upon her. Two were on their knees massaging her feet, giving her the world's greatest pedicure. Two more were at her hands giving her a manicure. Someone else was rubbing her neck. Another, was giving her a facial. She'd never felt so good in her life and couldn't help but sigh with pleasure. If this was "complete truth," sign her up.

She open her eyes and spotted Cody across the marble room. He held another movie script and wore a silk robe as a dozen servants waited on him. But he had changed. Instead of being young and gorgeous, he was now old and ugly. Instead of being his kind, thoughtful self, he was screaming, "I wanted this robe in white! Not ivory! WHITE!"

"But my lord—" one of his servants answered.

"No buts!" Cody yelled. "And tell the director I expect to play *all* the parts in this movie. Do you understand me? ALL!" To make his point, he threw the script at the servant.

"Yes, your highness." The servant bowed low and backed out.

Piper couldn't believe what she saw. And when Cody spotted her staring, he screamed, "What are you looking at?" Before she could answer, he yelled, "Get out of here, or you'll miss your weekly plastic surgery!"

Piper scowled, not understanding.

"And don't frown. You know how that makes you wrinkle."

Instinctively, her hands shot to her face. Her skin felt as taut as a rubber band about to snap. She spotted a mirror and motioned one of her servants to hand it to her. When she looked into it, she practically gagged. It was hard to tell her age because, staring back at her, was a creepy clown face, her skin pulled so tight from so many plastic surgeries that it was frozen in a grotesque perma-grin. The only thing worse was her giant-sausage lips from too many lip implants. Then there was her skeleton body. Not a trace of fat could be seen—only bones that jutted out. Finally, the skin that stretched over her arms, legs, and stomach was covered in scars from a hundred surgeries where they had cut and removed the slightest hint of flab. In her attempts to remain beautiful, she'd become a monster.

Behind her, in the mirror's reflection, she saw Zach lying on a couch. At least she thought it was Zach. She spun around and looked at her brother. His lean body had morphed into a ton of blubber with so much fat that she could barely see his face.

He was also yelling, "Make sure there's more chocolate in the next bite of pizza you chew for me!"

Piper looked on, trying not to retch. It was true, Zach was so rich and lazy that he actually hired other people to chew his food for him. They would take a bite of whatever food he commanded, chew it for him, and, you guessed it, spit it into his mouth so all he had to do was swallow it.

"And that is only the beginning."

Elijah's voice was speaking again.

"Here is the future. Here is the final truth."

The scene changed again. Suddenly, they were all standing on a cliff overlooking an ocean of fire. The heat was so intense that it made Piper's eyes water. And the smell reminded her of the time Dad cremated the hamburgers on the barbecue. The only thing worse was the screaming.

Screaming from the people who were burning in the fire.

She spun to Elijah and shouted, "I don't understand!"

"If you wish, I will agree and follow his master."

"And this will be the future?" Piper asked in a small voice.

Elijah said nothing.

Piper looked back to the people and the fire.

Elijah spoke again.

"This is the future for all who chose to follow Shadow Man and his master to their final truth."

"Final truth?" she repeated. "Would it also be yours?" She looked to Elijah. "If you followed, would this also be *your* future?"

He said nothing.

She tried again. "Are you saying that if you follow him, this would be *your* final truth?"

Elijah hesitated a moment, and then slowly began to nod.

Piper shuddered and stepped back. "No!" She closed her eyes against the screaming below. Louder and more strongly, she shouted, "No way! Absolutely not!"

Suddenly, she was back in her young, supermodel body, standing next to her movie-star boyfriend and her filthy rich brother.

"Are you sssure?" Shadow Man, who now stood beside her, hissed.

"Yes, I'm sure! Of course, I'm sure!"

"Really? Because I have ssso much to offer."

Once again she found herself standing on the giant

stage beside her brother's throne. Once again millions were shouting her name. For the briefest moment, she hesitated then caught herself. "No!" She closed her eyes again. "Don't do it, Elijah!" She turned to him. "It's not worth it! Don't do it!"

Elijah stared at her a long moment. It was almost like he could see inside her, like he knew what she was thinking. Maybe he could.

When he was satisfied she was telling the truth, he gave another nod.

Suddenly, they were back in Shadow Man's office. There was more blinding light, only this time it came from the tube in The Chamber's ceiling. It was exploding, filling the room with smoke and a thousand sparks.

"What have you done?" Shadow Man screamed. "What have you done?"

Chapter Ten

Wrapping Up

When he heard Shadow Man's cry, the ever-faithful Bruno barged in from the hallway. "What is it, Boss?! What's ...?"

That was as far as he got before he stumbled over Shadow Man and fell onto—"Oaff!"—Zach.

The good news was he didn't break any of Zach's bones. The better news was he *did* break Zach's chair. It hit the ground and broke into dozens of pieces, loosening Zach's ropes and allowing him to scramble free.

Bruno jumped up and would have nabbed him, but Bruno was too busy getting tangled up in the rope and falling over what was left of the chair—again and again. This gave Zach plenty of time to untie Cody and Piper, who managed to untie Elijah.

"Grab them!" Shadow Man kept shouting. "Grab them! Grab them!"

"Them?" Bruno cried in confusion. "Which them?"

A good question since, by now, they were all free and racing out into the hallway.

"Ssstop!"

At one end of the hallway stood a door leading outside. Unfortunately, that was also the end where Monica and Silas were sacked out on a bench catching some sleep.

Zach motioned the other direction. "This way!"

They all started to follow—except Elijah.

"Elijah?" Piper whispered. "What is it?"

"Come on, little guy," Zach urged.

But he shook his head and pointed the opposite direction, toward the door and past Monica.

"Forget it," Zach whispered. "It's too dangerous."

Again Elijah shook his head and motioned.

"No way."

"Zach," Piper whispered. "He's never been wrong before."

"Come on," Zach repeated and started forward.

But Piper didn't budge.

Neither did Cody.

Zach turned back and whispered, "Are you guys nuts?"

"Yeah," Cody agreed. "Probably a little. But your sister's right: he's never been wrong." With that he turned and started toward Elijah. Piper followed.

"Cody!" Zach hissed. "Piper!"

But they kept right on walking. Finally, with a heavy sigh, he turned and followed.

They continued down the hall as quietly as they could. Unfortunately, it wasn't quiet enough. They were right in front of Monica when she opened one eye. Then the other. "What's going on?" she demanded.

But instead of answering, Zach had a better idea. "Run!"

This time everyone agreed.

Monica leaped to her feet and was joined by Silas.

"Stop!" he shouted, pulling a weapon from his coat. "I've got a gun!"

The door lay ten yards ahead.

"We'll never make it!" Piper yelled.

But then she heard Bruno lumber into the hallway behind them—still dragging the rope and pieces of chair.

"Hang on," he shouted, "I'm coming!"

"No!" Monica cried.

"Don't worry, I'll help!"

"No, no, no!"

Fortunately, Bruno's idea of helping included arriving and tripping over his rope.

"Oaff!" he cried as he fell over Silas.

"Oaff!" Silas cried as he fell over Monica.

"You fools!" Monica screeched as they all crashed to the floor.

Cody was the first to arrive at the door. He threw it open and held it for Piper and the others to escape.

Once outside, they raced to the RV, just yards away.

"Hurry!" Zach shouted as Piper climbed inside.

Elijah and Cody followed. And finally Zach. He slipped into the driver's seat behind the wheel. (Piper felt no need to volunteer for the job).

The door to the building flew open.

Well, it *started* to fly open. But after only a foot it suddenly stopped. Piper could see Monica and her thugs trying to squeeze through, but for some unknown reason, it was stuck. Then again, maybe the reason wasn't so unknown. Because as Piper looked over to her little brother, she saw him concentrating very hard on that very door.

Meanwhile, Zach was trying to start the engine.

"Come on, baby," he coaxed. "Come on, come on." But nothing happened. He shouted over his shoulder. "Piper, pray!"

"What?"

"You heard me, pray!"

Normally, she wasn't crazy about praying in front of people, especially when "people" also included Cody. But since she was even less crazy about dying, she gave it a shot. She bowed her head and began. "Dear God, help us get out of here."

As she prayed, Zach tried the engine again.

Nothing.

"Please Lord, we really, really need to—"

Suddenly, the RV fired up. "Amen!" Zach shouted.

"Amen!" the others agreed.

Zach dropped the vehicle into reverse and it jerked backwards—throwing Piper forward into Cody's arms ... just like old times.

"Sorry!" she blurted.

"No problem." He helped her back up and smiled.

"Hang on!" Zach dropped the RV into drive, cranked the wheel hard, and hit the gas. This time Cody fell into Piper's arms.

"Sorry!" he laughed.

She tried to return the laugh, but it came out more of a nervous quack ... just like old times.

They bounced onto the dirt road and picked up speed.

"Are they coming?" Zach called.

Cody glanced out the back. "Not yet."

"They will," Zach said, "they will."

"Where to now?" Cody asked.

"Mom and Dad."

"We don't even know where they are," Piper argued. "How can we expect to find them?"

For once in his life, Zach had no answer.

No one did.

Except Elijah. The little guy was crawling up into the seat behind the table with the computer.

"What's up, buddy?" Piper asked. "You don't know how to work that thing."

It was true, he didn't. But he did know how to point.

Piper traded glances with Cody then moved into the seat beside her little brother to take a look.

●

"All right!" Willard cheered as they watched the blip move across the computer screen. "They're getting away!"

"Excellent," the hermit agreed.

Without a word, Willard reached for the keyboard and began to type.

"What are you doing?" the old man asked.

"Giving them instructions on how to pick me up." But he barely started before another address appeared on the screen:

Johnsonville Hospital

278 North Hampshire

"Where did that come from?" Willard asked.

The old timer scratched his head. "Hmm," was all he said.

Suddenly Willard reached over and hit the *Enter* key to send it.

"What are you doing?" the hermit asked.

Willard cut him a look. "Just saving you the effort," he sighed.

Epilogue

You let them get away?

Shadow Man felt the voice more than he heard it. But that was how it always happened here, deep in the cavern under the Compound. Here, where the Master made his abode.

"Not for long," Shadow Man thought back his reply.

Good, came the response. *I would hate to be disappointed. You know how I hate disappointment.*

Shadow Man knew full well how the Master hated disappointment. Over the centuries he had seen first hand how his fellow creatures had been tortured and destroyed. Actually, not destroyed, but tortured and imprisoned in the lake of fire. A fate so horrendous that they *wished* they had been destroyed.

Suddenly, Shadow Man felt the Master's invisible fingers grab his throat and lift him high into the air.

"Yesss," Shadow Man choked, "I know, I know how you hate disssappointment ..."

In an instant, he was flung into the air, flying across the giant cave until he hit the icy stone wall and slumped to the ground.

The time of The Enemy's appearance will soon arrive. We must prevent the boy and his partner from warning the others.

"Partner?" Shadow Man asked as he struggled back to his feet. "There isss another?"

According to The Book, there will be two. They will oppose me and call down the Enemy's judgments from Heaven. But you will not let that happen.

"No, Sssir," Shadow Man said, "absssolutely not."

Good, good. Now, tell me of your plan.

"Plan?" Shadow Man asked.

Suddenly he felt the cold fingers around his throat.

"Oh yesss, the plan, the plan, of courssse."

The fingers released, waiting.

Shadow Man's mind raced, trying to think of something. "We know they are going to ressscue the parentsss."

There was no reply.

Taking that as a good sign, Shadow Man continued. "I will sssummon darker forcesss to pursssue them."

Again there was silence.

Another good sign.

"Right now, right thisss sssecond, I will releassse them. I will order them to begin closssing in."

A chill spread through the layers of fat in his body. The Master was moving. To where, Shadow Man did not know. But he knew it was away. And he knew something else:

He must not fail again. He would use all of his powers to make sure that did not happen. If he did not ... he shuddered, refusing to think of the consequences, refusing to think of what could only be his fiery future.

•

"How much further?" Zach called from behind the wheel.

Piper stared at the computer screen. "Three, maybe four miles."

"Are they behind us yet?" Zach asked.

Cody looked out the back window. "Still no sign of them."

"Maybe we lost them," Piper said hopefully.

"Maybe," Zach said, though it was obvious he didn't believe it. Glancing into the rearview mirror, he spoke to Elijah. The boy sat beside Piper, quietly humming away. "Sure wish you felt like giving me some more clues, little guy."

"Clues?" Piper asked.

"Yeah. When we were in Shadow Man's office, Elijah was talking to me like a mile a minute."

"To you?" Cody said.

"Yeah. He was showing me the future, testing me to see if I wanted to follow Shadow Man."

"*You* were being tested?" Piper said. "I was the one being tested. He was talking to *me*."

"Yeah, right," Zach laughed. "He was talking to me the whole time. In fact, he even took me to a fiery lake and said that was Shadow Man's final truth, whatever that means."

Piper's jaw dropped. "He showed me the same thing."

"No way."

"Guys ..." Cody tried interrupting.

"He sure did," Piper argued. "And he showed me a giant stage and a palace and what we could look like if ..."

"Guys ..."

"That's what he showed *me*."

"GUYS!"

Piper and Zach turned to Cody.

He cleared his throat a little embarrassed. "Actually, that's what he was showing me, too."

All their eyes slowly turned to her little brother. The RV grew very, very silent—except for the hymn Elijah was humming softly. Was it possible? Had they all been through the same test? Each one, without the others knowing it?

"Hey, check it out," Zach exclaimed. Something in the night sky had caught his attention, and he craned his head for a better look.

Piper and Cody moved to a nearby window to see.

At first Piper thought they were black, swirling clouds. But as she looked closer, she saw they weren't clouds at all, but crows. Thousands of them. All circling the RV.

"What's that about?" Cody asked.

"Do you think ..." Piper kept her eyes glued to the window. "Do you think they're coming after us?"

"Relax," Zach said. "They're just crows."

"Yeah." Piper swallowed and gave a nervous nod. "Just crows."

"Except ..." Cody said.

She turned to him and he continued, "When was the last time you ever saw crows fly at night?"

Piper looked back out the window. The sky swarmed with darkness—so thick it blotted out the stars.

"I wonder what's going on?" Zach said.

Piper threw another look to Elijah. She wished she hadn't.

Beads of perspiration had formed on his face. And, instead of humming, his lips had started to silently move, as if ... as if he were praying.

Zach saw him too. "You all right? Elijah, everything okay?"

But Elijah didn't answer. Instead, he closed his eyes and continued moving his lips.

Piper watched. She wasn't sure what was next. It probably would be tough and pretty scary. Still, from what they had been through, she knew they would be safe. Whatever was out there could frighten them, yes. And it could definitely put them to the test. But if they kept obeying and staying connected to God, then whatever evil they faced would never be able to harm them. That much she knew.

So, like her little brother, Piper Dawkins bowed her head and started to pray.

We want to hear from you. Please send your comments about this
book to us in care of zreview@zondervan.com. Thank you.

ZONDERVAN.com/
AUTHORTRACKER
follow your favorite authors